D0175068

HUNTER'S
MOON

HUNTER'S MOON

A NOVEL IN STORIES

PHILIP CAPUTO

HENRY HOLT AND COMPANY   NEW YORK

Henry Holt and Company
Publishers since 1866
120 Broadway
New York, New York 10271
www.henryholt.com

Henry Holt® and ® are registered trademarks of
Macmillan Publishing Group, LLC.

Library of Congress Cataloging-in-Publication Data

Names: Caputo, Philip, author.
Title: Hunter's Moon: a novel in stories / Philip Caputo.
Description: First edition. | New York: Henry Holt and Company, 2019.
Identifiers: LCCN 2018038302 | ISBN 9781627794763 (hardcover)
Subjects: | GSAFD: Suspense fiction.
Classification: LCC PS3553.A625 L56 2019 | DDC 813/.54—dc23

LC record available at https://lccn.loc.gov/2018038302

Our books may be purchased in bulk for promotional, educational, or
business use. Please contact your local bookseller or the Macmillan Corporate
and Premium Sales Department at (800) 221-7945, extension 5442, or by
e-mail at MacmillanSpecialMarkets@macmillan.com.

First Edition 2019

Designed by Meryl Sussman Levavi

Printed in the United States of America

1 3 5 7 9 10 8 6 4 2

For Erin Caputo and Patricia Esralew

CONTENTS

HUNTER'S
MOON

BLOCKERS

1.

Tom lets a brief silence lapse before he asks, "Soooo—how is the pilgrim progressing?"

He doesn't mean to sound snide and dismissive—it's become his natural way of speaking, probably from cross-examining so many impeachable witnesses—but Lisa takes it as intentional, reproves him with a scowl, then lowers her glance to quarter the potatoes. "Fine. Doing just fine," she answers, each word sliced off clean, as if her vocal cords are moving in synch with the knife. Fine *chop* doing *chop* just *chop* fine *chop*. "Took out a couple of term life policies last May, right after he hit the big five-oh. The insurance company said he had to have a physical. Passed with honors. The usual back problems, but he's good to go for another half century."

"Lisa," Tom says, throwing a lift into the last syllable.

She motions impatiently at the bowls and pans on the kitchen counter and says with a trace of irritation, "Have you talked to the pilgrim himself about his progress?"

"Called him from Lansing to tell him we were on the way. And there's some blah-de-blah, and he asks if we're bringing any wine for ourselves, and I say no, we'll drink sodas with dinner, don't want to make things tough on him. And he goes, 'No problem, dude. Not one drop since Hazelden. I'm dry as the Sahara, sober as the Imam of Baghdad.' That's what made the buzzer buzz. Sober as the Imam of Baghdad. Know what I'm saying?"

She doesn't and turns to me, eyebrows furrowed. Thick, black, unkempt, they give her a glowering look.

"He means that I've-got-the-world-by-the-balls way Bill puts on when he's bullshitting," I tell her.

Lisa brushes a mustard sauce on the potatoes with strokes suggestive of painting Easter eggs, then lines them up in a roasting pan, pulls a pork loin from the refrigerator, soaks it in a marinade, and returns it to the fridge. She is a tall, big-limbed woman fifteen years younger than Bill, though her slumped shoulders and the lines at the corners of her mouth make her appear closer to his age. She'd learned to endure, growing up on a hardscrabble farm downstate, but, I suppose, marriage to Bill Erickson would wear on the sturdiest woman, in the same way that friendship with Bill Erickson wears on his friends.

Her preparations finished, she lights up, swoops out from behind the counter, shirttails hanging out of her Levi's, coarse, rebellious hair flouncing on her shoulders, and falls into an oversize chair, flinging her legs over its arm. She sits there, puffing on a cigarette, staring out the French doors toward the lake, not saying a word.

"Okay," Tom says into the disquieting quiet. "This isn't something you want to talk about right now."

"I was going to get into it, so it might as well be right now. He wasn't bullshitting, not completely."

She gets up, goes into the bathroom, and comes back holding a small brown bottle capped with a dropper. She sets it on the counter. The label reads: ZOLOFT (SERTRALINE) 60 ML. "All right, you two, do you swear on your mothers' graves that this stays between us?"

Our mothers are still aboveground, but we swear anyway.

"He *was* dry after Hazelden, went to A.A., but you know, all those people babbling about one day at a time and how it's all in God's hands—not for him." She jerks her head at the wall above the fireplace, where medals in a shadow box hang beside a photograph taken aboard an aircraft carrier during Desert Storm: Bill in a flight suit, helmet tucked under one arm, mounting a ladder to the open cockpit of a two-seat fighter jet. He didn't fly the plane, although the picture makes it look that way. He'd failed to qualify for pilot in flight school but had passed the test for bombardier, the "G.I.B," as he called it—the Guy In Back.

"But he stayed off the stuff," Lisa is saying. "It must have been in March that he started getting these . . . these mood swings. He'd be his old self for a while, then the spells. Of depression. I'm not going into any details, okay?" She pauses and tilts her chin to exhale. "They were bad enough that I nagged him into seeing a shrink in Marquette. He told me that she told him that he'd been medicating himself with booze for so long, going off of it had sent him into a tailspin. She prescribed talk therapy and this stuff." Gesturing at the bottle. "He saw her for, oh, maybe two months, then, Bill being Bill, he stopped and took himself off her meds and put himself back on his. No hard stuff but wine was okay."

"Knew it," says Tom, shaking his head, as wide and round as a soccer ball and almost as hairless.

"Doesn't take much," Lisa goes on wearily. "One glass he's

launched, two he's in orbit, half a bottle and he's on Apollo Twelve."

"So . . . Houston, we have a problem."

She corrects him—"That was Apollo Thirteen"—and turns defensive, offering all sorts of reasons for Bill's modified tumble from the wagon. The *Register* was still in the red, and old Four-M (her shorthand for Media Mogul Myron McNaughton) was constantly on Bill's ass to buck up the paper's bottom line. Plus, Allison, the younger daughter, had been accepted to Stanford, so now he'd have both girls in private colleges—*what the hell's wrong with a state school?*—and every dime earned from the Erickson Trust, what was left of it, and from his Navy retirement pay was going to alimony, so his ex could maintain her lifestyle out there in sunny California, and to tuitions, so his girls didn't have to take out student loans. If it wasn't for Lisa's casino job, they'd fall behind on the mortgage payments, and then all this . . . She makes a sweeping movement to take in the house, the guesthouse, the ten acres of woodland with four hundred feet of lake frontage, rubs her palms together, and sighs, "So I guess he figured the vino would sand the edges, y'know?"

Her lips part in a mirthless quarter smile. "Except it didn't. Know what I did? I got the prescription refilled and started spiking his orange juice every morning, and that seemed to help," she confesses with a brittle laugh. "He thought it was the wine doing the trick. Up to about a week ago, we were in the old rut. Nothing stronger than coffee before six, then he'd hit it and end the evening speaking in tongues and then shake off the effects like a retriever shakes off water. And all the time, I was trying to convince myself that it's better to live with a functional drunk than a dysfunctional one."

She doesn't deserve this is what I'm thinking when I ask what changed a week ago.

"We had a knock-down drag-out. End result? He promised he'd try again. Promised he wouldn't drink while you guys were in camp, a new start. And he hasn't touched a drop since, sort of getting himself in shape. I'm counting on you two to see that he keeps his word."

Tom folds his hands on his ample belly. "Great! Looking forward to it!"

"The meds will help," she replies, in a reassuring tone. "They keep the black dog in the kennel, and if it's there, it's easier for him to resist. One dropperful. I do orange juice because the concentrate clouds water and he'd notice."

"Wait a sec," I say. "You want us to . . ."

"I can't be there." She presses the bottle into my hand. There is in her touch an intimacy, a trust; it's almost as if we've shaken hands on a solemn contract. "Squeeze the dropper, stir it with a spoon, takes half a second. He'll never know the difference."

We leave when she begins to set the table, release our dogs from the back of Tom's GMC, then bring our overnight bags into the guesthouse, a one-room, prefab log cabin too finished to look authentically rustic. The bottle in my shirt pocket has a weight disproportionate to its size. I unpack my shaving kit and tuck the Zoloft inside.

We join the dogs, racing up and down what had once been lakeshore, across mudflats that had once been lake bottom. A long way out, duck blinds picket this year's shoreline. Once upon a time not very long ago, you needed a skiff to reach them; now you can do it on foot, if you're willing to slog through a hundred yards of muck. Hardly any snow has fallen the past three winters, depriving Lake Michigan of the spring runoff that had replenished it since, I suppose, the Ice Age. In the house, we'd seen yesterday's edition of Bill's newspaper. It carried the headline LAKE LEVELS AT RECORD LOWS. EXPERTS BLAME MILD

WINTERS ON CLIMATE CHANGE and a photo of a dredger deepening the ship channel into Manitou Falls harbor. The caption reported that similar excavations were going on as far south as Chicago and Gary. That—the lake's slow evaporation—was one of the things we'd been talking about before Tom flipped to the subject of the pilgrim's progress.

I'm allergic to change. I've been married to the same woman, living in the same house, and teaching the same courses at Michigan State for twenty-two years and hope to continue for another twenty-two. Aside from reuniting with my two oldest friends, the whole reason I come back to the Upper Peninsula every fall is the familiarity of its unaltered landscapes. No suburban sprawl, no interstates, the two-lane blacktops and woods and rivers—all the landmarks of my boyhood—are pretty much as I remember them. Now this—dry land where there'd been none in living memory. Walking where I should be wading, I get the feeling that things are out of whack, that we're on the edge of an epochal alteration in the order of the world. I picture the lake in the distant future: an enormous ditch littered with the hulls of long-sunken ships and pleasure craft and birch-bark canoes, anthropologists studying the exposed bones of drowned children, sailors, fishermen, voyageurs gone under in unrecorded gales.

"So what do you think?" Tom asks.

I don't answer, lost in my vision of slow-motion catastrophe.

He carries on. "The only thing I'd rather do less than slip Bill a mickey every morning is crawl on my bare knees over broken glass. Spells of *depression*? I don't remember that that guy ever had a down minute in his life. What the hell would he have to be depressed about?"

Mallards and black ducks, alarmed by the dogs, fly out of a pothole, wings rowing the quiet air.

"Depressed people aren't depressed about anything in particular," I say authoritatively. Not that I am an authority. I'm a professor of Russian literature. My knowledge of mental disorders doesn't go much beyond what I've read in Dostoevsky. "It's a chemical imbalance in the brain, short circuits in the neuro-transmitters."

"Yeah. I guess a lifetime of boozing *would* fuck up your neurotransmissions. So who spikes the OJ? Or do we take turns?"

"Well, she gave the meds to me, so I'll play nurse. The other stuff—making sure he doesn't nip on the sly—we play by ear."

"Shit and double shit. I really hoped we wouldn't have to play watchdog this trip."

"We're not doing it for him. It's for her sake."

He shambles along, hands in his pockets, and gives me a sidelong glance. "The way you look at her sometimes, I might think you've got a thing for her."

"Yeah, but not in the way you think. More of a brotherly thing."

"If you say so."

*　*　*

Bill comes home about half an hour before dinner. Inside, we find him, jacket off, tie loosened, sitting at the kitchen counter with Lisa while his English pointer, Rory, licks his hand. Lisa's clandestine doses must be working; he's not the morose character I'd expected, after all her talk about shrinks and mood swings. "Dudes!" he shouts, and jumps off the stool, grinning, growling, calling out his usual greeting—*"Buju! Shagunashee wadukee!"*—which he claims is Ojibwa for "Hello, crazy white men." He hasn't aged, trim as ever, hair still thick, the silver in it barely distinguishable from its original platinum blond. At a distance, you'd mistake him for thirty. His splendid genes have seemingly shielded his looks from the carpet-bombing of his addiction. His eyes remain clear; there is no boozer's flush or red map of a riverine delta in his cheeks.

He hooks his long arms around our necks, asking, "How's Cheryl? How's Julie? How're the kids? Goddamn, love ya, great to see you guys again." He has more than the normal share of human contradictions—self-centered but generous, often considerate, sometimes thoughtless. But I don't doubt his sincerity. He really does care about our wives and kids—no other male I know remembers to send birthday cards to Cheryl and my two boys—and he does love us, so it's hard not to respond in kind. Harder for me than for Tom, who stiffens and pulls away from the smothering embrace. We've been charged with keeping Bill sober for the next week; this is no time for sentimentalism, no time to be taken in by the warm welcome, his rough charm.

In the long northern twilight, we sit down at the table, which Lisa has set to Martha Stewart standards. She always does when we show up—crystal, silverware, china, shine and sparkle in candlelight.

"We're gonna have a great week!" Bill exults, presenting a hand-drawn map a friend has given him of a honey hole way back in the boonies, loaded with grouse. "We're gonna come back with enough birds to feed the whole damn town!" Again, the good cheer strikes me as a little forced, and his filling and refilling of our wineglasses while he confines himself to sparkling water seems theatrical. *Look at me; I'm in complete control.*

But his craving, like some night-blooming plant, flowers in darkness. As the evening wears on, he grows fidgety and a little irritable after Tom brings up the story in his newspaper.

"Global warming is getting the rap for everything but prostate cancer," Tom remarks. "Lake Michigan isn't, for Chrissake, going to disappear."

"That's *not* what the story said. What the fuck, are you one of these flat-earth nutballs who thinks it's all a hoax?"

They spar for a few minutes, then Bill does an odd thing—reaches across the table and, with an unsteady hand, tips the empty wine bottle into his empty glass, raises it to his lips, and gulps air. When Lisa brings out the cake and ice cream, he repeats the pantomime twice more, as if the motions of taking a drink might quench his need for the real thing. How, I'm asking myself, did he get through twenty years as a naval aviator? This guy who once flew through flak over the Iraqi deserts was now struggling to pilot himself through dinner. Tom and I watch to see if he makes it. Lisa launches into a story, maybe to distract us, about her dealings with the tribal council that owns the Northern Suns casino on the reservation outside town.

"White chick came up with a marketing plan to pull in high rollers from downstate and Chicago," she says, comically mimicking a throw of the dice. "What we get are loggers and mill workers blowing their paychecks, blue-hairs playing the slots when their Social Security checks come in. The idea is that we start with a junket to Foxwoods to see how the big boys do things. The council has to approve the funds for the trip, the whole plan. White chick gives a terrific PowerPoint. She's seen too many movies where Crazy Horse gives the orders and his braves obey, but things don't work that way in the real world of real Indians. The council chairman isn't Crazy Horse. The decision has to be made communally, y'know? Consensus. But nobody wants to be the first one to raise his hand and say, *Let's do it*. She tries to fire them up. *We'll go to Foxwoods! The big leagues! Catch a few floor shows, maybe a prizefight!* And they all go like this . . ." She purses her lips and shyly bows her head. "Not a peep. They're, like, embarrassed? Like somebody just farted."

Tom and I laugh. Bill, who's probably heard the story before, makes another grab at the bottle. Lisa grimaces like someone stabbed with a bellyache. "Darling, *please* . . ." She pushes his hand gently aside.

Only then, blinking two or three times, a corner of his mouth twitching, does he realize what he'd been doing. "Night-night for Billy Boy," he says, lays his hands flat on the table, and stands, announcing that he'll see us in the morning. It's a little past eight-fifteen.

"I do the same thing every time I quit smoking," Lisa says after he's gone into the bedroom and we help her clear the table. "I get so tired of fighting the urge that all I want to be is unconscious."

I say, "You don't have to apologize for him."

"I wasn't. Just explaining."

I put an arm around her waist, and her ample body yielding, she leans into me and I hold her a little longer, a little tighter than a brother would. "Don't worry. We'll watch out for him."

"Like always," Tom says.

2.

"He used you," Tom's mother scolded after the accident. "I don't care what that big-shot father of his did to make things better. He used you, and what makes me hopping mad is that you let yourself be used." She then turned to me, there on her back porch. "You, too, Paul. He uses both of you. You're not your brother's keepers."

I'd played fullback, Tom right guard, those two seasons when Bill quarterbacked for the Manitou Falls Norsemen and led us to the state championship in our division. I carried the ball on short-yardage plays; otherwise, I was a blocking back, assigned to shield our star from some slab of blitzing beef who'd penetrated the line. Like Tom and the other offensive linemen, I suffered collisions with little regard for my own health. We were all guardians of William J. Erickson, a football prodigy with a quick eye wired to a quick, strong arm. Total yardage, number of completions—he broke school records going back forty years. His talent didn't come from effort—he never tossed footballs through spare tires in the off season, that sort of thing; no, what he had was more like the grace the ministers preached about in church.

He had other unmerited blessings: son of Augustus Erickson, lawyer, state senator, later publisher of the *Register;* grandson of Olav, a Norwegian immigrant who'd ripped millions out of the northwoods by cutting them down; insufferably good-looking—six-three, with high, sharp cheekbones that lent an Ostrogothic tilt to his light-blue eyes. "A poster boy for Hitler Youth, a Nazi's wet dream," was how Tom had described him back then, smuggling a detraction into a compliment because he wasn't handsome or a born jock; he'd had to sweat to make the varsity, had to sweat for everything, his father a mill hand at the Mead paper plant. But nature had compensated for Bill's luck, making him heir to the family curse. Gus Erickson had been a legendary binger; his boy could down quantities of beer that would have left any other sixteen-year-old a puking mess, and because his capacity was coupled with a predilection for risk, the cool judgment he'd displayed on all those autumn Saturday afternoons often deserted him for the rest of the week. He liked to see what he could get away with. And he got away with quite a lot, thanks to his gift (for the gifted are usually forgiven their sins) and to his father, whose influence had been a Jaws of Life, extracting him from several wrecks. The most serious involved a certain girl in the senior class who was out of school for a few weeks after an operation, the nature of which was known but never mentioned, not in a small Midwestern town in 1972. It had been arranged and paid for by Senator Erickson.

The old man pulled Bill out of trouble; the task of preventing him from getting into it fell to Tom Muhlen and Paul Egremont, his closest friends, his blockers on and off the field. We assumed the role willingly. For one thing, it seemed natural; for another, it bought us dates with girls who otherwise might not have had anything to do with the sons of a mill worker and a hardware salesman: the daughters of Manitou Falls's tight little aristocracy of bankers, doctors, and heirs to timber and mining fortunes. We were always welcome in the Ericksons' seven-bedroom house on Michigan Avenue (which didn't resemble its Chicago namesake but nonetheless served as the town's gold coast) and were occasionally invited to stay for dinner, when we could listen to Mrs. Erickson chatter about the musical she'd seen on her last trip to New York or to the senator's tales of skippering his yacht in the Mackinac Race. This was glamour and high society to our teenage, provincial minds, and what a privilege to share in it. So, yes, it was just fine with us to be the keepers of our fortunate brother.

We'd fallen down on the job only once, on a rainy night the summer after graduation. In Tom's '63 Chevy pickup—bought with earnings from his summer job at Mead—we'd crossed into Wisconsin to celebrate the news that Bill had won a full ride to Central Michigan. Enlightened Wisconsin, where the legal drinking age was eighteen. Somehow, Bill ended up behind the wheel on the return trip, and on a deserted stretch of Highway 35 he skidded into a ditch to avoid hitting a deer. The quart of

Schlitz we'd been sharing sloshed all over us and the front seat. We climbed out unhurt and stood at the roadside to flag down a car. Two passed by; the third pulled over in a flashing of roof-rack lights. After smelling the interior, the Michigan state trooper ordered each of us to walk a straight line, then to close our eyes and touch our noses with our fingertips. Our performances made a Breathalyzer test superfluous. "Whose truck?" the trooper asked. "Mine," Tom answered. License. Registration. "You were driving?" Tom and I waited half a beat for Bill to say something, but he had lockjaw. We knew what he was thinking, because it was what we were thinking: if he was convicted, his scholarship might be revoked. Not that he needed it. Tom slurred, "Yes, sir, I was," and I confirmed the lie with an emphatic nod. Gus Erickson returned the favor by getting the charges dropped and picking up the tab for repairs to Tom's truck.

3.

Before breakfast, practicing under Lisa's supervision, I adulterate Bill's orange juice with the Zoloft.

We load the GMC and drive north through Seney, past obsolescent logging and railroad towns, through spruce and tamarack bogs, gloomy as Saxon fens even on gorgeous days like this one. Across the east branch of the Fox River, the land rises gradually, topping out in a hardwood ridge from whose crest Lake Superior shows as a blue triangle wedged between the oaks and maples crowding both sides of the road that winds downhill into Vieux Desert. The whole town is easily encompassed by the eye from above, its clapboard and shingle-sided houses, its diner, IGA, gas station, two churches, and two bars crouched along its namesake bay, aquamarine in the brilliant October light. The big lake beyond is indigo, a mock ocean reaching toward the Canadian shore, two hundred miles away.

We fill up at the gas station and buy staples at the grocery before heading toward camp along the road that skirts the bay. Superior's shoreline, unlike Lake Michigan's, hasn't advanced. I'm pleased to see it where it's supposed to be and that the town looks as charmingly shabby as it did last year and the year before and the year before that.

Bill's cabin, built for his grandfather in the late 1920s by Finnish loggers—unemployed because nearly every profitable tree in the area had already been cut down—lies at the end of the two-track, on a low bluff above the Windigo River. Varnished cedar logs; pegged, not nailed. A barbecue grill and picnic table. An outhouse. A toolshed. All of it is surrounded by an incongruous lawn maintained by a caretaker.

Tom and I lug duffels up to the loft, its rail eye level with the head of an eight-point buck mounted above the stone fireplace. Smaller racks decorate the walls, along with trout and grouse and ducks caught or shot in the long ago and an ancient photograph of Bill's grandfather, standing in the snow beside a felled white pine. The hewn trunk reaches to the top of his head, and he'd been over six feet.

In brush pants and hunting vests, we troop downstairs, where Bill is practicing gun mounts with his new 28-gauge side-by-side: a custom-made Arrieta with bouquet-and-scroll engraving on the receiver plates.

"Ready to roll, except for one thing," Tom says. "The case of wine."

Bill snaps the gun to his shoulder and swings the barrel smoothly right to left, left to right. "Bring it in."

"Sure you're cool with that?"

Bill lays the gun on his bunk, fetches the case, and sets it on the kitchen table. "Let's go."

Heading out, the crated dogs whine in anticipation. We feel

it, too—the old quickening that I've stopped trying to explain or justify to my faculty colleagues, many of whom consider my fondness for blood sport a character flaw, if not downright criminal. Reminding them that their supermarket hamburger and chicken breasts once had heartbeats has proven futile; so now, when some politically correct tyrant asks how I can shoot innocent creatures, I answer, "Can't help it. I'm less evolved than you."

We park near a jack-pine plantation, facing a plain speckled with black-cherry thickets and islands of spruce and aspen. The dogs are off, the beeper collars on Tom's Jasper and on my Erica squawking. Rory wears a bell collar because Bill is a traditionalist, even though his pointer makes long casts that take him out of hearing range. True to form, Rory sprints away, the bell's sweet jingle fading off into silence.

"That dog should be issued a passport," Tom mutters.

We find him stock-still at the edge of an aspen grove, outstretched tail rigid as a pipe. Jasper and Erica lope toward Rory and honor the point. Golden leaves trembling like candle flames, three dogs in tense arrest. It's a sight I've seen a thousand times, and the effect never varies. My pulse rate rises; a slight quivering passes through my knees. We walk up, Bill's long legs carrying him ahead. A woodcock pair whistles into the air, crossing left to right. He downs both. Rory retrieves the birds, and just as he drops the second at Bill's feet, Erica freezes out in the open. Two more woodcock take off. Tom fires twice and misses; I hit one with my second shot and am walking to it when another flushes wild almost from underfoot and flies behind me. I spin, but Bill is in the line of fire, the woodcock streaking straight at him, as though it means to poke out an eye with its long beak. It passes a yard over his head, and as it veers sharply to the left, he pivots, swinging the gun like it's his arm, and I know the bird is dead before it tumbles, trailing brown feathers. It was a tough shot that Bill made look easy. He makes everything he does look easy, except one thing.

"Well, goddamn," says Tom. "We haven't been out twenty minutes and you've got your limit of woodies."

"A flight must have come in," Bill says, meaning migratory rather than local birds. "You'll have plenty more chances." He stuffs the woodcock into his game pouch with the first two. "Had your head off the gun. That's why you missed."

"Helpful hints from Heloise."

We hunt through the morning and into the afternoon. A flight has indeed come in, riding a nor'wester down from Canada. I get my limit of woodcock, but Tom's slump continues. He practices a lot on the skeet range, labors at his shooting as he did at high school football, in the expectation that he'll one day shoot in the field like Bill, not only with accuracy but with style. On the hike back to the truck, Bill repeats his critique: "You're not tight to the gun! Damn, do you want me to shoot your limit for you?" Tom snaps that he sure as hell doesn't, and, in an anger born of frustration, finds the competence he's been seeking. When Rory points a double, he cracks both and snorts, "Shoot my limit for me, Jesus Christ."

* * *

At the cabin, we clean and pluck the birds and listen to a Green Bay game on the radio. *"Favre rolls out of the pocket . . . Connects to Driver . . . But Driver is dropped two yards short of a first . . ."* Tom groans. He's got a hundred on the Packers and three points with a friend back in Lansing, but now, late in the fourth quarter, they're losing by seven to the Giants.

"Favre will pull it out," Bill says confidently. "The last-minute miracle man. He gets better every year." There is a wistfulness in his voice.

He hadn't fulfilled expectations at Central Michigan. A concussion and a back injury benched him for one season and part of another. He healed in time but never recovered his former brilliance. I wonder, listening to his praises of Brett Favre, if he's thinking about might-have-beens. Might have been drafted into the pros. With his telegenic looks, a career as a commentator might have followed. Big money and TV glamour and no worries about squeezing a profit out of a hick newspaper with a declining circulation.

Gus Erickson, widowed and dying of liver cancer, had summoned his son from California back to Manitou Falls eight years ago to help save the *Register* from bankruptcy. I guess Bill answered the old man's call because he'd been at loose ends out on the West Coast—Joanne had left him and he'd left the Navy, having put in his twenty and been passed over for promotion twice. The senator died, and the paper fell into Bill's hands. He was going to sell it and give California another try, until a woman named Lisa Williams came to his office looking to take out a full-page ad announcing the grand opening of the Northern Suns casino. She changed his plans. When McNaughton Media offered to buy the *Register* and to keep him on as editor in chief, he said yes.

He phoned Tom and me down in Lansing to tell us that he'd returned. We were surprised to hear that the Gulf War hero, the seagoing flyboy who'd sent postcards from places like Bangkok and Naples, had moved back to our old hometown. After all, the whole point of our young lives had been to get out and stay out. We didn't see him until the following year, at our twenty-fifth high school reunion. There he was in the hospitality suite of the

Holiday Inn, his new wife at his side. He looked a little abashed, as if he thought that his repatriation had diminished him in our eyes. Or maybe the diminishment was in his own eyes. He'd lived large; now he was living not so large, a Midwest burgher with all of burgherdom's required badges—Rotary, Lions, VFW. Still, much of his old magic remained; ex-teammates and cheer-leaders, now in sagging middle age, flocked to him, Tom and me among them. We relived our youths, that time when we were all bulletproof and everything seemed possible. Tom mentioned that he and I got together to hunt birds every fall, and the next thing we knew, we invited him to join us the next season.

Adolescence is a condition no one recovers from completely. You've probably heard a story about ex–high school sweethearts who meet decades later, discover that the emotions of first love haven't faded, divorce their spouses, and pick up where they left off. In the same way, Tom and I found that our relationship with Bill hadn't changed. We fell right back into our guardian roles. For a week of nights for six autumns in a row, we made sure he didn't do grievous harm to himself, dragged him out of bars, waltzed him into bed. It got on our nerves but was nothing we couldn't put up with.

Things got more complicated after last year's outing—we bought a stake in Bill's reformation.

I was in my office, advising a student who'd made a hash of a paper on *Notes from Underground*, when Lisa phoned. It seemed that a week earlier, at a Miami conference for the satraps in McNaughton's media empire, Bill had guzzled too many vodka martinis during a poolside party and toppled into the deep end, whereupon he called for others to come on in, the water was fine. It seemed that when no one took him up on it, he climbed out, scooped the female editor of another paper into his arms, and leaped in with her, showering several onlookers.

They weren't amused. Nor was she. Well aware of Bill's problem, Four-M summoned him the next morning and said that
the only reason he didn't sack him on the spot was the difficulty
of finding a replacement—who would want to relocate to the
Upper Peninsula? Bill could spare him the trouble and keep his
job if he, one, apologized to the woman, and two, committed
himself to rehab.

He was "in denial," Lisa reported, resisting the second step:
a month in the Hazelden Clinic in Minnesota. Would Tom and
I please, *please,* come on up and help her talk him into it? And so
we did, the weekend before Thanksgiving. A root canal would
have been more fun. After she'd shown him the encouraging
brochures—*We don't just treat addictions; we restore and trans-
form lives*—he accused her of betraying a confidence by dragging us into their private affairs. Thanks but no thanks, his life
didn't need restoration or transformation. Goddamn if he would
ever submit to the ministrations of some therapist. This went
on until Lisa threatened to walk out, which prompted him to
punch a wall, fracturing his knuckles. She started crying. Bill
embraced her, blubbering, "Oh, baby, I'm sorry." Tom said,
"Fuck this and fuck you," and went outside. Lisa followed him
and was getting into her car to go who knows where when Bill
ran into the chilly night, calling, "For Chrissake, Lisa! Tom! All
right! I'll do it!"

* * *

Tom stuffs the woodcock with grapes, bastes them in garlic butter, and slaps them on the grill with the dramatic professional-
ism of a cooking-show chef. At dinner in the cramped kitchen,
under the light of a propane lamp, we talk about the dogs: the
prancing setters, the sinewy pointers, the well-trained, manage-
able ones, and the great ones that were just this side of out of

control, with a spirit and a character that training could never develop. Rory belongs to that class, his passion for the hunt bred in the bone, the look of the wolf in his eye.

Bill repeats the previous night's performance, cordially topping off our wineglasses, drinking water himself, and then tipping the empty wine bottle into an empty glass. He notices me looking at his trembling hands and is embarrassed. Long ago, his effortless proficiency drew me to him; now it's something else—the peculiar magnetism generated by the opposing poles of his mastery and this one vulnerability. I silently encourage him: *C'mon, anyone who can shoot the way you did today and who flew off aircraft carriers can do this.*

* * *

He sparkles like a showroom car the next morning, opening the propane fridge with cries of "Fuzz cutter! Bill want fuzz cutter!"

"Right there," I point at a striped glass on the table. I'd gotten out of bed early and crept down from the loft to mix the antidepressant screwdriver.

After bolting down Tom's Denver omelets, we set out into a crisp morning, hoarfrost sheathing the tree branches, shoot a few grouse, and return in the late afternoon, when the low, slanting light makes the birch and maple leaves glow neon.

The next two days are just as splendid. On the fifth, the wind shifts, cracking out of the northeast. Clouds bruise the sky, and it begins to rain. The rain turns to sleet, sleet to snow. Soaked and shivering, we shamble in early from the field. The drenched dogs flop down in front of the fireplace, where Bill builds a conflagration, whistling some Irish ballad. In his pre-rehab days, his Scandinavian ancestry notwithstanding, he would sing rousing IRA songs or melancholy airs about the green glens of Antrim as if he were an immigrant homesick for the old sod.

Amid the smells of wet clothes, wet gundogs, woodsmoke, and boot oil, we kill time playing five-and seven-card stud for quarters, enjoying the snugness of the cabin, the maple logs popping and snapping in the fireplace while the wind rattles the window frames.

"So much for global warming," Tom says when a flurry smacks the glass with a sound like spent birdshot.

"Don't start that again," Bill says.

I deal the next show cards. "Seven to the lady, no help . . . Pair of eights on the board . . . and a five to my six, possible straight. Eights are high."

Tom tosses two blue chips, representing fifty cents, into the pot and throws a challenging look at both of us. I fold. Bill stays in, draws a five, Tom a third eight. The hand progresses, and when the final hole card is dealt, Tom has the three eights and a six on the board, Bill a ten, a five, and a seven with the queen. Tom taps his skull with a forefinger while he considers if Bill, veteran of shipboard poker games, is bluffing or sandbagging him with a hidden hand. But he can't fold now and goes all in. Bill sees the bet, pushing his chips into the middle of the table. The eights are all Tom has. Bill flips his down cards. Two are queens.

"One lucky son of a bitch," Tom says, trying but failing to sound sporting and good-natured about it all. "You always were."

"Yeah?"

"Yeah."

"Well, I am. Lucky I met Lisa." He spreads his arms and reaches across the table to grip us both by the biceps. "Lucky to have friends like you two."

He is given to such mawkish demonstrations. I shove the deck at him. "Your deal."

"Yeah, friends. But sometimes friends . . ." He shuffles and sets the deck down, staring at it, forehead ridged.

"What's wrong? Find a marked card?"

"We've always been up front about everything, right?" His eyes, those eerie pale-blue eyes, swivel from me to Tom and back to me as he coaxes his lips into the half sneer, half smile that's his way of expressing an injury to his pride. It was the look he'd worn last November, when we'd shamed him into going to Hazelden.

"I saw you put something in my orange juice." He motions at his bed, from which he can see into the kitchen. "I'm pretty sure I know what and who asked you to do it and I need to hear if I'm right."

"You are," I admit after a silence.

"And I suppose she's been feeding it to me on the sly, too?"

"Right again."

"She told you everything?"

"She did," Tom says.

Bill draws in a deep breath and lets it out slowly, flapping his lips.

"Now maybe you can tell us something." Tom wedges his jaw between his fists and works up his best prosecutorial glare. "You think you're so lucky to have her, why make her—us, too—look after you when you won't look after yourself?"

"Y'know, Tom, every time you ask a question you sound like you're trying to nail a hostile witness."

"You suffer from terminal solipsism, that's why."

"Ante up," Bill says, and begins to deal. "Now, there's a word. 'Solipsism.'"

"It means self-centered."

"It means a theory that the self is the only reality that exists, but you're close enough." He passes out the first show cards.

"You don't know any more about what goes on between her and me than I do about you and Julie or Paul and Cheryl. But eff–why-eye, I do give a damn about her. And my girls. And, yeah, you dudes, too."

"You might rethink how you show giving a damn."

"Hey, listen, I'm taking care of all of them—Lisa and the girls and my ex. How's that for showing I give a damn?"

"Time out," I say, forming a T with my hands. I go upstairs for the Zoloft and plunk the bottle down in front of Bill. "All yours now."

He looks at the medication pensively, then unscrews the cap and, tilting his head backward, squeezes the dropper onto his tongue. "Tastes better without the OJ," he declares, teeth clenched into a slightly malignant grin.

*　*　*

Waking up after midnight, I get into my moccasins, switch on a flashlight, and shuffle outside to piss. The snow has stopped falling, but half an inch covers the ground. I make designs in it with my urine, the movement causing the light in my free hand to twitch back and forth. It illuminates Bill, in nothing but long johns, sitting on the top step of a staircase that leads down to the river from a small deck over the bluff. He turns as the light falls on him, squinting.

"Back was bothering me, couldn't sleep, so I thought I'd come out here and contemplate if life without a drink is worth living."

The attempt to sound jaunty doesn't quite come off. "Stay out much longer, you'll freeze to death and then you'll know."

He pats the step, inviting me to sit down. "Sorry for putting you on the spot today."

"Kind of a relief, you want to know the truth."

"Not my back. Made the mistake of calling my office voice-mail before I hit the sack. My biggest advertiser, guy who owns a heating-oil company, is having a bad year. Pulling his ads until things pick up. I'm an old jet jockey. Whatever made me think I could run a newspaper?"

I have no idea what made him think so. "It's a small-town paper. Gave you something to do," I suggest. "Run the family business."

"Doesn't answer the question. Christ, the *Register* is right back where the old man left it when he died. In intensive care. McNaughton wants to sell off his underachievers, and we're at the top of the list. He doesn't find a buyer, it goes belly up and me with it."

"You? You've got your retirement pay, the—"

"The trust?" A pause, a bitter chuckle. "Last couple of years, I've been peddling ad space at discount rates to keep everybody on board and pulling money out of it to make up the difference. Kind of embezzling from myself."

The question in my mind is, *Where did you come up with five grand for that shotgun?* What I say is, "I thought it was going to, you know, alimony, college expenses . . ."

"Lisa told you that, too? Well, it's not. It's propping up what you call the family business. That's not for public consumption. She doesn't know."

"I'm freezing my ass off."

We retreat into the cabin. He throws a log into the fireplace and blows on the embers to raise a flame. Tom is emitting snorts and gasps and whistles from the loft above.

"Paul," Bill begins in an undertone. "Have you ever . . . Did you ever feel . . ." He trails off and strikes a pose, looking down into the fire, palms flat against the river-rock mantelpiece.

"Did I ever feel what?"

"Ah, nothing. Forget it." He twists his head to look at me, one cheek in shadow, the other burnished in the quivering light. "Guess I was wrong. Favre didn't pull it out."

* * *

I wake up late, panic-stricken because I haven't gotten out of bed early to administer the Zoloft. Then I remember that I'm now free of that responsibility. Bill's emotional pendulum has made a wide swing, so wide that I wonder if he's experiencing a delayed reaction to yesterday's double dose. He's almost giddy, staging a comical show as he twirls the dropper over his orange juice with a magician's flourish.

After breakfast, he flies into the next room, opens a storage closet, and pulls out a gun we've seen him shoot only once or twice in the past: Grandpa Olav's shotgun, a 12-gauge L. C. Smith with double triggers and exposed hammers. It must be nearly a hundred years old. "A proposition, gentlemen! After yesterday's confinement, I've got cabin fever, so we'll have dinner in town. If I can't outshoot the two of you put together with this thing, chow and beverages are on me. Otherwise on you. Are you on?"

He cranes his neck toward me, fixing me with a direct and confidential gaze—it's as if Tom isn't even in the room. A coded message flashes in that look: he isn't expecting an answer to his sporting challenge; he expects me to keep last night's conversation to myself, and that's what I do.

4.

Friday night. A fleet of dirty pickup trucks and SUVs are nosed up to the front of the Great Lakes Brew Pub. Under the water-stained ceiling and the blind stares of a bobcat, a coyote, two ratty-skinned bucks, and a snarling black bear mounted on the walls along with vintage logging tools, more people than will be seen in church on Sunday morning are eating and drinking, playing pool, or watching football previews on the two TVs flickering above each end of the long bar: hefty middle-age couples visiting for a weekend of leaf-peeping, a few locals—commercial fishermen, pulp loggers—bird hunters wearing orange caps, and bowhunters dressed like Special Ops commandos in woodsy camouflage.

We stand near the door, waiting for seats to open up. Bill orders a non-alcoholic beer, Tom and I a couple of drafts. Bill drains his bottle in three long pulls, calls for another, and is halfway through it when four customers vacate the bar. We barge through the crowd to claim the empty stools. Bill lays down two twenties—he lost his wager, having shot two grouse to our combined three—and then goes off to the men's room. When he comes back five minutes later, Will Treadwell, the owner, takes our orders. Pizzas and drafts for Tom and me. Whitefish and another near-beer for Bill. Treadwell looks at him as if he hasn't heard right; he's known Bill a long time but doesn't know about his stay in Hazelden.

"I'm in recovery," Bill explains. "I was recently diagnosed with solipsism, and now I'm getting over it."

Treadwell clutches a bottle of O'Doul's in a fist that, many years ago, had done damage in Kronk's gym in Detroit and that, despite his fifty-four years, still looks capable of fracturing a jaw. "No idea what you're talking about, but congratulations anyway," he says, and spins away to tend to another customer.

By the time the food arrives, Bill has consumed two more O'Doul's and gone to the men's room again. He knocks back a third with dinner, and then, with his whitefish only half eaten, he pushes off for yet another pit stop.

"Better get your prostate checked," Tom says to his back.

While Bill's gone, Treadwell falls into an argument with Tom about the presidential campaign. Treadwell fought with the Marines in Vietnam and calls himself a "left-wing survivalist" to describe his politics and lifestyle—he and his half-Ojibwa wife live in the woods, sustaining themselves on what she cans and what he shoots or hooks. Tom, the ardent Republican—he's running unopposed for a second term as Ingham County prosecutor—is carrying on about the Swift Boat Veterans for Truth, exposing Kerry "for the fraud he is." Treadwell counters that they're neither truthful nor swift and probably aren't even veterans, "like your chubby vice president, the guy who didn't go to Vietnam because he had other priorities."

Tom sputters, "He's *your* vice president, too. Or have you renounced your citizenship?"

"I might do that if Bush and Dickbrain get reelected."

Tom has no comeback. Treadwell bares large, straight teeth in a cartoon smile. "You rose to the fly like a retarded brook trout."

"Ha!" Bill, returning from the men's room, bangs his palm on the bar. "Tha's good! Retarded brook trout! A nighty-nightcap, Will. One more bottle of your finest Irish fakery."

"Finest Irish" comes out as "fineish arish," and Treadwell looks at him quizzically as he dips into the cooler. The bottle is soon drained, "a dead shoulder," Bill proclaims, and waves an index finger to and fro as he sings, *"Now we are all dead and gone, for we are the arish, now we are all dead and gone, for we are the arish shoulders . . ."*

A young, hulking bowhunter in a knit cap and jacket printed with leaves and branches looms over the jukebox, punching buttons. "The Wreck of the Edmund Fitzgerald" drowns out Bill's Celtic ditty . . .

> *The legend lives on from the Chippewa on*
>> *down*
> *Of the big lake they call Gitche Gumee . . .*

"Hate thish fucking song."

It's now perfectly clear that Bill's prostate isn't what's been sending him to the bathroom. Tom snarls in disgust, "*Goddamn* you, Erickson," as Bill spins off the barstool and lurches to the jukebox . . .

> *The lake, it is said, never gives up her dead*
> *When the skies of November turn gloomy . . .*

. . . and, reaching behind the machine, jerks the plug.

"Fuck Gordon Lightfoot! I give you Longfellow!" he hollers into the sudden quiet, and begins to recite *The Song of Hiawatha* at bullhorn level. "*From the forests and the prairies/ From the great lakes of the Northland/ From the land of the Ojibways . . .*" Slurring the "j" and every "s."

Some customers look at him nonplussed; some giggle at the impromptu show. The bowhunter and his buddies aren't laughing. Tom and I aren't, either. Maybe we would be if we hadn't gone through the trouble of getting him into rehab, if we hadn't made that pledge to Lisa; now, watching the failure of our mission, we feel that Bill is making fools of us as he makes one of himself, flinging his arms like a nineteenth-century thespian. "*From the land of the Dacotahs/ From the mountains, moors, and fenlands/ Where the heron, the Shuh-shuh . . .* the Shuh-shuh . . . the wha'ever the fuck . . ."

"Let's get him home," Tom says, acid in his voice.

But before we can get to him, the brawny archer stiff-arms Bill into a wall. He slides to the floor, bellowing, "The Shuh-

shuh-gah! Tha's it, the Shuh-shuh-gah . . . *Feeds among the reeds and rushes . . .*" while the bowhunter muscles the jukebox with the ease of a furniture mover, plugs it back in, and pumps quarters into the slot. With Gordon Lightfoot again mourning the *Edmund Fitzgerald,* he stomps back to his table. Treadwell comes out from behind the bar and points an aluminum billy at him. "No trouble out of you, friend."

The bowman gestures at Bill. "That asshole's the trouble."

Tom and I are wrestling Bill to his feet, and in the struggle a hip flask falls out of his jacket pocket. Treadwell picks it up, and with the billy jammed in his belt, escorts us toward the door, past the bowhunters' table. I'm nearest to it, Bill between Tom and me. I don't see the Gordon Lightfoot fan stick out a leg, only the insolent look on his face as I stumble and Bill crashes facedown onto the pine-board floor.

"Hey, dickhead," Tom says. "You made your point before."

He jumps up, all bulk and youthful leverage. "You want a problem, here I am."

What amazes me is that Tom is ready to go toe-to-toe with him. All I can think of is how undignified it will be for a district attorney to appear in court and a professor of Russian literature to return to classes with their eyes blackened or noses broken in a northwoods bar brawl, when Treadwell intervenes. Pushing Tom aside, he bangs the club on the table.

"You've got the problems. You're eighty-sixed. Pay up."

You can almost see the bowhunter's brain making quick calculations. One old man versus four of them. But the club, the heavyweight's shoulders, the scarred knuckles, the bared forearm thick as an average man's calf, bearing a tattoo of a bayonet thrust through a skull's eye sockets, and the banner under the skull's jaw—*USMC. Death Before Dishonor*—counsel discretion. He slaps a twenty and a ten on the table and leaves with his fellow archers. The jukebox is now mute, the whole place as hushed as a theater at curtain rise.

A waitress scoops up the bills, glances at the tab, and groans, "They owed thirty-six fifty."

Treadwell promises to make up the difference and add a tip, then gives us a hand hauling Bill into an upright position. He grins stupidly, a red lump rising on his forehead. Treadwell twists the cap on the silver flask engraved with Bill's initials, shakes out a few drops into his palm, and licks. "Scotch" he says, handing the flask to me. Then to Bill: "No private stock allowed. You're eighty-sixed, too."

* * *

He is the last out of bed—no surprise there. He shambles to the small mirror above the kitchen sink, delicately presses the bruise above his right eye with a forefinger, and claims to have no memory of how it got there or of the events preceding its acquisition. I'm skeptical about the amnesia but give him a summary nonetheless. Tom introduces the evidence. Exhibit A: the flask. Exhibit B: a bottle of Johnnie Walker, half empty.

"Found the scotch in your duffel last night. Didn't have time to get a search warrant, sorry."

"All right, all right."

"The part I like was that sanctimonious speech. About being up front? I really like that."

"I said, *all right*."

"We promised Lisa, so it's not all right," I say. "It's about three time zones from all right."

"We would've gotten our asses handed to us if Treadwell hadn't been there." Tom points the bottle of scotch in his face for emphasis. "You're a selfish guy, Bill."

"Terminally solipsistic, right."

Tom's upper lip quivers, and though it's chilly with no fire going, beads of sweat glitter on his scalp. "Booze isn't your problem. You're a poor little rich boy, that's your problem. You've always had somebody to run interference for you and clean up behind you. Your dad, your wives, your friends. Who did that when you were a flyboy? Some enlisted flunky?"

"I apologize, okay?" says Bill sullenly. "Sorry for letting you down. I . . ." He frowns as if in thought, then grabs Johnnie Walker by the neck, empties it into the sink, and dramatically holds it over the trash can before dropping it in. "My last drink, solemn promise."

It sounds more like an appeal than an oath. Tom, in the righteous tones of a cuckold telling his wife they're through, says that it's a little late for promises.

Bill asks, "Are you done now?"

Tom shrugs and smirks, petulantly, it seems to me.

"I'll take that as a yes," Bill says. "Last night was last night, and today's today, and it's our last day." He goes to his jacket, hanging by a peg above his bunk, plucks a map from a pocket, and waves it around like it's a winning lottery ticket. "The honey hole I told you about. Let's try to close out in style."

* * *

Low clouds, patched with blue, glide on a light northerly breeze. Clear sky shows far out over Superior, ruffled with whitecaps. The climate inside the truck is far darker. Tom, at the wheel, doesn't speak. He's not quite through punishing Bill, letting him know, through his silence, that he's been betrayed. Remembering his readiness to trade punches with the bowhunter, a thought enters my mind: his attachment to Bill is more complicated than mine. He likes playing the part of his anointed-but-wayward brother's protector, however much he complains about it. Bill's weakness is, as it's always been, the one thing that makes Tom feel superior.

Ten or twelve miles south of town, we turn onto a wide dirt road that runs straight as a surveyor's transit across a plain studded with the stumps of white pine cut down decades ago. Two miles in, the desolation ends in a forest of beech and maple. Tom slams the brakes, the truck slewing in the mud. Leaning between the two front seats, I see what appears, at first glance, to be a doe, facing us from the road some fifty or sixty yards ahead. Then it turns broadside, long-legged, gray-black in the dull light, furred tail pointed like a semaphore.

"Paul! My camera! In the bag on the floor!"

But by the time I pass it to Tom, the wolf is gone. A moment later, as he fumbles to snap a long lens into place, two more cross the road at an easy lope, and then another and another.

"A pack!" Tom shouts. "A whole pack in broad daylight! I've never seen that before!"

The acid in his mood has been neutralized, the toxic atmosphere dispelled. For the next couple of minutes, we babble excitedly about our good luck. We're friends again, which inclines me to regard the sighting as less a matter of luck and more as a blessing, the wild's benediction.

Following the crude map, we leave the gravel road and bounce down a rutted two-track that hits a dead end where decked pulp logs lie rotting. The dogs are sprung, and we set out on foot into a woods still damp from melting snow, cross a swamp thick as split-pea soup, and hike up a hardwood ridge. Below, an archipelago of spruce and aspen stands mottles a broad pale-brown meadow. And that, says Bill, is the honey hole.

The dogs quarter out ahead, Rory way in front. He stops

dead in front of a hazel thicket. Jasper and Erica honor, all three studies in complete concentration. Bill stands well behind Tom and me, making up for his bad behavior by giving us first crack at the bird. It goes up with the thundering sound characteristic of grouse, a sound that never fails to startle. At Tom's shot, it tips sideways and falls. The dogs remain staunch. A single explodes from the thicket. Two shots, two misses, and still the dogs hold fast. This is astonishing—there must be two coveys in the thicket. Bill cocks the hammers on his gun, figuring that he's been gracious enough. Two more birds take off, going straightaway, and he drops them. Half a second after he's reloaded, another pair bursts from cover, streaking over the meadow, one just behind the other. Bill shifts his stance, twists his body, and the gun barrels seems to paint the sky in a smooth, elegant stroke, the shots following so closely that they sound almost as one. Both birds tumble in a fall at once thrilling and tragic. To shoot a grouse pair with a modern firearm is rare; to shoot two consecutive doubles with an antique is a feat that we'd talk about for years. Watching him pull that off so effortlessly was like seeing him, years ago, rifle a pass through double coverage. If we hadn't already forgiven him for last night, we did now.

Two hours and some miles later, he kills a fifth for his limit. Tom and I have four each, all but two mature birds, fat as chickens, their black-banded tails fanning out to a hand's span. We take a break.

"A honey hole all right," Tom says, picking a burr out of Jasper's coat. "Look, Bill, what I said this—"

Sitting against a hemlock, Bill waves a hand to say, *Forget it*.

"Helluva day. The wolves; you dropping two doubles in a row. One *helluva* day."

"Can't imagine having a better one," Bill murmurs, then stands and drapes a comradely arm over Tom's shoulders. "You guys need one apiece for your limit. That'll make it el perfecto."

We hunt our way back toward the truck, and after covering most of the distance, Erica and Jasper stop hunting seriously, contenting themselves to trot in a straight line. Rory, catching some scent on the wind, jogs across a cranberry bog and vanishes into the woods beyond. We follow his ever-fading bells to the T-junction of two skid trails, one leading toward the truck, the other into an overgrown clear-cut, a treacherous snarl of aspen sticks dense as a bamboo jungle, of brush-filled potholes, slash piles, hidden stumps, felled tree trunks. The wind has risen; leaves swirl in the air. Rory's bells have gone silent; either he's run out of hearing range or he has another point.

"All yours," Bill says.

"Forget the limit," I say. "We're done; our dogs are done. No way we're going to tromp through that crap."

Bill stares into the clear-cut for at least five seconds before he says, "Well, I'd better go find him. Wait for me here."

5.

The investigator's name is Ron Jankowski, and he's built like a snowman—no chin, no neck, round torso squeezed into a chair facing Tom's desk. A file folder lies open on his lap, and a small notebook is lost in his huge white hand.

"Let's start," he says, and places a tape recorder on the desk. "All right, so, you saw Mr. Erickson step into a pile of . . ." He looks down at the Schoolcraft County sheriff's incident report. ". . . a pile of slash. It covered a hole, kind of like camouflage over an animal trap. It gave way under his weight, he tripped, the shotgun struck the ground, and it discharged into his chest. Is that right?"

From behind his desk, flanked by the American flag and state flags, Tom scowls thoughtfully. "Not quite."

"How 'not quite'?"

"We didn't *see* it happen."

Jankowski snaps a finger against the report. "This says you witnessed the accident."

There is a note in his voice that encloses the last word in quotes.

"Well, I suppose that's just a figure of speech," Tom explains. "On the sheriff's part, not ours."

"This scenario, then, it's speculation on *your* part?"

He glances my way as he asks the question. I'm seated on the sofa, beneath Tom's framed law degree and photographs of him with the governor and assorted dignitaries. More than a week has passed since the memorial service, at which Tom and I delivered eulogies and tried not to look at Lisa, sitting in the front pew next to Bill's daughters. Jankowski wanted to interview us separately, presumably to catch inconsistencies in our accounts. Tom insisted that he talk to both of us in his office in the Ingham County building. It would put him on the defensive: the flags, the photos, the view of the state-capitol dome, the nameplate on the door. But Jankowski—he's a freelance private eye who snoops for several insurance companies in addition to Midstates Mutual—doesn't appear to be on the defensive. Not on the offensive, either. Only doing his job, which is to save his client a great deal of money.

"It's what made sense to us," I reply. "We heard a shot, then another, not as loud. Like he was farther away. Like he'd fired at a bird and missed and chased it for a re-flush. When he didn't come back, we went in to look for him, and when we found him, we figured he'd stepped into the slash pile and fell or tripped and the gun went off . . ."

Tom had rehearsed me—he's an expert at witness preparation—and I'm telling the same story I told the sheriff and Bill's own newspaper—and Lisa. I've told it often enough that I almost believe it myself.

"And he had a bad back, you know," I add. "So it could be that when—"

Jankowski interrupts with a dismissive gesture. "He was an experienced hunter. He didn't have the safety on?"

This gives Tom an opportunity to discourse on antique firearms. Bill, he explains, would have cocked the exposed hammer on the second barrel before shooting. When he stumbled and the gun butt hit the ground, the impact tripped the hammer, or a branch hooked the trigger. Either way, it was just terrible luck that the barrel was pointed at his chest.

As if he's pleased with his show of expertise, a faint smile passes across Tom's lips, then fades, quick as smoke. Jankowski scribbles in his notebook. His eyes are hidden, tiny lumps of coal buried in his snowman's face. I can't tell if he finds the story plausible.

* * *

After we'd found Bill's body, we dragged him out of the entangling brush, his mouth wide open, teeth bared, a ragged cavity in the middle of his chest, about the diameter of a grapefruit; it looked as if some small, ferocious animal had gnawed through him from the inside out. My experience of violent death limited to the blank pistols fired in Chekhov plays, to the decorous expiration of the mortally wounded Prince Bolkonsky, the sight made me sick; yet my eyes were manacled to it, for there before me was a body that mere minutes ago had been someone I'd known all my life, who could think and speak and feel and was now only insentient matter. Tom was calm, inappropriately calm. True, he'd seen worse things, but this wasn't a stranger in a police photograph or on a morgue slab. He removed his belt and buckled it through Rory's collar for a leash and handed it to me. I wiped the gore from Rory's nose with a bandanna. It would have been nice if, like a dog in a fairy tale, he had lain down faithfully beside his fallen master instead of lapping up his blood, but he was only a dog, thirsty and starved for protein after so much hard running.

A minute or two passed in total silence until Tom, pointing at the slash pile—it would not have deceived an experienced eye—said under his breath, "He would've known better than to step into that with a cocked hammer."

His thoughts were running ahead of mine. Really, I was too stunned to think at all, but when he asked, "When did Lisa say he took out those policies?" my brain unlocked.

"May; I think she said May," I said. "He might have been in worse trouble than we knew about."

"How so?"

I lifted the embargo on the late-night conversation I'd had with Bill. No point in keeping it secret any longer.

"There's going to be questions," Tom said after he'd digested my intelligence.

He walked around the corpse, pausing to study some detail with the dispassion of an evidence tech examining a crime scene. When he finished, he looked off into the middle distance, then went into full lawyerly mode and crafted the narrative we would present to whoever had those questions.

"Are you with me, Paul?"

I answered that I was. After all, his version sounded more believable than the alternative. Bill couldn't have choreographed the whole thing, planned it out ahead of time, planned to have Rory run off into those woods.

"There's still going to be questions. The books are full of stories about guys who'd been thinking about it for a long time, then all of a sudden drive off the road at sixty miles an hour right into a tree. It might have gone down something like that. He saw the circumstances were just right, and time was running out. Our last day. He knew he could count on us."

"That's why he told us to wait for him, that's why he fired the first shot?" I asked.

"Listen, none of that makes any difference, and maybe it *was* an accident. . . ."

"I don't think it was, Tom. And neither do you."

"Whatever, let's keep Lisa and his girls in mind. We're gonna say what we're gonna say for their sakes, not his, okay?"

Breaking the news to Lisa had been the hardest part. It was the hardest thing either of us had ever done. I'll never forget leaving her in that house alone, with what I knew to be a lie. If she believed it, it was only because she needed to. Bill may have convinced himself that he was doing the best thing for her and his daughters, but there was no more forgiving him.

* * *

Jankowski has stopped writing. He clicks his tongue, looks at Tom. "How would you describe Mr. Erickson's state of mind?"

"His what?" Tom asks, feigning surprise.

"If you don't mind, Mr. Muhlen. I've done my homework."

"Then you know what the coroner's report said. Death caused by blah-de-blah due to the apparent accidental discharge of blah-de-blah."

Jankowski stabs the air with his pen. "That wasn't my question."

Tom ponders for a couple of seconds. "Well, only an hour

before, he said he'd had the best day of his life. What does that tell you about his state of mind?"

Tom is improvising, spinning Bill's actual words, certainly the truest he'd ever spoken. Jankowski turns to me, leaning forward as far as his bulging gut will allow. "And what did you hear him say, Mr. Egremont?"

It is Lisa I have in mind; it's her stricken face I see when I answer.

GRIEF

The photograph was taken the summer after his father's war. It's a black-and-white that shows the family on the beach of a northern lake, pine trees picketing the background. Jeff's mother wears a one-piece swimsuit that hugs her like a girdle; his father is in baggy patterned trunks. Between them, in a diaper, Jeff stands on bowed, chubby legs. His parents hold him by the hands, and because both are tall, his arms are raised high, as if in surrender to the adults towering over him.

"Look at you, a little guy. Couldn't stand on your own long enough to pose for a picture," Hal says. "That beach, that's where you took your first steps. Right there." He taps the strip of sand in the foreground with a finger. Emphatic taps, as if he's indicating the site of an event worthy of a historical marker: HERE, IN JULY 1946, JEFFREY HAVLICEK TOOK HIS FIRST STEPS. "You waddled three, four feet, then flopped back down to all fours and crawled to the water like a goddamn little turtle."

Jeff presents a hesitant smile, certain that the affection in

Hal's voice is for the toddler in the photo, not for the man he grew up to be.

Father and son are in the motel dining area—with its self-service counter and paper plates and cups, it can't be called a dining room—eating the "free hot breakfast" advertised in the lobby. They are on their way to hunt deer in the Upper Peninsula, but the point won't necessarily be to shoot anything. The point will be to give Jeff's younger brother and sisters a break from looking after their difficult father. All three live near their childhood home in Bloomfield Hills, which Hal refuses to leave for the retirement community they found for him in Florida. Golf course, activities, the company of people his own age. "A nursing home is what it is," he said, and nobody was going to kennel him in some goddamn nursing home where seniors watch TV not knowing what's on. For the past year, Jerry, Jennifer, and June (it had been their mother's idea to give her kids names beginning with "J") have made sure that he gets a call from at least one of them every day. They've taken turns inviting him to dinner on Sundays, when the woman who does his cooking and cleaning is off; they've chauffeured and shopped for him and put up with his complaints. And what has Jeff done? Nothing more than phone every now and then from New York. Time he did his share. *Take him with you.*

Jeff objected at first. He and Hal don't get along, haven't for, oh, it must be forty years now. And besides—hunting? With a man of eighty-five with failing eyesight? But his siblings wore him down. It would do the old man good to get out of that house. He'd loved to hunt when he was younger. Maybe, in the woods, he'd forget his loss for a little while. A kind of holiday from grief.

Jeff's plan had been to drive due north and across the Mackinac Bridge into the U.P., but when they left, yesterday morning,

Hal demanded that they go the long way, around the tip of Lake Michigan, past Chicago, and up through Wisconsin. He wanted to make a pilgrimage to the beach at Lake Gogebic and—if they found it—stand where he'd stood with his wife and infant son nearly sixty years ago. Jeff didn't see how that was going to help him forget, but he agreed just to be agreeable.

All they have to guide them on their quest are Hal's unreliable memory and the photograph. Hal lifts it from the table and, holding it at arm's length, tilts his chin to focus through his trifocals.

"She was a beauty, wasn't she?" he murmurs.

"You were pretty good-looking yourself," Jeff remarks, trying to steer the conversation in another direction.

"With that face and that figure and the way she could swim—boy, could she swim!—she could've been another Esther Williams."

"But then she would've gone to Hollywood, run off with Tarzan. The guy who played Tarzan, the swimmer."

"Johnny Weissmuller. Won the Olympics. Esther Williams wasn't in Tarzan. Maureen O'Sullivan played Jane."

"A joke. I meant, if Mom became a movie star, you'd never have met her."

"How the hell do you know? Some things are meant to be, no matter what."

Jeff decides not to argue with destiny.

"It was her father," Hal goes on. "Kept her under lock and key. Those brothers of hers could do as they pleased, but not her. She wanted to try out for the Aquacade, like Esther Williams did. He wouldn't let her." Jeff cannot remember how many times he's heard this story. "I don't know, maybe in those days, if I had a daughter that pretty, I'd've done the same thing. Look at her."

He does as he's been told, as though he's reverted to the

obedient boy he'd once been. At first, he tries to find in the Hal of today—the bottle-bottom glasses, the stooped shoulders, the horseshoe of gray hair over his elongated ears, plugged with hearing aids—some resemblance to the Hal of the photo. If it's hard to see any, it's impossible to connect the last image he has of his mother—her body wasted by cancer, her mind by dementia, her vacant eyes staring from a face veneered in translucent flesh—with the glamorous young woman he's gazing at now. Her blond hair, dazzling in the sunlight, partly veils one eye, so that she appears to be winking; that and the slight cant of her head and her coy smile give her the coquett-ish allure of a 1940s pinup girl.

Jeff, of course, had never thought of his mother as a sexual being. Now, looking at her as she was, he can imagine the effect she must have had on Technical Sergeant Harold Havlicek when, on a weekend pass from Fort Leonard Wood, he met her at a USO dance in St. Louis. The urgent desire, heightened by the war.

Ellen Fancher, only daughter of a prominent St. Louis lawyer, came home gushing about the tall blond-haired sergeant with whom she'd danced every dance. She and Hal dated every week-end he could get away. Her father warned her not to do any-thing foolish. The war was making young people crazy, and she was very young—eighteen. She paid no heed, and in the autumn of 1944, when Hal's engineer battalion was ordered to France, they decided to get married. He asked for her father's blessing. Differences in class and background meant something then, and Roland Fancher, Esquire, refused. His baby girl marry the son of bohunk immigrants? A soldier-boy she hardly knew, and not even an officer?

They eloped about a week before he shipped out. That was the story they'd told, the story their kids believed all their lives, until Jeff and one of his sisters, Jennifer, discovered it wasn't true.

He hands the photo back to his father, who sticks it in a greeting-card envelope and into his jacket pocket.

"Good thing this breakfast is free. That's the right price," Hal says, stabbing the scrambled eggs with his fork. "They're rubbery as nutty-putty. Powdered eggs. Just like the eggs they dished out in the service."

He makes one of his distinctive gestures, a little bit of a wave, a little bit of a swat, that expresses his disgust not only with his breakfast but with the world in general. Nothing, absolutely nothing, has been right since his wife's death.

"Powdered eggs on a plastic plate, and you eat them with a plastic fork. Everything's artificial."

"Finish up, Dad. We need to get going."

"What's your rush? If that beach is still there, it's still there. It's not going anywhere."

Hal is a contrarian even with himself. Instead of taking his time, he digs in and in about two minutes polishes off the inferior eggs, the substandard sausage patties, and the English muffin, which he gives a one-star customer review.

* * *

Near Green Bay, Jeff leaves the interstate to follow a two-lane westward. The road is an artifact from the days of tailfins and chrome bumpers, and the towns it passes through are likewise relics, each one with a sign directing travelers to its HISTORIC BUSINESS DISTRICT, where little in the way of buying and selling is conducted nowadays, commerce having long since migrated to the malls in larger towns or to the Internet. Patches of woods flash by; harvested cornfields mown to stubble or with stalks still standing, dry and brown. They are cultivated by corporate farmers, those fields. The family farms he remembers from his boyhood, when his father took him on hunting trips, vanished years ago.

The last pilot Jeff pitched for a new crime series set in El Paso died in the womb. *Not edgy enough,* the network execs said. *Would've been fine in the eighties, but now it would come off as quaint.* And sometimes did he detect, in the way the industry's young, tech-savvy up-and-comers spoke to him, a kind of respectful condescension? Two shows he'd produced for cable had been nominated for Emmys; but, like an aging quarterback, he was esteemed for past glories, emphasis on "past."

His father's voice intrudes.

"Wausau. That's where we lived the summer after Gogebic." He flaps a hand at a highway sign: CLINTONVILLE 9 MI. WAUSAU 65 MI. "You wouldn't remember. That boardinghouse I had to put us in till I found a rental. Loggers stayed there when they came out of their winter camps, and—"

"Mom was pregnant with Jerry and the only woman in the place, besides the old lady who ran it," Jeff interrupts to remind Hal that this is another tale he's heard before. "Everybody ate at the same table, and the lumberjacks couldn't take their eyes off Mom, but they were real gentlemen. Never made any moves on her, never used bad language in front of her."

"I'd be at work, she'd be taking care of you. Nobody to talk to except that old lady. But she made the best of it. You remember that cabin on Lake Chetek? You gotta remember that. You weren't a baby by then."

"I was eleven."

They fall into a call-and-response.

"No indoor plumbing. A jack-handle pump over the sink," Hal says.

"The outhouse stunk. Shit and lime."

"Power going out in storms. Kerosene lamps at night."

"And bears knocking over our garbage cans."

"She made the best of that, too. Sometimes I felt rotten, putting her through all that, a girl who'd grown up in a house with four bathrooms and a cook and a maid."

Hal had been a semi-itinerant machinist for the Standard Container Company, working in its Detroit plant in the winter, on the road from May to October, journeying to canneries and breweries in Wisconsin and Michigan to service the machinery that filled Standard's cans with the land's bounty, its bottles with beer. In June, his wife and children joined him, spending their summers in whatever place he'd found to rent in whatever territory he'd been assigned. And that was how the lawyer's daughter had gone from a life with a cook and a maid to the Wausau boardinghouse and a succession of cabins and cottages in the sticks.

"She was a saint to put up with it," Hal rolls on. "If I'd gone to college on the G.I. Bill, got an engineering degree, I'd've given her a better life."

"Well, you did later on, in your own way." The beatifying of his mother somehow annoys Jeff. "Hey, can we make a pact not to talk and talk about Mom for the rest of the trip?"

"You don't want to talk about your own mother?"

"I want you to get your mind off her for a little while."

"Jesus H.! We were married for sixty-one years! And I'm supposed to get my mind off her?"

Sixty years, Jeff thinks.

He and Jennifer had been going through their mother's things after the funeral, deciding what to keep, what to give or throw away, when she came across some old letters, bundled in a shoebox with a marriage certificate, signed by a justice of the peace and dated October 17, 1945, soon after Hal returned from overseas.

"Well, holy sweet Jesus. I always knew you were a bastard, now I can prove it," Jennifer said after they read the letters, those from their mother bearing the return address of *Evangeline Home for Girls.*

He was surprised but not shocked. In fact, because he'd always considered his parents boringly conventional, it thrilled him to find documented evidence of one kink in their otherwise ruler-straight lives. Drama being his business, he couldn't resist casting a cinematic light on them and himself, the love child born of a wartime romance.

What did shock him was the secret concealed by the secret of their marriage, the box within the box. Ellen's father had cloistered her, expecting that she would give up her baby for adoption. It seemed that she and Hal agreed that that would be best. Then, only weeks before her due date, she'd had a change of heart, writing that she couldn't go through with the adoption, Daddy's wishes be damned, Daddy be damned. Jeff could almost hear the plea that she'd been too demure, or too wise, to state directly. Hal wrote back from the battlefield, pledging to *do the right thing* as soon as he got home.

That explained why the Havlicek children had seen so little of their maternal grandparents when they were growing up: their father had compounded the sin of knocking up Roland Fancher's baby girl by marrying her. But the find raised more questions than it answered. Did Hal feel that he'd been trapped into marriage? And what would his, Jeff's, life have been like if he'd been adopted? And did his parents perpetuate their fiction of elopement not because they were ashamed of his illegitimate birth but to hide the fact that they'd been willing, almost up to the moment he came into the world, to give him up?

"Don't you dare ask him; don't you even think of mentioning we've seen this stuff," Jennifer said, drawing a finger across her lips. "Promise?"

* * *

They drive without talking into Clintonville, then turn north on U.S. 45. After another sign appears—GOGEBIC 10 MI.—Hal breaks the silence.

"Y'know, I'm not sure you ever appreciated your mother the way you should."

"Don't start."

"You didn't cry at her funeral. And that eulogy you gave. It sounded like . . . You sounded like . . ."

"A newscaster reading the obituary of somebody he didn't know. You've told me that. More than once."

Out of the corner of his eye, Jeff catches the movement—the half wave, half swat—and it comes to him that his failure to show sufficient sorrow—another of his shortcomings as a son—is what the old man has been leading up to all along.

"I didn't get all choked up because I was relieved that she didn't have to suffer anymore," he explains, bothered that he has to, knowing that his reasons were more complicated than that.

"She wasn't suffering. She didn't know what the hell was going on. Maybe you were relieved that you wouldn't have to fly in from New York every month to visit her."

Jeff feels a flush of anger, which he represses. "Are you trying to piss me off?" is all he says.

"We piss each other off."

There isn't the slightest suggestion in Hal's remark that things could ever be any different between them.

The time when they were different has been all but lost to memory. Jeff has fuzzy recollections of himself as a small boy, running to the front door when his father came off the road in the fall, crying out, "Daddy's home!" and feeling the strong hands raise him into the air, the stubbled cheek rubbing his. Or, some years later, calling from curbside as he watched Hal march in a Memorial Day parade, "Hey, Dad! Over here!" to make him turn so others would see the medals arrayed on his chest, the proud shine of the "V"-for-Valor device pinned to his Bronze Star.

*   *   *

At a gas-station convenience store in Gogebic, Jeff picks up a map of the lake. They drive around it for the next hour; it isn't small—twenty miles of shoreline, the map notes. Hal sees nothing familiar, no landmarks to jog his memory. All he remembers is that the lakeshore was less developed in 1946; now it's ringed by resorts, cottages, summer homes. He falls into a morose silence, feeling disappointed and cheated. Jeff, determined to come through for him, despite his misgivings about this expedition, returns to the convenience store with the map and the photograph.

"The woman inside said it's probably the beach at the county park," he says when he's back in the car. He opens the map and points to a spot on the north side of the lake. "She told me we probably missed it because you can't see it from the main road."

It takes a quarter of an hour to drive to the park. Hal gets out of the truck in stages: he plants one foot firmly on the ground and holds on to the open door to make sure he has his balance before he tries the other foot. His first few steps are a shuffle, until he's worked the stiffness out of his knees and is able to pick up a stride.

They walk through a campground for trailers and RVs— only one site is occupied, by a camper-truck—and onto the beach.

It, too, is deserted, except for a young couple scanning the lake with binoculars. "Oh! Goldeneyes," the woman says, pointing at ducks paddling in a reed bed. Birdwatchers.

Hal shambles to the water's edge and looks up and down the shoreline and across the lake. Rippled by a light breeze under the dull November sky, it resembles a sheet of corrugated tin.

"So is this it?" Jeff asks.

His father nods, then calls out, "Ellen, it's Jeff and me. Do you see us?"

Lowering her binoculars, the young woman turns toward him. "Pardon?"

Hal ignores her and starts walking along the beach. She throws a puzzled look at Jeff, who pauses and signals her, with a flutter of his hand, to pay no attention.

"I thought he was talking to me," she says. "My name is Helen."

"It's Ellen. He said Ellen," Jeff answers, without explaining that Ellen is a ghost.

He catches up with his father, still engaged in the one-way conversation. He's telling the ghost that he found it . . . the beach on Lake Gogebic where their oldest took his first steps . . .

Jerry had prepared him for something like this. *He'll be watching TV or eating dinner, whatever, and he'll start talking to her. It's like a séance, except the spirit doesn't answer.* But Jeff was not to be alarmed; their father wasn't losing touch with reality. *He'll say a few words to her, then snap out of it and go back to whatever he was doing.*

And as Hal falls into small talk—the weather, what he'd seen on the drive, the motel's crummy breakfast, sounding as if he's on the phone—Jeff is not alarmed, just a little anxious that if he allows him to go on much longer, the old man *will* lose touch with reality.

"Okay, we got here," Jeff interrupts. "Mission accomplished. Let's get back on the road."

Hal hesitates, glancing up at migrating ducks strung out like tendrils of drifting smoke. Then he turns on his heel and heads off, back toward the birdwatchers.

"Why in the hell did God have to take her before me?"

Jeff is unsure if the question is addressed to him and if he's expected to reply.

Suddenly, tossing his head backward, Hal shouts at the sky in a quavering treble, "You sonofabitch! Why did you take her? Goddamn you!" then falls to his knees, sobbing.

For this, Jeff isn't prepared. His father doesn't believe in the deity he's cursing, nor has he ever been given to such extravagant, and public, displays. The couple stare in the perplexed, embarrassed way people do when they see a madman raving on the street.

Jeff hisses, "Dad, for Chrissake . . ."

He goes on, weeping and hurling epithets at an unjust God. "Stop it! Get hold of yourself!"

Hal chokes out a "go to hell," and Jeff is immediately ashamed to have spoken so harshly. Because he now sees why his father insisted that they come to this place. It's for the same reason he won't sell the house haunted by her absence. He must, *must,* rip at the scab and make the wound bleed afresh. It's a way of keeping her alive.

Jeff slips his hands under Hal's arms and attempts to pull him to his feet. It's like trying to lift a sack of concrete—Hal weighs in at 220 pounds. The young man, a bulky guy in a quilted vest, takes a step toward them. "Can I help?" Jeff waves him off, and just then, as abruptly as he'd lost it, Hal recaptures his composure. He stands and brushes the sand off his knees and says in a hoarse whisper, "Let's go."

* * *

On the drive north, he dozes fitfully. His head droops; he snores and twitches, then opens his eyes, looks around for a few moments, and nods off again. Grateful for the silence, Jeff heads up U.S. 45 and crosses the state line into the U.P. He's mulling over the outburst on the beach. Maybe it wasn't as out of character as he'd first thought. It's natural for Hal to be angry with God; he's been angry for as long as Jeff can remember—and perhaps not without reason. His best friend died in his arms as their squad of engineers bridged some contested river in France.

On nights after work, he toiled in the garage behind the family's bungalow in Livonia, hunched over a draftsman's board papered with mechanical drawings, or turning out parts on his lathe, grinding them mirror smooth, measuring tolerances with his micrometer. He came up with a few improvements to canning equipment, submitted his ideas to Standard Container, and was rewarded with modest bonuses, mentions in the company house organ. He'd hoped for more, like a promotion off the shop floor into the engineering department, but it never materialized. When he wasn't kicking himself for not going to school on the G.I. Bill, he fumed about the college boys in the front office, toward whom he felt a combustible mixture of envy and contempt. Thought they were so goddamn smart just because they had a piece of paper.

After he designed a new machine, there in the garage—it would manufacture milk and juice cartons faster than anything else in the industry—he took a leap into the dark. He applied for a patent, quit the company, and started his own firm, HH Engineering. But the leap was preceded by a distasteful step: he begged his father-in-law for start-up capital. Hal's argument—if his venture was successful, Ellen would have the life her father thought she deserved—persuaded Roland Fancher.

He set up shop in an abandoned warehouse off Eight Mile Road, hired a couple of machinists and tool-and-die makers, and poured out torrents of sweat for the next few years. He missed his sons' Little League games and his daughters' recitals and hardly ever took a day off (opening day of deer season an exception). He couldn't keep up with orders, hired more employees, then expanded into designing bottling equipment for microbreweries and midsize soft-drink companies. A million dollars in revenue, then five, then twelve . . .

Hal moved the family out of the Livonia bungalow into a ten-room house on an acre and a half in Bloomfield Hills. The Georgian with its white-pillared portico and fairway of a lawn had three bathrooms instead of four, no cook, and a cleaning lady in place of a live-in maid—but it was proof in brick and stone that he'd climbed the ladder to Roland's rung.

But if her restoration to privilege made any difference to Ellen, she didn't show it. Maybe she'd known all along that it had never been about her.

Success did do two things to Hal: it honed his sharp edges outside the home and made him an autocrat within it. As the story has come down to Jeff, Hal flew to St. Louis to pay off the loan in person. But he and his father-in-law, more alike than either of them would care to admit, vied for who could be more ungracious. "This is from the son of bohunk immigrants," Hal said, handing over the check. Roland said that stealing his daughter was a debt that could never be repaid, to which Hal replied, "Well, we're square now. And you can go to hell."

Beneath his own roof, Hal mandated what the family would eat for dinner and which TV programs they would watch and, on the rare occasions when he took them to movies, which films they would see. He never raised his voice to his wife, was always protective and solicitous toward her, but, many years later, Jeff heard her complain that as a girl she'd lived under a father's tyranny, as a woman under a husband's benign dictatorship.

For his children, it wasn't so benign. They were afraid of him, afraid of the loaded silences that often came after he'd suffered one of his war nightmares and the quick bursts of temper—"Hal-storms," they called them—as well. And they always felt his hand when they acted up or sloughed off in school.

Jeff was a junior in high school when his future was laid out for him as if it were already an accomplished fact: "You're going to UM, you're going to get a degree in engineering, then I'll teach you the business from the bottom up, and when I retire, you'll take over." Persuading himself that his father's ambitions for him were his own, Jeff marched off to study mechanical engineering at the University of Michigan, hated every day of it, and flunked out at the end of his freshman year. To keep his student deferment and avoid the draft, he enrolled in theater arts for the following term, mostly because he'd gotten an A in an elective, drama.

The experience of defying his father's wishes was as terrifying and exhilarating as a parachute jump. They almost came to blows. "I was handing you the chance I wish I'd had, and you've pissed on it!" Hal raged, and then he cut Jeff off.

Jeff thought then that Hal would get over his hurt and disappointment and they would go back to being father and son but on a more equal footing. But it didn't work out that way. Hal had loved him for what he'd hoped to make of him, as if his eldest child were a piece of metal to be fashioned on a lathe into something useful. When Jeff failed to measure up, Hal seemed to stop loving him. Jeff tried to do the same. But they were never

able to completely sever their connection. They built a relationship of mutual antagonism, poking and jabbing each other face-
to-face or on the phone. Big things and little things: politics
and Vietnam and the Detroit race riots; Jeff's divorce and remar-
riage; Hal's love of stupid sitcoms; his constant bitching about
the Detroit Lions. They became like a divorced couple who make
a marriage of their estrangement.

*   *   *

Jeff turns off the highway onto a bumpy gravel road that shakes
Hal out of his slumber. He smacks his lips and blinks at the
woods—fir trees dripping grandfather lichen, congeries of aspen
and hardwoods stripped bare except for a few oaks and beech,
the last to shed their leaves in the fall.

After two miles of this, Hal says, "When do we start sing-
ing 'Ninety-nine Bottles of Beer on the Wall'?"

They come to a junction, where a varnished sign, nailed to
a tree and bearing the word CHAMOUN, points up a sandy two-
track. Jeff shifts into four-wheel and turns.

"What's that mean? Chamoun?" Hal asks.

"It's Danny's last name. Remember? I told you yesterday. I
went to Michigan with him. Danny Chamoun. He's Lebanese."

"Oh, yeah. Some kind of ambulance chaser, you said."

"Trial lawyer is what I said. Try to be civil, will you?"

"The other guys are who? Remind me."

"Craig Ungar and Will Treadwell. Craig's an emergency-
room doctor in Grand Rapids, and Will runs the bar and micro-
brewery in town."

Most northwoods deer camps make sharecropper shacks
look luxurious. Danny Chamoun's, situated on a knoll above the
tannin-browned Windigo River, could be a lodge advertised

in an Orvis catalog. Hal emits a low "woo-hoo" and cracks, "Ambulance chasing must be good these days."

Jeff lets it go, trusting that his father's resolve to be obnoxious won't survive meeting his friends. The three men rise from the back deck, stride to the car, and greet the old man with warm handshakes, addressing him as "Mr. Havlicek" until he invites them to call him by his first name. Danny, who has a fleshy face that he can manipulate into a cavalcade of expressions—an asset sharpened by years of winning juries' sympathies—composes a solemn look as he says, "Jeff told us about your wife, and we're sorry for your loss." The sentiment sounds a little canned, like a condolence card, but Hal is touched. Then Craig, six feet five inches tall, a fitness fanatic as buff at sixty as an athlete half his age, totes Hal's duffel and cased rifle into the house. He's the guest of honor, Danny tells him, and has been given the master bedroom downstairs. There is only one bathroom, and it's also downstairs, so he won't have to negotiate the winding staircase in the middle of the night.

"I still piss a pretty good stream," Hal says jocularly.

Before dusk descends, they head out in Danny's pickup to a makeshift range to zero their rifles. Ever the man's man, Hal is happy to be in masculine company. He hasn't had much in years. His friends from the hard old days are gone, like the smokestack Detroit they'd lived and labored in: the boys from the plant he'd hunted and fished with on weekends, drunk with in corner taverns when the shift was done, work-thickened fingers clasping shot glasses raised to choruses of *skoal nazdarovya mud-in-your-eye,* emptied in a gulp, and slammed down hard on the bar—all are gone into graves or nursing homes. He talks the brewing business with Will, banters about firearms with

Craig, a gun nut who admires Hal's .30-06, an iconic Winchester Model 70. The conversations—the right temperature for brewing ale, the advantages and disadvantages of bolt actions over semi-automatics—don't interest Jeff, but he's glad that he no longer has to keep his father distracted all by himself.

The range is an abandoned gravel pit a few miles outside the town of Vieux Desert. Craig hangs a target of a silhouetted buck in front of an embankment, while Danny stacks two sandbags atop a weathered picnic table that now serves as a shooter's benchrest. Will, whose rifle is already sighted in, stands behind a spotting scope mounted on a tripod and trained on the target a hundred yards away. Danny muffles his ears with a headset and goes first, followed by Craig and Jeff, Will calling out corrections in windage or elevation, the gunshots sharp and crisp in the quiet air.

The bullet holes are taped, and now it's Hal's turn. He sits down and lays the Winchester's barrel on the sandbags, grimacing as he bends his arthritic neck to sight through the scope, liver-spotted hands quivering as he adjusts the focus and loads three rounds. Twenty years since he's pulled a trigger. Jeff feels a vicarious embarrassment when all three miss completely, spattering dirt high and to the right of the cardboard deer.

"Down five clicks," Will calls. "And you'd better come . . . *way* left."

Hal, as good as stone-deaf with the muffs on, takes them off and looks at Will, who repeats the correction. He turns the scope's windage and elevation knobs with a dime inserted into the center slot, but even through his glasses, he can barely make out the tiny, grooved increments, the arrows indicating up or down. He's all over the place with the next three rounds. The first clips the deer's antlers; the last two whip off far to the right, hitting the hindquarters.

"You're jerking the trigger," Jeff says. Because he has to shout, it comes off too sharply.

"Suppose I don't know that, you've got to tell me? I taught you to shoot."

The old man's barometer is falling; a Hal-storm threatens, the last thing Jeff wants the others to see. He backs off. Craig, also the son of a temperamental father, senses the tension, grasps the rifle barrel, and calls for a break to let it cool.

Hal tries to slough off his performance—"Getting on in years. But the good thing about having birthdays is having them." No one laughs or smiles. The doubtful look that crosses Danny's face expresses the question on all their minds: the woods tomorrow, opening day, will be full of hunters. What if Hal shoots somebody?

Maybe it was a mistake for Jeff to bring him along, a mistake for the others to agree to it. But something else is spoiling the companionable mood of minutes ago. None of them are young any longer, and Hal, with his fumbling hands, his dimming sight, his lost skills, is too clear a reminder of what they have to look forward to.

Craig has a stoic philosopher's cool detachment. It's a useful trait for an emergency-room doctor. He knows, because Jeff has told him, that Hal was once a crack marksman. He sits down and begins to revive the memories interred in the older man's muscles and nerves. "Breathe . . . aim . . . squeeze . . . exhale as you squeeze," he intones. Six more rounds are fired, the final three forming a respectable group high up on the target. Craig reaches across the table and adjusts the elevation. Hal loads the five cartridges remaining in the box. He cheeks the stock, squeezes one off, and locks in another, his movements as he flips the bolt smooth and unhurried. His transformation is wonderful to see.

After the fifth round, Will squints through the spotting scope. "Do that tomorrow, and there's venison in the freezer."

Jeff takes a look: all five have punched holes in a tight pattern slightly above and behind the deer's shoulder, any one a killing shot.

Hal is exultant. "Hell, I just needed to get the rust out. And you were my WD-Forty," he says to Craig.

Jeff gives him a bump on the arm. "You had us worried there for a minute."

Casing the Winchester, his father says in an undertone, "Good bunch of guys. How the hell did you ever get to be their friend?"

It's partly meant as a joke. Jeff decides to ignore the part that isn't.

*　*　*

They're awake well before dawn, and then come the smells of frying bacon, coffee brewing in an enameled pot. At breakfast, Hal chuckles at the camouflage outfits worn by his son and his friends. "You guys look like you're going on a raid in Afghanistan." He's garbed in the hunting apparel of a bygone era—a wool cap with earflaps laced on top, twill trousers, a black-and-red checkered mackinaw.

Outside, their breath plumes in the cold. The sound of the Windigo quarreling with a boulder rises from below. A solitary star sparkles low over the woods across the river, and the patches of the Milky Way shining through the gaps in the trees could be mistaken for thin, moonlit clouds. Jeff never sees skies like these in New York.

Craig and Danny hike toward their stands. To spare Hal's legs, Will drives him and Jeff to theirs on an ATV, following a jeep trail upriver. Beneath the dense overstory, it's as if they're

riding an ore car through a mineshaft. The headlight illuminates a strip of orange forester's tape hanging from a branch.
Will parks and, as the sky begins to brighten, guides them down
a footpath to a giant white pine overlooking a clearing. Planks
nailed to the trunk make a ladder to a platform, like the floor to
a tree house, twelve or fifteen feet above. That will be Jeff's stand.
The climb would be too dangerous for Hal; he will shoot from
a blind at the base of the pine—a three-sided frame of two-by-
fours thatched with pine boughs and furnished, incongruously,
with a ripped lounge chair hemorrhaging foam rubber.

"An eight-pointer's been hanging around here," Will whispers. "I've got baits out in the clearing. See you at the four-wheeler,
noonish."

He's a man of bearish bulk but a fine woodsman, and he
walks off toward his stand without cracking a branch. Hal settles
into the lounger, the Model 70 across his lap, and mumbles that
all he needs now are a TV and a beer. Jeff ties a parachute cord
dangling vine-like from the platform to his rifle's trigger
guard; then, after scaling the makeshift ladder, he pulls the
rifle up to his perch. He sits down to wait, back against the tree
trunk. He isn't fond of stand shooting. Too impatient for it,
preferring to stalk on foot. Nor does he approve of baiting
game. If it means the difference between putting meat or
mac-'n'-cheese on the family table, fine. Otherwise, it's unsport-
ing, more like sniping than hunting. The baits, like the ground
blind, are there for his father's sake.

The sky lightens from the gray of old asphalt to oyster and
snuffs out the stars one by one until all are hidden in a canopy
of brilliant blue. A hoarfrost glitters on the brown bracken fern
matting the clearing, across which the white pine's shadow lies
like a fallen spear. Jeff stares past the open space into a maze of
balsam fir and paper birch, his glance flitting side to side, alert

for movement. The sun climbs, chopping off lengths of the pine's shadow. After two hours, expectancy gives way to restless boredom. He falls into a fantasy of sex with his new girlfriend, Diane, a fortyish divorcée who sings airline commercials for a living and adores being taken from behind in front of a mirror. He's getting a hard-on, a fairly rare event these days, when a doe materializes at the clearing's edge. A big doe, her coat winter gray. She stands statue-still beside a leaning birch, its bark peeled back in scrolls, then steps out into the open space, bows her head, and begins to graze on the bait, a pile of apples and carrots. In a moment, a smaller doe joins her.

Ever so slowly, Jeff lifts his rifle off his lap and rests it on the platform's rail. The rut is on. If these two females belong to the eight-pointer's harem, he, too, will have his mind on sex. He'll come crashing out of the woods, his better judgment overcome by lust.

Three or four loud snorts, followed by a teakettle whistle, cause the does to jerk their heads upright. They stare at the noise for an instant, then bound off, white tails flagging. The snorts and snuffles and whistles don't stop. Jeff climbs down into the blind and, after shaking his father awake, cups his hands around his mouth and the old man's ear.

"You were making enough racket to scare every deer in the Central Time Zone. I've got a thermos of coffee up there. You want some coffee?"

"It'll just make me piss myself inside out. Stay down here. Gimme a poke, I start to nod off again."

Jeff clambers back up, lowers his rifle, comes down, and nestles into the blind. He sits on the ground on his folded jacket—the weather has turned warm—and resumes his watchful waiting. It's more or less going through the motions. No buck with an ounce of buck sense is coming anywhere near, not now.

Fifteen or twenty minutes pass. Hal leans over the arm of the chair and says in a low voice, "Know what I was thinking earlier? When the stars faded out? That's what happened to your mother's brain."

Jeff motions to keep still.

"Like there was a little man up there, a kind of electrician in her brain, throwing circuit breakers, turning out the lights one after the other."

Jeff produces a prolonged sigh. "Another time, not now."

But the image—vintage Hal, the brain as machine—starts a series of mental quick-cuts: The lights of memory and recognition. *Out.* Jeff's mother, on one of his monthly visits, confuses him with her father and asks his permission to leave the house. The light of bodily functions. *Out.* Ana, a Polish hospice nurse, is hired to bathe and change her. The light of speech. *Out.* Ellen is able to make only unintelligible sounds as Ana combs her hair and puts on her makeup and fusses over her as if she were an infant, which is what she's become. *Ya, my Ellen, I make you real pretty, okay?* She sits in the living room, coiffed and looking pretty and mute as a mannequin, nothing behind her eyes, no flicker of human consciousness, already gone, Jeff thinks—her soul, or whatever made Ellen Ellen, has fled her body. Her cancer, in remission for two years, roars back. Hal wants to bring her in for a radical mastectomy. His three younger children, as wary of opposing his wishes as when they were kids, are going along. Jeff phones her doctor and convinces him to convince them that an operation not only would be futile, it would be torment, for her, for all of them. Another thing his father holds against him. *Might have given her a few more months.* The light of motor control. *Out.* She's moved into a bed in a spare bedroom, where she lies, respirating and drugged on a Demerol drip, until the little electrician, at last showing some tender mercy, flips the master switch.

Two distant gunshots, echoing through the woods, return Jeff to the present.

Hal mutters, "I looked up her nostrils when she passed."

"You did *what*?"

"I was kneeling by her bed. I wanted to feel her last breath on my face, and I looked up her nostrils, and they were pink. Pink and clean, like a baby's."

He wants to say that this is one of the weirder things he's heard, but he restrains himself and pleads, "Stop talking."

* * *

On the morning of the fourth day, a morning that brings snow and high wind, Jeff, Hal, and Will return early to camp, where they see a six-pointer hanging from the meat pole. Its gutted cavity, gaping like an enormous mouth, breathes steam and drips dark blood that stains the snow pink. While Craig skins the carcass, Danny stands aside, his hands and sleeves splattered with gore. The buck is his. First one in three years, he says, molding his lips into a jubilant grin. Jeff suppresses a flash of envy and congratulates him.

Craig works with surgical care, peeling back the hide. The sight of the exposed flesh is one Jeff has seen before, and it always awakens a shameful fascination. The carcass is lowered to the ground. Craig saws it into quarters and stuffs them into burlap game bags. The wind rumbles through the trees; the snow swirls in the wind.

Will has to attend to business in town. He offers to deliver the antlers to the taxidermist, the meat to the butcher at the IGA, who will complete the deer's disassembly.

"How about me and Jeff tag along?" Hal asks. It's more

demand than request. "I'd like to get out of these woods for a while. Grab some lunch."

"Sure. We dish out a mean chili," Will says.

His establishment, the Great Lakes Brew Pub, occupies a long, shingle-sided building facing the main street and Lake Superior. The bar and grill are in front, the brewery in back. Hal asks to see it. Will ushers them through a hallway into a room where gleaming copper vats sprout pipes that lead to pumps and stainless-steel tanks. To Jeff, it's a bewildering rat's nest of metal, but it makes perfect sense to his father, who converses with Will about mash kettles and lauter tanks and automatic superblocks. Machinery. Hal turns nostalgic when they sit down to lunch, carrying on about the machines he worked on and the men he'd worked with back in the day.

"When 'we were makin' Thunderbirds,'" Will says.

From Hal, a puzzled squint.

"It's a Bob Seger tune. All about the times when we made stuff in this country."

"Now we buy it from the Chinese with money we borrow from them." Hal shakes his head in dismay; but he's in a good mood. "Never heard of this Bob Whatchymacallit."

"Seger. A real Dee-troit boy. His old man worked for Ford," Will says with a certain civic pride. Will had grown up in Detroit, one of only five white boys in his high school, a fact that gave him an incentive to become a boxer. He claims to have sparred in Kronk's gym with Tommy Hearns, the Motor City Cobra. "I've got one of his CDs in the office. I'll give it to you. Bob Seger and the Silver Bullet Band."

The waitress stops by, a blue-eyed blonde with Valkyrie breasts and hands that would look more comfortable gripping a lug wrench than a pad and pencil.

"Decided what you'd like, hon?" she asks, addressing Hal first.

The word "hon" encourages his flirtatious streak. Composing what he must think is a rakish smile, probably imagining that he's still the flat-bellied young sergeant who won a girl's heart, he casts a glance at her bosom.

"Not on the menu," she quips in a breezy, bantering voice that declares that she doesn't mind the attention, even if it's coming from an octogenarian. Jeff remembers that women always had been drawn to his father, though he's never fully understood why.

After she's delivered their orders—three bowls of chili, three pints of Moose Sweat, as Will has labeled his oatmeal stout—Hal watches her walk away.

"Always did grow 'em substantial up north," he observes. "Keeps a man warm on nights when it's forty below, isn't that right, Will?"

He wouldn't know. His wife, who is half Ojibwa, is "skinny as a fly rod."

"How long've you been married?"

"Going on twenty-five years."

"Kids?"

"One from my first marriage, one of our own."

Hal scoops a spoonful of chili, blows on it. "I don't know about your generation. First marriage, second, third. I'm not criticizing, but, damn, whatever happened to 'till death do us part'?"

Will clears his throat nervously. "Uh . . . in my case, it did. My first wife died in a car crash."

"Oh . . . I didn't . . . Um . . . I didn't know . . . If I'd known, I'd've, well, y'know . . ." This is the best Hal can do by way of apologizing. "I meant number-one son over here. Two marriages, two divorces, no kids. My wife died last year, and we got married when FDR was president."

Will arches his eyebrows in appreciation for the feat of mat-rimonial longevity. Jeff, smarting, yearns to correct Hal's boast by saying, *Not quite. Harry Truman was in the White House.* It would be worth it just to see the old man's reaction.

"Sixty-one years!" his father continues. "And not because of me. It was all her. She put up with a lot that ninety-nine out of a hundred women wouldn't have. I don't know about all that heaven-and-hell crap. Personally, I think that when the shovel-ful of dirt hits your coffin, that's it. But if there is a heaven, let me tell you, she's there." He gulps his beer, then looks toward the pressed-tin ceiling. "Isn't that right, Ellen? If there is an up there, you're up there."

Ah, time to reopen the wound. He hasn't mentioned her in three days. Fearing that a repeat of the beach performance is imminent, Jeff stretches a leg under the table and gives Hal a gentle kick.

"What's that for?" Then to Will: "He thinks I'm crazy because I talk to her. Sure I do. After she passed, I thought I'd hear from her somehow or other, maybe see her, that maybe she'd visit me in a dream. But there's been nothing, nothing. You don't know what you've got till it's gone, and she's gone. The shovelful of dirt. That's it."

He speaks with a kind of delighted bitterness, as if he's been waiting to pour out his feelings into ears that haven't heard them. Will, plainly uncomfortable, fumbles for something to say and finally excuses himself to fetch the promised CD.

His departure doesn't deter Hal, who just keeps talking. Jeff steals a glance at his cellphone, hoping for an urgent text from his production assistant, a voicemail from Diane. But there's nothing. He looks out the window at Superior, heaving in the northwest wind, hurling waves into Vieux Desert's harbor jetty. What are the springs, he wonders, for his father's self-flagellation, his obsessive need to beatify Ellen? It's over the top. He doesn't dispute that she was everything Hal says she was, but there was a side to her that would disqualify her from sainthood.

He remembers what she did to sabotage his second marriage, which had been shaky enough on its own merits. To Will's mother, Laura, a soap-opera actress, had been the home-wrecking Jezebel who'd come between her son and her former, beloved daughter-in-law, Melissa. On holiday visits, she treated Laura with a chilly correctness, except when the chance to criticize her presented itself. Her taste in clothes. Her sloppy housekeeping. Her tendency to utter banalities in her soap-star voice. *You speak beautifully, dear. I don't think I've ever heard anyone who can say so little so well.* When the inevitable end came, she phoned him in New York. *I wish I could tell you how sorry I am, Jeff, but you're well rid of her. If you get mixed up with another tramp, promise you won't marry her.*

His father, meanwhile, reprises the conversation they had in the car five days ago. How lonesome he'd been in those early days, on the road in the spring before his family joined him, in the fall after they left. The hardships he'd subjected Ellen to in boondock cabins with no indoor plumbing. He segues into the trips she wanted to take after he'd retired. Cruises to the Bahamas. A cruise of the Danube. He had the money, but being a son of the Great Depression, sailing the Danube seemed an extravagance. They never went.

"Should've given her that much." He contemplates his empty beer glass for a few moments. "Sometimes I hate myself."

Jeff is practically grinding his teeth. "For God's sake, lay off."

The wave of disgust. "You're no help. Never were, never will be."

Another slap uncalled for, and this one stings more than the first. It shouldn't, but it does. He's sick of hearing about his fail-

ures. He notices Will, emerging from his upstairs office, spread
two fingers to indicate that he'll be along in a couple of minutes. It comes to him right then, all in a burst, and he feels as
he did his year in engineering school, when the answer to some
opaque equation would suddenly manifest itself.

It is the lingering sting that moves him to lean across the
table and ask, "How many were there? Just one? Or were there
more?"

"How many what?"

"When you were on the road all by yourself. I'm just curious. I'm not going to pass judgment," Jeff answers in a confidential tone, the assurance subverted by an accusatory note,
faint but audible.

Hal hesitates; then, the meaning becoming clear, a startled
expression drops over his face. He recovers immediately.

"That's good," Hal says. "If anybody doesn't have a right to
pass judgment, it's you."

He stands, resting his hand on the chair to steady himself.
"Where's the men's room?"

Jeff points toward the rear of the bar.

"Never pass up a chance to take a piss," his father says.
"That's my advice, now that you're an older man."

* * *

Hal is silent on the drive back to camp and silent as he and Jeff
trek to the stand for the late-afternoon hunt, silent at dinner and
afterward, as they all sit around the fireplace, sipping Danny's
whiskey. It's impossible to ignore him. He radiates a discontent
that, more than the heat from the fire, more than the smoke
from Will's cheap cigar, makes the room feel oppressive. Danny,
ignorant of the cause of his sullen mood, makes a stab at cheer-
ing him up. *You've got three more days; that big eight-pointer is*

bound to show up. With a gesture of disinterest, Hal mumbles that he's shot plenty of deer in his time; one more or less won't make any difference.

Danny resorts to the TV for diversion. He scrolls through the channels to a night football game, the Lions against the Bears. But something, possibly snow on the satellite dish, interferes with the signal. The only clear channel is a local one out of Marquette. It's showing a reality series about EMTs. A jerky handheld follows paramedics wheeling an accident victim into an emergency room while nurses babble medical jargon. Will solicits Jeff's professional opinion about reality TV. *The last refuge of mediocrities,* he replies. *Every bozo gets to be a celebrity, second-rate writers who can't write a bad check get a job, and cheapskate networks don't have to pay scale for talent.*

"The Emmy-winner speaks!" Danny says.

Jeff corrects him—he was not nominated, his shows were, and they didn't win.

"Why don't you produce a series with Craig as the star? *Emergency-Room Doctor.*"

"There's already a series called *ER.*"

"You're a smart guy. You could think of another title."

"Whatever you call it, I won't be available," Craig says; then, with his usual phlegm, he makes a surprise announcement: he's quitting medicine as of the first of the year.

"You're kidding! What're you going to do?" Danny asks.

"As little as possible."

"Christ, you're the guy who graduated numero uno from med school, and you're packing it in early?" says Danny, sounding genuinely distressed by Craig's failed promise.

"I hated med school and I hate medicine and I hate patients."

From out of a balloon of cigar smoke, Will says, "Definitely a problem for a doctor."

"Put up with it all this time, so I've earned the right to be an underachiever."

Something in what Craig has said animates Hal. He pokes his head from out of his burrow. "If you hated med school, how did you graduate top of your class?"

"Force of habit," Craig answers, and elaborates: his father, a world-class eye surgeon, had raised a brood of what Craig terms "über-children." Three boys and a girl, all expected to excel at everything they did, and what they did was dictated by him. "I was the oldest, so I had to follow him into medicine. No questions asked."

"Wonder what his secret was." The example of a patriarch's successful tyranny draws Hal out entirely. He's also had a little too much scotch. Tiny red veins fracture his florid cheeks. "I tried like hell to put Jeff through engineering school. He was going to run my firm one day," he says, as if Jeff is absent. "He had the brains for it, but . . . Keg parties, frat-boy hijinks, and he flunks out and winds up studying"—he raises both arms in a flourish, his hands fluttering, and puts on a stagy accent—"thee-ah-ta!"

Jeff bristles; he feels a fullness in his ears. It would give him deep satisfaction to smash the old prick in the mouth. This is ridiculous. Almost five months into his sixty-first year, and he's reacting to a father's censure like an angry adolescent.

"Well, Jeff won two Emmys," Danny chimes in, coming to Jeff's defense. "How many guys can say they have a son who's won two Emmys?"

Now it's Hal who corrects him, albeit incorrectly. "He was nominated; you might say he finished second in a game where only first counts." He pours another shot of single malt into his glass and drinks half, swishing the whiskey like mouthwash. "We went to those ceremonies, both of 'em, my wife and me.

Never felt so out of place. A thee-ah-ta full of fagolas dressed up like penguins, handing out little gold statues. For what? Playing make-believe."

"Fagolas?" Jeff says, forcing a lopsided, sarcastic grin. "Last time I checked, I was straight."

"I didn't mean you."

"What did you mean, then?"

"For sure, not to hurt your feelings." A pause, another sip. "If you've got any. A guy who doesn't cry at his own mother's funeral."

He must be drunk, letting go like this, as if no one else is around.

"You're feeling sorry for yourself, not her," Jeff says. The others aren't present for him, either. He and Hal are, as it were, alone in a cage of their own making. "Like you're the first man in the whole fucking history of the human race to lose his wife."

Hal launches himself from his chair, as if rage has instantly cured his arthritis, and crosses the ten feet of space between him and Jeff, who thinks for a moment that his father is going to slug him. He jumps to his feet, ready to block the punch. It doesn't come. The two stand there, nearly nose-to-nose, the scarlet veins spreading across the older man's cheeks like cracks in a windshield.

"Don't you dare talk to me like that!" Hal shouts.

Craig and Will are dumbstruck; Danny is rummaging through his inventory of facial expressions but can't find one appropriate for the occasion.

"You've never done one goddamn thing for me. Name one goddamn thing," Hal says.

"I brought you here! That's one thing. I've listened to your whining and crap for nearly a week. That's another!"

"Like that's some big sacrifice? You've got a perfect record, because shit is what you've done for me, you son of a bitch."

At that moment, Jeff wishes a massive stroke would drop his father lifeless to the floor, and it could be the sincerity and depth of that wish that compel him to break his promise.

"Bastard is more like it. I was born one," he says, in a voice as hard, flat, and cutting as he can make it. "Yeah, that's the word you want. 'Bastard.'"

And it silences Hal, takes all the fight and fury out of him, like a blow to the liver.

"You want to hang our dirty laundry in public?" Jeff continues. "Okay. I've got more skid-marked skivvies to hang. If Mom hadn't changed her mind the last minute, I wouldn't be Jeffrey Havlicek, would I?"

Hal's eyelids flutter, his lips flap to make reply, but there is none to make. Jeff almost feels sorry for him.

He says, "Why don't you go to bed, Dad?"

"Maybe we all should," Danny says.

* * *

In the morning, everyone tries to pretend that nothing happened. Neither Hal nor Jeff says anything beyond *pass the salt, pass the butter.* Danny, appointing himself master of the hunt, volunteers to organize a deer drive. He theorizes that with so many hunters scouring the woods, the wise old eight-pointer has chosen to hunker down and avoid exposing himself. So, he proposes, Will, Craig, and he will beat the woods and push the buck out of his hiding place into Hal's or Jeff's crosshairs. Jeff guesses his thinking: *Let's do all we can to get this sour old man and his son their deer so they'll go home and we won't have to witness any more psychodramas like the one last night.*

A topographic map is rolled open on the table, a plan is worked out, two handheld radios are tested. Jeff takes one, Danny the other; then he and the other two men, donning bright-orange vests to reduce the chances that they'll be mistaken for deer, head out for the logging road from which they'll start their sweep. Jeff mounts the ATV, his father beside him, and drives upriver to the trail that leads to the stand. They wait there, in the frigid darkness, for Danny to call on the radio. They don't speak, both afraid that the things they said have opened a breach too wide to be bridged, each thinking the other should be the first to apologize. It is Jeff who takes that step.

"You're eighty-five, I'm sixty," he says. "It's sort of stupid to be carrying on like this, isn't it?"

Hal nods and asks, "When did you find out and how?"

Jeff tells him about the discovery—the letters, the marriage certificate. He says, "You hid it all these years. What for?"

"I don't even remember anymore."

"Oh, come on."

"It was one those things that got started . . . After you were born, your mother moved in with a girlfriend and . . . A single mother in those days, not like now. So she told people that her husband was overseas. And after I got home, we took it from there."

"So that I'd never know you almost handed me off?"

"Maybe. Are you glad we didn't?"

"You make it pretty goddamn hard sometimes. How about you?"

"You don't make it so easy, either."

Hal pauses, staring at his boots. "There's one other thing, the question you asked me in the bar. If you've got to know, there was one other a long time ago. It didn't mean anything. It was just loneliness."

"Did Mom know?"

"I think so, but she decided not to know. I broke things off, anyway. I couldn't stand the lies and her pretending that I wasn't lying."

"Okay. I shouldn't have asked."

"But you did, and now I've answered, and we're square."

They fall silent again. They aren't reconciled. This isn't peace; more like an armistice between combatants who've run out of ammo.

Morning twilight comes. They hear from Danny; the drivers are in place and ready to start. Hal and Jeff hike to the ground blind and settle in, Hal in the lounger, Jeff on a tree stump he's rolled inside to keep his butt off the frozen ground. He raises Danny, reports that they're on stand, and sets the radio on the stump. They wait and watch the sun, rising over the trees across the clearing, go from red to orange to a yellow-white that bleaches a skein of low, wispy clouds. Hal removes his glasses and wipes them with a bandanna. It's not, Jeff sees, the warming air that's misted them. Her ghost, unbidden, has come calling. He leans over to lay a consolatory hand on his father's shoulder. The movement is stiff, awkward, like that of an aging athlete whose body only half-remembers what to do. Maybe there was some truth in what Hal said last night about his lack of feeling. Maybe he's spent so much of his life reacting to the contrived emotions of TV that he's forgotten how to respond, gracefully, to the real thing.

The ghost departs; the spell passes. Hal cautiously leaves the blind to piss. Just then, Danny calls. They have moved a deer. They didn't get a good look at it, but it is a buck. Jeff motions his father to finish up, get back inside.

Minutes later, the buck emerges from out of the woods, head high and prancing—not the magisterial eight-pointer, only a six.

But he'll do. Jeff lets out a soft whistle to stop him. He pauses, turning his head to locate the strange sound. Hal leans forward in the chair, snapping the rifle to his shoulder. But he hesitates—the sun is in his eyes. Sensing danger, the deer whirls and lunges for the sheltering trees. Hal swings the gun for a lead and fires. The animal tumbles, regains his footing, and vanishes into the woods.

"I hit him! I hit him good!"

But maybe not good enough, Jeff thinks. He sprints to where the deer fell and finds bright blood speckling the dull brown ferns. His father is behind him, breathless from excitement. Jeff says, "You'd better stay back. I'll track him."

Hal shakes his head. "My responsibility."

They climb over windfalls, thrash through a willow thicket, following the blood trail. It's faint at first—a few splotches here, a few there, stain fallen leaves, patches of snow. They find more at the base of a ridge forested with oak and beech. It's no longer bright; it's almost black. Liver shot, Jeff concludes; he traces the blood trail with his eyes as far as he can and spots the buck partway up the slope. He's kneeling, facing away. Catching scent or sound of his pursuers, he tries to rise, pushing up on his forelegs. The wound is too grave. His hind legs do not respond. The two men climb and, when they're about twenty-five yards from him, circle around for a broadside shot. The deer struggles, front hooves pawing the ground. He twists his neck to look at the men who have done this thing to him, and his valiant efforts to flee, to live, and the look of dumb animal pain in his eyes are heart-breaking.

"Now I . . ." Hal begins. Though they haven't come far, less than a quarter of a mile, he's gasping. "Remember why . . . I quit hunting."

Jeff raises his rifle. His father nudges the barrel aside and says, "Clean up my own messes." He flops into a sitting position for a steadier aim and fires the finishing shot. The buck's forelegs crumple, thrash, and then stretch out, still.

Hal starts to stand but falls back onto his seat. "Help me up."

As Jeff grabs his outstretched hand, he groans. "Feeling a little . . . sick. Like I'm going to puke."

"Sit right there. Get your wind back. I'll dress him out."

Skinning knife drawn, he hasn't gone ten feet toward the dead animal when he hears another moan, much louder than before. Hal sits doubled over, forehead on his knees.

"Dad? What is it?"

"Jesus H. Can't catch my breath." He taps his sternum and brushes his fingertips across his chest to his left shoulder. "Like somebody's tightening a belt in there."

Breaking out in a sweat, Jeff goes to him. "Lie down," he says, at the same time pushing him gently onto his back. His face is ashen. "Lie down. Take deep breaths. Deep breaths now."

He isn't sure if this is the correct treatment. It's the only thing he can think of. He reaches into his coat pocket for the radio to call Craig. Craig will know what to do. The radio isn't there. He left it at the stand.

He cannot drag or carry his bulky father out of this wilderness. He tries to think of a sensible course of action. He needs to clear his mind, clouded by guilt; it's as if, in some unredeemed part of himself, he's willed his wish of last night to come to pass.

Hal's chest swells, sinks, swells, sinks. "Hurts when I do that. Goddamn, the big one . . ."

"Listen. Keep trying!"

Jeff takes out his GPS, turns it on, and waits for it to acquire satellites. It's taking longer than it should; the tree cover is hindering the signals. As he waits, he tightly clasps his father's hand. Hal's fingers enfold his, requiting the pressure.

"How is it now?"

"Maybe a little better. What're you doing?"

Jeff explains: he's going to pinpoint their position, then run a GPS track—electronic breadcrumbs—back to the stand and call the others on the radio. He'll need their help, especially Craig's. Craig will know what to do.

At last a green miniaturized topo map flashes on the screen. Jeff lets go of the hand and presses the button to mark the way-point. Hal rolls his head aside and raises his eyes, magnified by his glasses. The plea in them is clear enough to make his next words superfluous.

"Stay beside me, Jeff. It'll be all right."

"No, it won't."

"Can think of worse ways," he says in a weak voice. "Worse places. Some nursing home . . ."

"I'm not going to let you die here, even if you want to. Can't break my record."

"Record?"

"It's one more thing I'm not going to do for you."

DREAMERS

I t was past the lunch hour and Jerry's Dew Drop Inn was empty except for the bartender, the cook, and a customer, an old man wearing a blaze-orange shirt and cap with a mottling of black camouflage. He sat at one end of the bar, sipping a beer between bites of a cheeseburger and fries in a plastic basket.

At the other end, Lonnie the bartender and Mike the cook stood watching World Series highlights on a TV on a shelf above the bar. Mike was a big man, bearded and shaggy-haired; Lonnie was undersize, with a long nose and the predacious eyes of a feral terrier. He wore a military haircut, shorn close above his ears but longer on top, and his wiry arms were so covered in tattoos they looked like the sleeves of a tight-fitting paisley shirt.

The old man called for another draft. Lonnie went to the taps, poured, and set the glass down in front of him.

"How did this town get its name? Germfask?" the customer asked.

Lonnie said, "No idea. You're about a week early for Halloween. All that orange you got on, you look like a pumpkin."

"Are you new around here?" asked the old man amiably. "It's bird season, and bird hunters wear orange. State regulations."

"What about your hat? What's with the black camo stuff? That state regs, too?"

The old man grinned. He had crooked teeth. "It's to fool the grouse. It's to make 'em think I'm a camouflaged pumpkin instead of a hunter."

"You're hilarious," Lonnie said. "And just so you know, I'm not new round here."

He turned back to the World Series. Two guys in suits were analyzing last night's game. He lit a cigarette and had smoked about half of it when the old man said, in the loud voice of someone hard of hearing, "Excuse me, could I ask you to put that out?"

"Sure," Lonnie answered. "Go ahead and ask."

"Hey, Lon," Mike said. "No mouthing off."

"Ah, fuck him. I'll smoke if I want to."

The old man motioned at the sign hung above the cash machine. "No smoking in bars anymore. State law," he said. "And I'm allergic to tobacco smoke."

"The allergic pumpkin. You're kinda big on these state laws and regulations."

"C'mon, dude," said Mike under his breath. "You're lucky Jerry gave you this job."

"That's what you call it? Lucky? Some luck this is."

"You're young, so maybe you never heard of the saying *the customer is always right*?" the old man said.

"This time the customer is wrong."

Now the old man looked angry and scared at the same time. He said, "Well, you've lost this customer. What do I owe?"

Lonnie snubbed the cigarette in a coffee saucer, snatched the bill, and slapped it down next to the beer glass. "After you pay up, you can go outside and breathe all that fresh air."

"I don't know if you're obnoxious or just plain ignorant."

"Obnoxious? Ignorant? You can add an apology to the tab."

"Maybe nuts is what you are," the old man said.

As he turned slightly to reach for his wallet, Lonnie's right arm shot out and smashed the old man in the mouth, knocking him off the barstool. He staggered and grabbed the barstool to keep from falling. Lonnie vaulted over the bar, swung wildly for his jaw, missed, and stumbled into him, both sprawling backward, Lonnie on top, flailing with his fists and screaming, "I'll show you nuts, you old fuck!"

Mike ducked under the counter, ran over to the two men rolling around on the floor, and locked his arms around Lonnie's chest. As big as he was, he had trouble pulling the smaller man off. Lonnie writhed and kicked until Mike lifted him off his feet, body-slammed him, and then, straddling him, pinned his shoulders to the floor.

"Chill!" he shouted into Lonnie's face. "Chill, or I'll . . ."

The old man—he looked to be sixty-something—had got to his feet. He was leaning against the bar, wheezing, blood drooling from a corner of his swollen lips.

"Hey, mister, if you can walk out of here, do it," Mike said, still sitting astride Lonnie. "If I was you, I'd walk out of here right now. Lunch is on the house."

* * *

All three were jammed so tightly in Will Treadwell's pickup that nothing short of a head-on collision could have dislodged them. Will was six feet two and two forty, and each of his clients matched him in size, although their weight was better distributed than his, they being half his age and in gym-rat condition:

Chicago cops who belonged to some sort of tactical unit that tracked down gangbangers and crack dealers. They were on vacation now, off the mean streets and in the woods to hunt bear with bow and arrow. It was their first time hunting bear. They had shot deer and elk, and Will hoped they were as good with their bows as they claimed. He did not want to track down and kill a wounded bear, as he'd had to do last year on a moonless night, his client shining a flashlight on the blood trail, the bear, an arrow buried to the feathers in its gut, rising to its hind legs from behind a deadfall, its eyes glowing a preternatural green in the flashlight's beam. Will put a round from his .45-70 into its chest. The beast screamed and thrashed in the underbrush before it died. He could hear it still—that half-human scream— and he'd been thinking to quit guiding bear hunters. Sometimes it made him feel like an accomplice in murder.

He left the highway leading out of Vieux Desert and headed up an unpaved forest-service road toward one of his stands, on the verge of a cedar swamp.

"I've got a boar coming in there," he said. "Fattening up for winter. He'll go four-fifty at least."

"That's what we want!" said the white cop, whose name was Kevin Walsh. Hands crossed on his lap, shoulders hunched, he sat squeezed between Will and his black partner, Lamont Lewis. "So guiding is your sideline?"

"More like a hobby that pays a few bucks," Will answered. "Gets me out in the woods. The woods are good for my head. The bar business drives me crazy sometimes."

"We ride with the guide, guides on the side, does his mind good to be in the woods, it's his hobby . . ." Lewis's palms beat out rap percussion on the dashboard. "Kev, gimme a word rhymes with 'hobby.'"

"'Lobby'?" Walsh suggested. "'Snobby'? 'Knobby'?"

"How about this: ain't no jobby, it's his hobby, a fine line from a sideline . . ."

"Beautiful," Walsh said. Then to Will: "It's what we do on stakeouts. Make up rap lyrics."

"Because a stakeout can be as boring as hangin' drywall," Lewis said.

"Not the last one," Walsh said. "No drywall on the last one."

"What happened?" Will asked.

"I'll give you the abridged version," said Lewis. "We were in hot pursuit—I'm talkin' on foot—of a badass Mexican, Eduardo Morales. He was what the Mexicans call a *sicario,* an assassin, for the Latin Lords gang. They're kind of the sales force for the Sinaloa Cartel in Chicago. We spot him, we get out of the car to pop him, and he takes off running like he's got an afterburner in his ass down an alley in Pilsen. That was onetime a Czech neighborhood, now it's all Latino—"

"Hey, abridge, Lamont. Abbreviate," Walsh said.

"Kev is a little way behind me. I'm maybe five yards from collaring Morales when he spins, reaches behind his back for his piece. Mine's already out, so I send him to his own funeral. It's SOP—you cap somebody, no matter who, no matter what, no matter why, Internal Investigations gets into it. The IID guy is interviewing me, and he asks, 'Why did you shoot him *thirteen* times?' And I go, ''Cuz I ran out of bullets.'"

Walsh gave a short, sharp laugh. "''Cuz I ran out of bullets.' Lamont is a legend for that one."

Will said nothing. He supposed that a bear would be a piece of cake for these two.

"Don't know what Morales was thinking," Lewis said. "Like he's gonna get away with shooting a cop? Had to be Mexican machismo."

"Nah. It's because he was Catholic," Walsh said.

"What's that got to with it?" Will said.

"Those Latino gangbangers go to confession every week, no shit. It's like, *Bless me, Father, for I have sinned. Since my last confession, I missed mass, and, oh, yeah, I killed a guy.* And the priest is like, *Say ten Our Fathers and ten Hail Marys. Your sins are forgiven, name of the Father, the Son,* et cetera. Morales must've figured, *I kill this cop, I'll go to confession; he kills me, I'll go to heaven.*"

Distracted, Will did not see the deep washboard rippling the road as he rounded a curve. He banged over it before he could brake, the tailgate to his old pickup flew open—it had a faulty lock—and the bear baits tumbled out of the truck. He pulled over, and they climbed out to retrieve the baits: two five-gallon buckets of kitchen scraps and grease, a bucket of fermenting crab apples, and a beaver carcass rank and rotten enough to make a man gag.

"I ain't touchin' that," Lewis said. "God*damn*, what a stink."

"It'll smell like prime filet to a bear." Will put on his gloves, grabbed the beaver by its tail, and tossed it into the bed of the truck. The lid to the apple bucket had come off in its fall; crab apples were strewn down the road. The three men walked along, picking them up one by one. They looked like a farm crew. As they were returning to the truck, Lewis paused to gather a few apples they'd missed. Just then, a Ford F-250, jacked up and tricked out in tongues-of-fire decals, spotlights racked on its roof, sped around the curve behind them, slammed over the washboards, and veered sharply toward Lewis. He leapt aside, the Ford shooting past him without slowing down.

"Lonnie! You sonofabitch!" Will hollered, ineffectively: the Ford was already a hundred yards away, churning up funnels of dust. He turned to Lewis. "You okay?"

He nodded.

"Man, right now you look whiter'n me," Walsh said.

"No shit. You coulda slipped a credit card between that dude's door handle and me. You know him, Will?"

"Lonnie Kidman. Our village asshole."

They wedged themselves back into the cab and drove on.

"That looked a little on purpose to me," Lewis said. "It looked personal."

Will shook his head. "He lost control hitting that washboard. Thirty is fast on this road, and he must've been doing fifty-five."

"What I'm sayin' is, my face is the only black one I've seen since we got north of Milwaukee."

"Whatever else Lonnie is, he isn't a bigot," Will said. "He hates everybody—white, black, brown, or in between."

"He hate you?"

"I'm part of everybody. He worked for me for a few weeks last year. Dishwasher. I fired him, so maybe he hates me a little more."

* * *

They sat in the tree stand all afternoon, Walsh and Lewis with steel-tipped arrows notched, and waited for the reek of the baits to entice the bear out of the swamp. They waited until dusk bled toward night and then climbed down and tramped through the darkening woods to the truck. Will dropped the hunters off at their motel in town and said he'd come for them in the morning, an hour before sunrise.

"We'll be ready," Lewis said. "Sure do hope your village idiot won't be on the road that early."

That reminded Will. Instead of checking up on things at the brew pub before going home, he phoned Madeline and told her to keep his dinner on the stove; he would be a little late. He took the highway south to Seney and a gravel road out of Seney to the Kidmans' place, a seasonal deer camp that Lonnie's father, Angus, had rehabbed into an all-weather cabin without detracting one bit from its original shabbiness. Just the two of them, living in male squalor. Mrs. Kidman had fled ages ago, and most people wondered why she hadn't done it sooner.

Lonnie's redneck wagon wasn't there, but a light was on and Will could hear a TV inside. He stepped up to the porch and knocked. No answer. He knocked harder. Someone turned down the volume on the TV and called, "Who's there?"

"Will Treadwell."

Angus opened the door. "To what do I owe this honor?"

Like his son, he was a slightly built man who might have topped out at five feet eight. Will looked over his head into the room with its buckled fiberboard paneling and wood-stove, behind which an assortment of animal traps were piled in a corner and shotguns and assault rifles stood in a makeshift case. Angus drove a logging truck for a living; like a lot of people on the Upper Peninsula, where food stamps were good as gold and far more prevalent, he did a little of this, a little of that, to make ends meet. The little of this and that he did was to shoot game out of season and net whitefish and trap beaver without a commercial license and peddle whatever he'd shot, netted, or trapped to whoever was willing to pay and ignore legal niceties.

"Mind if I come in?" Will said.

"Hell, yes, I mind."

"Lonnie around?"

"See his truck, eh?"

"Is he here is what I asked."

"Nope."

"Where can I find him?"

"What d'you want him for?"

"He damn near ran over one of my hunters this afternoon. He was coming down a forest-service road like it was I-75 and swerved and came right at him. Would've killed him if he hit him."

"Where'd this happen?"

Will told him. Angus tilted his head aside and half-closed one of his wide, protruding eyes and looked up at Will with the other.

"So you're a traffic cop now? Gonna give him a ticket or what?"

"If I was, I might cite him for attempted vehicular homicide. My hunter thought Lonnie was *trying* to run him over. Because he's a black guy."

"Don't see many nig-nogs up here. Coulda been Lonnie got curious and wanted a closer look."

"I'm falling down laughing," Will said.

"He was prob'ly just blowin' off steam. He got fired yesttidy. From Jerry's place in Germfask. Guess he beat up on a customer. Some old fart pissed him off."

"Why doesn't that surprise me? That boy of yours has got the ugliest temper I've ever seen."

"Ain't no boy. He's twunny-five. What d'you expect me to do? Whip his ass?"

"From what I've heard, you did enough of that when he was younger. I'll be out there tomorrow, so what I expect you to do is tell him I'd appreciate it if he watched his driving."

"I'll be sure to do that. Now I expect you to get off my porch and the hell off my property."

"Pleasure talking with you, Angus."

* * *

Despite Angus, when Will pulled into his driveway, the sight of his house, its lighted windows cheerful and welcoming against the backdrop of black woods, immediately cast him into a better frame of mind. It stood on twenty acres he'd bought for a small fraction of what they would have cost in the resort lands on the Lower Peninsula. Across the drive was a pole barn and a log hut with a paneled sauna inside. He'd built much of this place with his own hands—he'd worked construction for three years after his discharge from the Marines—and looking at it always gave him a feeling of satisfaction: the barn and the sauna, the house with its steep roof that shed the snows of northern winters, its screened-in porch where he and Madeline sat in the long summer evenings.

His pair of springer spaniels, Chesty and Roy, slobbered him as he went into the mudroom behind the kitchen. His hunting clothes threw off hints of the bear baits' stink, and Maddie told him he would have to shower and change if he wanted dinner. Upstairs, he peeked in on Alan and ordered him to put down his phone and open a book. The command lacked sternness; he felt too good to play the role of strict father.

Will was sixty years old and in fine health, if somewhat overweight. He had a good woman's love. Dakota, his daughter by his first marriage, was teaching handicapped children downstate, and the son he and Maddie had together was doing well enough in high school, a star on the hockey team. Will was happy, and he clung to his earned joy now. For there'd been a long period in his life when he could take pleasure in nothing, when the memories of Vietnam, jabbing his brain, told him that he wasn't entitled to happiness or even simple contentment. He dwelled in a dark place that grew darker after Janine was killed in a car accident and he found himself a widower raising a child alone. His devils hadn't been exorcised so much as tamed. Maybe all he'd done was to keep putting one foot in front of the other, like the grunt he'd been.

"Much better," Maddie said when he came down scrubbed and in fresh clothes, his sparse reddish hair combed.

She rewarded him with a kiss and a bowl of venison stew. He poured a glass of wine and sat down to eat. She sat across from him with a cup of tea. Madeline had been a heavy drinker once—the Indian curse, though she was only part Indian, an Ojibwa on her mother's side—but had quit a couple of years after she and Will married. She'd been dry ever since and was a counselor at a drug-and-alcohol rehab clinic in Newberry, a calling to which her personal experience proved more useful than her degree in psychology. They'd joked about the ways they made a living—he served booze, she was paid to get people to stop drinking, and if ever she succeeded they'd have to turn to crime to pay the bills.

"What kept you?" she asked. "Did you have to track down another wounded bruin?"

He caught the note of disapproval in her voice. In her recovery, she'd become a born-again Christian, but she retained vestiges of her mother's traditional beliefs: the bear was a sacred animal, its powerful manitou held the secrets to healing sickness, it was not to be killed for frivolous reasons.

"I went to see a guy in Seney," Will said.

"Who and what for?"

He gave her the story.

"Lonnie Kidman? Doesn't ring a bell."

"That jerk who washed dishes for me a while back," he

reminded her. "He was looking for a job after his discharge, and I got sentimental about hiring a vet. Y'know, *Thank you for your service, here's a job.* I had to can him."

She glanced off to the side, crinkling her forehead. "Oh, yeah. I remember now. Something about him blocking a customer's car."

"The guy asked him to move his truck, Lonnie said when he felt like it, the guy asked him again, not so polite the second time, and Lonnie jumped on him like a pissed-off wildcat. I guess he got fired again for doing the same kind of thing. Beat up some old man."

"So he's one of these post-traumatic stress cases?"

"Is there such a thing as *pre*-traumatic stress?" Will said. "Because he never went to Iraq or Afghanistan. He was all hot to go, couldn't wait to shoot some Arabs, but Fort Benning, Georgia, was as close to the war as he ever got. He's never gotten over that."

"Schizo? Bipolar? There's got to be a reason for somebody behaving like that."

"Maybe. He's a mean little bastard with a vicious temper."

"How did we get on this?"

"You wanted to know what held me up. Let's talk about your day."

"Can't say much. The usual."

As she looked at him, the brightness of her gray-blue eyes startling in her coppery face, Will thought she was beautiful, better-looking at fifty-two than when she was younger and best friends with a gin bottle.

"Then let's not talk at all," he said, with a huskiness in his voice that made the suggestion plain enough.

She pointed at the ceiling to indicate that Alan was very much awake.

"At my age, moments of lust have to be taken advantage of right away," he said.

"Save it for later. So tell me a little about your clients. The Chicago cops. A black bowhunter—pretty unusual, isn't it?"

"A first for me. They're funny guys."

"Do you mean weird funny or funny funny?"

"Funny funny," he answered, then related the tale of Lewis's encounter with the gangbanger, the remark he'd made to the investigator.

She frowned and passed a hand through her hair with an abrupt movement and said, "Guess you had to have been there. What's so funny about taking a human life?"

"Look, it's like when I was in Vietnam. We made jokes about stuff that would curl most people's hair. It's a way of dealing with things. Otherwise, you go crazy."

"There is a divine spark in all of us," she said with evangelical fervor. "Even in the worst of us."

One of his old devils opened archival footage in Will's memory: two Marines from his squad shoving blocks of C-4 under the piled bodies of North Vietnamese soldiers, lighting the fuses, heads and limbs blasting skyward, raining down, strips of flesh and entrails hanging from tree branches, like streamers at some bloody festival.

"Sometimes it goes out," he said. "Even in the best of us."

* * *

Less than twenty-four hours later, Will was in the emergency room in the hospital in Newberry, sitting up in bed in a hospital gown, one arm connected to an antibiotic IV drip. He'd been given a local anesthetic before fragments of windshield glass had been plucked from his face. There was still some numbness, but he was beginning to feel a throbbing in the sutured cuts.

The curtains were drawn, creating an illusion of privacy. Madeline stood at his bedside with the doctor and a nurse, the doctor showing Will CAT scans of his head while assuring him that his injuries were superficial; the fragments had not penetrated to the bone or damaged any nerves. The wonder was that his eyes had escaped the spray of glass entirely. Maddie squeezed his hand and exhaled with relief.

"We're going to keep you overnight for observation," the doctor said. He was tall, slim, and freckled and looked too young to be a doctor. "You're a lucky man, Mr. Treadwell. Any questions?"

One question he had, the doctor could not answer. No one could. Why had he been so lucky while Lewis and Walsh had not? He'd heard an old saying once: luck is the residue of design. Meaning that you make your own luck. Vietnam had demolished whatever faith he'd had in that proposition. One hundred fifty-two men from his battalion had been killed during his tour. Why them and not him? The war had been a lottery, drawing its winners and losers blindfolded. He supposed that was true of life in general, the great difference being that in war it was immeasurably more obvious and that much less deniable.

"What time is it?" he asked, his voice slurry, the way it sounded after a novocaine shot in the dentist's office.

"Two-thirty," Maddie said. Her clinic was next to the hospital, and she'd run over to the ER as soon as she'd heard. It was she who'd told him that Lewis and Walsh, arriving in a separate ambulance, had been pronounced dead, a superfluous announcement. He knew they were dead. He'd seen them die.

"There's a police officer outside who wants to talk to you," the nurse said. "Are you up to it?"

He was. While they waited, he said to Madeline, "Y'know, I

felt really happy last night, really good, looking at our place. I should have known that something was going to happen."

"Sorry, I don't get it."

"In Vietnam, when you were coming in off patrol, when you were out of the bad bush and thought you were in friendly territory, and you were hanging loose, smoking smokes, grabassing around, happy as hell you made it through another one, that's when you got ambushed."

"I wish you wouldn't . . ." she began, then stopped herself, knowing that he knew what she was going to say: she wished he wouldn't look at life through the distorting lens of the war. "What are you saying? That happiness is dangerous?"

"I'm saying that you shouldn't put any faith in it."

The cop came in—Bromfield, a deputy sheriff—looking for a statement from Will, as full and complete as he could make it. The one he'd given to the officers who'd responded to the 911 call had been pretty sketchy. Understandable, considering . . .

"You're our only witness, you're it," Bromfield said.

"You've caught him?"

They had not. Sheriff's deputies had surrounded the Kidman cabin earlier, about the time that Will was being wheeled into the ER. Lonnie's truck was there, but Lonnie wasn't. Nor was his father. Angus had been miles away, delivering a load of logs to a mill, and when the police contacted him, all he said was that his son had left early in the morning to go hunting.

"Yeah, that's what he did, all right," Will said.

"It looks like he grabbed some warm clothes and survival gear from the cabin and ran off into the woods on foot," Bromfield said. "We've got officers from three counties beating the bushes for him, and a team of tracker dogs from the state police. We don't catch him today, we will tomorrow. He's not going to last long in those woods."

Will turned to Madeline. "Pack some things, get Alan after practice, stay in town tonight."

"You don't think he'll—" she began.

"We're too isolated out there. It'll make me feel better, okay?"

"But he's on foot, twenty miles away, cops and dogs chasing him."

"Please, Maddie. *Please.*"

After she left, Bromfield dragged a folding chair into the enclosure, spoke into a small digital recorder—*statement of Willard Treadwell, recorded on,* et cetera—and placed it on the bed. Then he sat down, a notebook in his lap.

"Okay, from the get-go, best as you can remember."

Will took a few moments, trying to assemble his fractured recollections.

"We got to the junction a little before first light," he said. "Where Forest Road 24 meets a jeep trail that leads to my stand. You can't drive it—it's blocked off by a berm. Right there in the headlights, we saw this black F-250 in the turnout where I usually park."

"Kidman's vehicle," Bromfield said.

"Can't miss it. Flames painted on the hood, jacked up, tires that look like they came off a road grader, spots on the roof. A badass redneck truck. Y'know, cruise around for trailer-trash chicks in tight jeans that don't leave much to the imagination."

"Please stick to what happened," Bromfield said. "Where was Kidman at this time?"

"Standing outside the truck, looking at a GPS. In a camo T-shirt. How do you figure? Thirty degrees and he's wearing a T-shirt."

Bromfield motioned his impatience with this irrelevant detail. "In your earlier statement, you said you asked him what he was doing there. Right?"

"Right, and he said he was going bear hunting. And I said back, 'Not here. It's my stand.' I knew right away what was going on."

"Which was . . . ?"

"You know about the talk I had with his old man last night?" Bromfield nodded.

"Well, I made the mistake of telling him that I was going to be there this morning. That's how Lonnie knew where to find me."

"You mean this wasn't just an accidental run-in? He was looking for you?"

"I can't say for sure. But Angus keeps tabs on where guides have their stands. He's a professional poacher. He'll poach just about anything except an egg, and knowing where baits are out makes his life easier. You can get up to three grand for a bear's gallbladder on the black market. His son is his understudy—"

"Then why did you tell Angus where you were going to be?" asked Bromfield, in his best suspicious-cop tone.

"Like I said, a mistake. I screwed up. So my guess is, he told Lonnie that he was going to be busy today and to get out real early and shoot the bear before I got there."

"Stacks up with the evidence," Bromfield said. "We found a spotlight and night-vision goggles in his truck. But what I'm asking is, do you have some reason, something Kidman said, for thinking that his real motive wasn't to shoot a bear but to ambush you?"

"You ask my opinion, yeah."

"I don't want your opinions, just what you saw and heard," Bromfield said sternly. "All right, you told Kidman that he was trespassing. Then what?"

"I lowered my window and told him to clear out. Lonnie went into a routine, y'know, made like he was looking around for something, and he said, 'I don't see no sign says, RESERVED FOR WILL TREADWELL. We had words."

"What kind of words? What did he say? What did you say?"

Will's face felt stiff from the stitches, as though there were bits of cardboard sewn to his skin. But he was pleased with himself for the way he was handling things, for the calm, composed manner in which he was answering the deputy's questions.

"Lonnie goes, 'I hear you don't like the way I drive.' I go, 'I don't like the way you park, either.' Then he says, 'And I hear you're spreadin' it around that I tried to run you over, you and the Uncle Remus you've got with you.' So I told him for the second time to get in his truck and go somewhere else."

"And what did Kidman do then?"

"Started shooting, that's what. He pulled a rifle from out of his truck and—"

"What kind of rifle, if you know."

"An AR-15."

"Walsh and Lewis were off duty but they were carrying their service pistols. Did they try to defend themselves?"

"Never had a chance. They never got their guns out of the holsters. We were crammed in the front seat like sardines. Could hardly move."

"All right. So you told Kidman to leave and he opens fire, just like that?"

"I left a part out. First off, he blows his stack, yells something at me—something like, *You're the one who's going somewhere, motherfucker*—and then he opens the passenger door on his truck, swings it open like he wanted to tear it off the hinges. That's when Lewis and Walsh tried to get their guns out, like they knew he was going for a weapon. The next thing I saw was the rifle . . ."

Bromfield scribbled with one hand while gesturing with the

other for Will to go on. But his memories of the following seconds, however many there'd been—Five? Ten? Fifteen?—were
as shattered as the windshield. The sounds of the rifle, of breaking glass, of bullets hitting metal and flesh, merged in his mind
into one sound. He remembered Walsh's body slumping against
him but had no recollection of how he'd managed to open the
door, roll out of the truck, dash across the road, and dive into a
culvert. One moment he was in the cab, the next in the ditch,
as if transported there by magic. Yet one memory was clear, and
it pained him to summon it up. As he lay in the culvert, he heard
Lewis cry out, "You shot me enough! Don't shoot me anymore!"
and then two or three more rifle cracks.

"I stood up. I don't know what I thought I could do," Will
continued, watching Bromfield's ballpoint skip across the page.
"I thought I saw Kidman trying to pull Walsh's body out of the
truck. I couldn't see much because of the blood running into
my eyes. Kidman spotted me, or heard me rustling the brush
when I got to my feet, and he spun around and I guess I'd be
with Lewis and Walsh now if he had a round left."

Because I ran out of bullets, Will thought as he spoke. "I took
off running, and that crazy little bastard reloaded and ran after
me, shooting into the woods, and yelling that he'd get me yet. I
knew where I was. I knew that Johnny Bugg—he's an Ojibwa I
know from my bar, a pulp logger—has a place out that way, with
a phone. And that's where I went, and you know the rest."

Bromfield flipped through his notes, clicking his tongue.
Then he stood, handed his card to Will, and said, "If you think of
anything else, anything you might have missed, give me a call."

Will slipped the card into the plastic bag containing his wallet and clothes. He saw the bloodstains on his shirt. The flecks on
his collar he assumed to have come from him, the large blot below
from Walsh, after he'd slumped, without a sound, into his lap.

"There's one other thing," Will said. "When I told you that I told Kidman to get out for the second time, that's not exactly what I said."

"Exactly what did you say?"

"'I heard you like to beat up on old men. If you don't get your skinny ass out of here, you can try your luck with this old man, you scum-licking little shitbird.' I was pretty pissed off, taking lip from a scumbag. I should've known better. It doesn't take much to set him off. Maybe if I'd . . ."

"I wouldn't worry about that," Bromfield said. "I wouldn't think about it."

"I'll try not to," Will said.

* * *

Will was wheeled to a private room, as if he'd been crippled, and hooked up to a machine that monitored his blood pressure and heart and pulse rates. It seemed that a lot of fuss was being made over a patient with superficial injuries. The doctor was probably erring on the side of caution; the hospital in Newberry, Michigan, population two thousand give or take, didn't admit many shooting victims.

The anesthetic had worn off, and Will felt as if a tormentor, hidden from sight, were poking thorns into his forehead, cheeks, and jaw. The nurse administered a shot of morphine. In minutes, it duplicated a sensation he'd had nearly forty years ago, on a hospital ship off the coast of Quang Nam Province: a liberation of mind from body. His conscious self floated into midair and looked down on his physical self with the detachment of someone observing an injured insect.

He had no awareness of time passing, so he didn't know how long he'd been hovering there, between the ceiling and the bed, before Lewis spoke to him—not as a voice remembered but as if he'd entered the room, a kind of unseen visitor. *Forget it, Will. Don't give him what he wants.* Lewis had uttered those same words this morning, right after Will had called Kidman "a little shitbird" and right before Kidman grabbed the rifle. But what did he want? An excuse to commit cold-blooded murder? Doubtful. Kidman's violence wasn't the sort that needed excuses.

Speaking spirit to spirit, Will asked Lewis, *Well, what did he want, or what do you think he wanted?*

He was a soldier, Lewis began, *and so were you, so you ought to know that soldiers are dreamers. . . .*

Suddenly, the room phone's ring yanked Will back into his body, and contact with Lewis was lost. He lifted the receiver. It was Madeline. She and Alan were going to stay the night with the Magnusons. How are you feeling, darling? *Soldiers are dreamers.* Those words, vaguely familiar, teased his brain. Will, are you there? How do you feel? Like I've been shot in the face with a dozen pieces of safety glass, he answered, his voice thick and slow from the drug. Did you tell Alan that I'm okay and that I'll be home tomorrow? Yes. If you've got a TV in your room, it's going to be on the six o'clock news tonight. No, thanks. I've got a pretty good idea of what happened. The police are going to call off the search till tomorrow. It'll be pitch black in the woods pretty soon. Everybody in town is locking their doors. *Soldiers are dreamers.* Where had he heard or seen that line before?

* * *

Sitting against a tree, rifle in his lap, Lonnie looked through the trees. He'd been waiting here, in the woods at the edge of a roadside rest stop, since before dawn. The sky was paling now, and he could clearly see the parking lot, a picnic table, two outhouses, and the highway beyond, Michigan Route 28. This part of it, called the Seney Stretch, thirty-odd miles of two-lane shooting straight as a railroad track through spruce bog and tamarack swamp, bore little traffic even at midday. At this hour, it was almost deserted. So far, only two cars had passed by.

Lonnie shivered in the late October chill. Besides cold, he was hungry and wet, having slogged through a marsh yesterday to throw the dogs off his scent. Tired, too. He'd slept maybe two hours, after breaking into an empty deer camp last night.

Another car went by, then a semi-trailer. Ten minutes passed, fifteen. Daylight washed over the woods and the rest stop and the highway. He knew he could not wait much longer before he would have to plunge back into the wilderness and dodge the search parties and the dogs. Ten more minutes. At last, a car turned in, a white Jeep Cherokee. He watched a man climb out and walk into one of the outhouses. Lonnie rose and moved quickly to the rear of the outhouse, then around to the front. He didn't have a high opinion of Jeeps. Not as fast or as rugged as his V8 Ford or a Dodge Ram. But beggars couldn't be choosers, could they? Not that he intended to beg.

* * *

Madeline drove Will home in the late morning. They listened to the NPR station out of Marquette, waiting for the news to air. A classical-music program was playing, violins and cellos making a bizarre soundtrack when they were stopped at an intersection by a state-police roadblock: two patrol cars, flashing lights strangely festive; four cops carrying shotguns. One of them gave their license plate a quick look, peered into the window for a moment, and let them through with a brusque wave.

Will called Bromfield on Maddie's cell. His was in his truck, and his truck, impounded as evidence, had been towed to the sheriff's department in Manistique.

"Hey, it's Treadwell," he said after Bromfield answered. "What's going on? The state cops have a roadblock at 28 and 77."

"Yeah. Roadblocks all over the U.P. A closing-the-barn-door-after-the-horses-are-out kind of thing."

"What're you talking about?"

"You don't know? Kidman hijacked a car."

"Holy shit!" He turned the phone to speaker so Maddie could hear. "Where? When?"

"The rest stop on the Seney Stretch, a few hours ago. Nobody was there. A guy pulled in to take a leak, a liquor salesman. Kidman cornered him in the men's room at gunpoint, took his car keys and wallet, and then whacked him over the head with a rifle butt and drove away. Kidman didn't take his cell, so when the guy came to, he called nine-one-one."

"Pretty good head start," Will said. "He's got to be—"

"Out of state by now. Figure three hundred miles."

"You said yesterday that you'd have him today. Doesn't look promising, does it?"

"Uh-uh," Bromfield said, as if this were of no great concern. "But there's a lot of today left, and he's got police departments from here to North Dakota looking for a white Jeep Cherokee with Minnesota plates GIN2408. You know his reputation. This isn't some ice-cold professional we're dealing with. A dumb hot-head. He'll fuck up. He's desperate."

"He seems to be doing just fine so far," Will said, annoyed by Bromfield's casual confidence.

"Listen to this. The liquor salesman is five-nine, thin, got dark hair, twenty-nine years old."

"Kidman will try to pass himself off?" Will said. "He'll use the guy's credit card to buy gas, and that's when he gets nailed?"

There was a rushing sound on the phone—Bromfield sighing, like a teacher exasperated with a slow student.

"You're almost there. The rest stop was deserted, remember? If Kidman were Mr. Frosty killer thinking ahead, he would have shot the guy, then dragged the body into the woods. He's got his wallet and ID and car. How long before anybody finds the dead liquor salesman? How long before he's identified? How long before his murder is tied to Kidman? By that time, Kidman could be on the goddamn North Pole."

Will thanked him for the insight into the criminal mind and closed the phone. Madeline said, "Jesus God, it's like we're in a movie."

"I wish."

"All right. But now he's three hundred miles away," she said. "Can Alan and I sleep in our own beds tonight? Can we go back to normal? I want out of the movie. I want to feel normal again."

He gazed at the woods flashing by, the yellow aspen leaves flickering in a breeze, the red blooms of mountain ash. "All right. And you don't have to take the rest of the day off and nurse me. I'll be fine. Go to work, go grocery shopping, and I'll pick Alan up from hockey practice, like always."

"Nope. You're on painkillers. You shouldn't drive. I'll get him."

* * *

Will should have known he'd been too quick to congratulate himself; he'd been calm and composed merely because he was in shock. As soon as he came out of it, the reaction was bound to set in, and it did after Madeline dropped him off and he was alone in the house, with no one to talk to except Chesty and Roy.

Lying in bed, he played the shooting over and over in his

head, on an endless loop. The thin, tattooed arms in the headlights, the black rifle. He was helpless to stop it and sick with
fear, much as he had been decades ago, unable to sleep at night
because night was the time of maximum danger, his mind
refighting battles there in the room where he silently recited the
bedtime prayers of his childhood: *There are four corners to my
bed, And four angels overhead; Matthew, Mark, Luke, and John,
Bless this bed that I lay on.*

Now what frightened him most was the expression on Kidman's face, or, rather, the absence of expression when he opened
fire, eyes as blank as a rattlesnake's. Will questioned how he
could have observed such a detail with bullets drilling through
the windshield. Was this a true memory or a thing imagined?
Or a memory altered by his imagination? Whatever the case,
he saw those eyes now. The deadness in them caused him to
wonder if there were people in whom the divine spark had never
been lit: a kind of birth defect.

Four angels overhead. Yes, but what goblins lurked under-
neath, what bogeymen crouched in the corners, what dread fig-
ments cast their shadows on the walls? He got up and paced
the room, trying to settle his nerves. *Bless this bed that I lay
on . . . G'night, Mom. Good night, honey. Sweet dreams.* Then he
remembered: *Soldiers are dreamers* was a line from a poem he'd
read years ago. Odd. He didn't read poetry. He didn't read much
at all, beyond newspapers and sporting magazines.

He went downstairs and looked at the bookshelves in the living room, his gaze roaming over Maddie's textbooks and professional tomes, a few paperback novels and histories. There was
only one volume of poetry: *The Collected Poems of Siegfried Sassoon.* He opened it and read the inscription from an old Marine
Corps buddy, Tim Galloway, with whom he'd stayed in touch
after they'd rotated back to the States: *Christmas, 1977. Will—I*

*was blown away by this book. The poems are about WWI, but
they could be about our war, too. Merry Xmas and Semper Fi,
Tim (aka Dado).*

Will smiled as he scanned the table of contents. Their squad
leader, Sergeant Perkins, had given Tim the acronymic nick-
name Dado, for "Dumb-Ass Drop-Out," because he'd quit college to join the corps.

He found the poem "Dreamers" on page 76, read it through
twice, and the last four lines of the first stanza—

> *Soldiers are sworn to action; they must win
> Some flaming, fatal climax with their lives.
> Soldiers are dreamers; when the guns begin
> They think of firelit homes, clean beds, and
> wives.*

—spoke to him directly, as if he and Siegfried Sassoon had
shared a foxhole in the An Hoa Valley.

He remembered that while half the guys his age would do
anything to stay out of the war, he'd wanted to get into it, eager
for an experience terrible and great. He'd pictured himself, that
year he'd enlisted—it was 1968—dying in some valiant act, the
solemn notes of "Taps" drifting into the echoes of the honor
guard's rifle salute, eulogies in praise of his bravery following
him into a hero's grave. Boot camp and advanced infantry training conjured darker longings. The point of those ordeals was to
overcome certain inhibitions by instilling not only a willingness
but a wish to kill. Two months later, he rode a helicopter into
his first assault, a pack on his back, rifle in his hand, and in his
head lurid visions of winning a medal not for dying but for making an enemy soldier die in a hand-to-hand fight.

After he'd gotten a good taste of war, which had proved more terrible than great, after he had taken lives, albeit at a distance without certainty that his bullets had dropped the running figures two hundred yards away, the nature of his yearnings changed. On muddy monsoon nights lit by sputtering flares, a return to ordinary life, from whose dull rituals and routines he'd sought escape, became a beguiling fantasy seemingly beyond fulfillment, like imagining what he'd do if he won the lottery.

He was startled out of these recollections by the dogs' furious barking in the kitchen. He called, "Quiet down!" They kept on. He went in. They were up on their hind legs, forepaws on the windowsill, howling at an intruder: a spikehorn buck had wandered into the yard. It seemed to know the dogs weren't a threat and tiptoed around Maddie's vegetable garden, looking for a way over or through the deer fence. Finding none, it began to browse on the twig ends of a young red maple.

The angle of late-afternoon sunlight threw a coppery tone on the buck's gray coat, late afternoon at these latitudes being three o'clock. Alan would be done with hockey practice at four. Will went to the cordless phone to tell Madeline not to bother picking him up; he was feeling well enough. Not that he was; he simply needed to think about something other than what had happened to him.

The phone was dead. He smacked the handset in his palm, put it to his ear. Still no dial tone. The handset must have failed to recharge. He placed it back in its cradle and was about to go to the bedroom phone when in a single instant he heard two quick gunshots and saw the spikehorn spring straight up into the air, then fall. In the next instant, he threw himself on the floor, his heart banging against the tiles. Chesty and Roy were yapping and running in circles; to them, gunfire meant a downed bird they were supposed to fetch.

"Shut them fuckin' dogs up, or I'll kill 'em, too!"

The shout came from somewhere behind the pole barn. Immediately, without thinking, Will, on all fours himself, grabbed the spaniels by their collars and, crouching low, tripped the latch to the cellar door with an elbow, pitched them down the stairs, and slammed the door behind them. They would be safe there. The next shot smashed a window and ripped a chunk out of the wall. It hurt him almost physically to see that, what with the pride he felt for this place, the sweat and money he'd put into it.

"You know what I come here for, Will Treadwell! Let's get it done!"

In a panic, he lunged up the stairs to the bedroom. Yes, he did know now, which meant one more item could be added to his list of should-have-knowns. Should have known that he and Bromfield had misjudged Kidman as incapable of forethought or cunning. Collecting himself, Will grasped all at once what must have happened: Kidman had calculated that the carjacking, after it became known, would draw the search parties out of the woods onto the highways in pursuit of a white Jeep Cherokee. That was why he hadn't killed the liquor salesman. He'd taken the car into the backcountry maze of logging roads, forest-service roads, and two-tracks, which he knew from accompanying his father on poaching expeditions. Then he must have looked for a spot to hide the vehicle, remote enough not to be noticed by some wandering hunter or off-roader but near enough to Will's house to make his way there on foot. He'd arrived a short while ago and set the dogs to barking when he'd snipped the phone wires at the connection outside.

Another gunshot, this one from a direction opposite the last. It shattered a window in the living room, where the *Collected Poems of Siegfried Sassoon* lay on a lamp table. And another, from the back of the house. Kidman was circling the place, a raiding party of one.

Does he know I don't have my cell? Did he see it in my truck? Will thought, ducking into the closet. His home-defense weapon was propped in a corner: a semi-automatic police shotgun loaded with eight rounds of double-aught buckshot. He grabbed it. Was there any other choice? Even if he had his cell, he could not possibly summon the police to get here in time. He could flee, as he had yesterday, take his chances and run out the door and hope that Kidman would miss him again, but he sensed that in the act of seizing the shotgun, he'd committed himself to a single course of action that could have only one of two possible outcomes. He sensed as well that the random firing, the challenge to "get it done," were supposed to lure him outside, where Kidman, hiding in the woods surrounding the yard, would have a clear field of fire. Or maybe he'd lead Will into the woods, and the two of them would stalk each other. In his own mind, Kidman was at war. Will knew it, perhaps better than Kidman did himself. The experience had been denied him, so he'd started his own war.

He fired again, a burst this time, the rounds whacking into the clapboard siding. The noise heartened Will. The plotting he'd had to do to come to this point had exhausted Kidman's capacity for calculation; his natural, impulsive violence was regaining the upper hand. Sooner rather than later, frustrated by the lack of response from inside, he would be unable to bear the tension; sooner rather than later, he would be compelled to enter the house and bring things to their flaming, fatal climax. Whatever he'd wanted a day ago, that was what he wanted now.

Will hurried to the downstairs hallway and wedged himself into a corner. An evil, once it presents itself, is not half so terrifying as when it's imagined. He wasn't as afraid as he'd been less than an hour ago, lying on his bed. He wasn't afraid at all, and the release from fear exhilarated him. In a state of acute awareness, he could hear Oscar and Buster whining in the cellar below and the sound of footfalls on the back-porch steps.

A thud as the mudroom door was kicked open. He pictured Kidman, lost in a fantasy, putting his boot to the door, rifle leveled, as he must have seen done a hundred times in news clips from Fallujah or some other nightmare place. And that image brought Will into a strange communion with the man who intended to kill him; he had a sense of the inevitability that arises when desire unites with necessity. What was about to happen had to happen because that was what he wanted, as much as his adversary did. Unconsciously, he'd wanted it since yesterday morning, running for his life, Lewis's plea echoing in his mind.

Kidman was in the kitchen now. In a moment, he would step through the entrance to the hall. Will eased the safety off and raised the shotgun to his shoulder.

THE NATURE OF
LOVE ON THE
LAST FRONTIER

I 've understood why a son might be driven to kill a cruel father, but a father murdering his son, no matter how delinquent, has always struck me as an unthinkable crime against nature, right up to the moment when my son made me think it.

I am on bear watch while Trey fishes, standing sideways to the current, his feet spread wide to keep his balance, the gray-green water making a V-shaped riffle as it pushes around his upstream leg. He's casting into a pocket across the river, just above the place where it necks down and dances over a rock-cobbled shallows before sliding into a long pool, smooth as an ice sheet and darkened by the spruce leaning out from both banks. In the far distance, a snow-cowled mountain shows blue in the long arctic twilight. It's late in August—the days at these high latitudes shed light quickly, each several minutes shorter than the one before; even so, the hours of full darkness are brief. The blackness that cancels dawn and dusk will not descend for another two months. I've experienced that perpetual midnight only once, the year I'd studied in St. Petersburg, then called Leningrad, and I hated it.

Trey makes a cast. Line and leader shoot ruler-straight behind him, then the forward cast unfurls in a tight loop. He stops the rod at the ten o'clock position, as I've taught him, and the leader inscribes a rough S in the air and the streamer flops into the pocket water, under a hanging alder branch. After mending the line to make for a natural drift, he follows the fly with his rod tip as it swings downstream, then strips in and casts again. *Nicely done,* I think. Sensing that the lift in my heart his finesse produces might presage forgiveness, I check it immediately. It's always a mistake to conflate the artist with his artistry.

The rod bows on the next drift; the line slashes crosscurrent into the shallow water above the pool.

"Big one!" Trey calls to me as I sit on the gray gravel bar and keep a lookout for bears. We haven't seen any so far, but they're around, fishing, too, because salmon and char are spawning now. Their huge tracks, printing the riverside mud, give me the same pause as signs that read: DANGER! NO TRESPASSING.

The tips of the tail and dorsal fins of Trey's fish show above the surface, and there must be at least a foot between them. I glimpse a flash of reddish belly, dark, speckled flanks: a char, a spawning male that might be six or eight pounds. Mud swirls when its belly scrapes bottom. Realizing it has swum into trouble, the fish turns suddenly into the pool and streaks downstream; all the line and then backing hisses off the reel.

"Jesus! Bigbigbig!"

Trey wasn't calling to me now; maybe to himself, maybe to the somber spruce immuring the river. Nature in Alaska is nothing like the housebroken nature in lower Michigan, where we're from. It's nature off the leash, stupefyingly vast, and its

wild soul whispers that you are a triviality, so you announce
your presence, you assert yourself with a yelp, a shout, a howl.

The pool is nearly as long as a football field. Tiring, the char
stops its run at about the fifty-yard mark. A quivering in the taut
line that throws tiny droplets into the air tells me that it's shaking its head to throw the hook. I picture it down in the emerald
depths, the streamer hanging like spittle from a jutting jaw. Trey
wades into the thin water to give himself firmer footing.

"Put the screws to him," I say, standing up. A lesser yellowlegs, alarmed by my movement, swoops toward my head, low
enough to make me flinch. "Cup the reel. See if you can turn
him."

"I know what to do."

"Then do it."

"I'm afraid I'll break him off."

"If you know what you're doing, you won't."

He follows my instructions—a rare thing—and clamps his
fingers on the spool to prevent the reel from turning and to
apply maximum pressure on the fish. It doesn't budge. The rod,
stiff enough for the grayling Trey caught earlier, is too light for
this beast.

It races off again, and Trey sprints with it, hopping along a
narrow shelf edging the right-hand bank, where the water is no
more than a few inches deep. He's trying to get below the char,
so he won't have to fight it and the current both. I follow him,
stumbling in my waders down the whole length of that pool, Trey
reeling up slack as he runs, staying tight to the fish. We round
an oxbow bend. The char stops again, and so do we, a good
thing; a sow grizzly with two yearling cubs occupy a gravel bar
no more than thirty, thirty-five yards downstream.

She is looking into the river, ready to pounce on any decent meal that swims by. Although we're downwind, she senses our presence, rises on her hind legs and stares right at us, as motionless as a stuffed bear in a museum, except for her cinnamon fur, rippling in the breeze blowing straight up the river from the direction of the mountain whose name I cannot pronounce. Every inch of eight feet, every ounce of five hundred pounds, she stands upright for three or four seconds, assessing if we're a threat, then drops back to all fours but continues to face us, her snout raised to pick up a scent. Grizzlies have poor eyesight, but she might consider it a challenge if I meet her gaze. Lowering mine, I notice how vibrant are the colors of the rocks paving the river bottom—green, gold, red—and this acuity of vision has something to do with the fact that a five-hundred-pound grizzly is taking a profound interest in my son and me.

Credit Trey with whatever is the opposite of attention deficit disorder. Or maybe it's the conviction, inherent in all twenty-year-olds, that he's indestructible. He's totally focused on his fish, which has lodged itself in a trough beside a boulder roughly halfway between us and the bear. Rick loaned me his .44 Magnum before we left camp. It's in a shoulder holster strapped outside my chest waders. No creature on earth is more implacable than a female grizzly defending her young. This one, probably, would be on us quicker than I can draw, aim, and fire a killing shot. Not that I want to kill her, but I want even less—much, much less; infinitely less—for her to kill Trey and me.

"Break him off," I whisper.

"No way. I—"

I snatch the line near the reel, give it a quick wrap around my fingers, and feel the line go slack as the leader parts.

"What the fuck . . . ?" Trey groans, reeling up as he reproaches me with a look.

The char enjoys its liberty for a second or two before the sow lunges into the water and, in a single movement, like a second baseman fielding a slow grounder barehanded and flipping it to first, swats the fish with a forepaw and tosses it onto the gravel bar. The cubs pounce on it.

We start to hike back toward camp, a half mile or so upstream. The river is low and braided, and the walking is easy over the exposed shoals, rocks milled down to pebbles by twelve thousand years of rushing glaciated water.

"That was a helluva good fish. Would've been the biggest trout I ever caught," Trey says, injecting rebuke into "would've been."

"A char isn't a trout, if that's any comfort."

"Well, it isn't."

"If that sow got it into her head that we were a danger to her cubs, she would have been on top of us in two seconds flat and in another five seconds turned the both of us into coleslaw."

Trey responds with what used to be called the silent treatment but is now known as passive aggressiveness. Being a male of the old school, the kind who prefers back slaps to bro hugs, I would welcome a mood of active aggressiveness, an air-clearing, spleen-blowing fight, albeit one that doesn't turn physical: Trey is one-ninety and is—I mean *was*—a varsity wrestler at the University of Michigan, while I'm a fifty-six-year-old Russian literature professor who hasn't been in a scrap since I was his age, and maybe younger.

When we come to the spot where I'd been watching for bears, the yellowlegs flies from out of the woods on another strafing run. She wings so close that she nearly knocks my hat off. Others join her—a squadron buzzing us with shrill cries. The avian attack is like a scene from Hitchcock's *The Birds,* but it's as comical as it is menacing. Laughing at ourselves as we duck and bob and weave, like punch-drunk fighters, we break into a jog to escape, staggering over the rocks. Finally, we're in the clear, except for a single bird that flies out ahead, one wing flapping erratically.

"What the hell was that all about?" Trey asks with a nervous giggle. Some of the tension between us has relaxed. Some, but not all.

"Must be a rookery nearby," I answer. "Protecting their chicks." I point at the lone yellowlegs with the spastic wingbeat. "She's pretending she's injured to draw us away from the nests, I guess in case the bombardment didn't work. Predators always go for the weak one, right?"

Trey shrugs and resumes his silence.

Three bell tents of brightly colored nylon sit like huge termite mounds on the tundra fell that slants upward toward the south face of the Brooks Range. Smoke rises in tendrils near the largest of the three, our mess-cum-supply tent. Rick and Elise are cooking dinner. Rick is a freelance wildlife photographer who is doing a photo-essay for a sporting magazine that appeals to outdoorsmen with seven-figure incomes. Elise is his girlfriend, but he always refers to her as his assistant, to preserve the fiction that their relationship is strictly professional. As for Trey and me, we're Rick's subjects—we are to begin hunting Dall sheep when the season opens tomorrow.

We slog across the fell toward camp. It looks cozy and welcoming, so long as we focus on it and avoid taking in the landscape, whose scale and wildness reduce it, and us, to nothing. In the Alaskan bush, you are constantly aware that a small mistake in judgment, or a stroke of bad luck, can have catastrophic results. Most state mottoes and nicknames are exaggerations or outright falsehoods. Michigan claims it's the Wolverine State, even though a wolverine hasn't been sighted there in a century. But Alaska really is what it calls itself—the

Last Frontier—and given its inhospitable climate and geography, is likely to remain so forever.

"Any luck?" Rick asks, stirring a pan in which the contents of a U.S. Army MRE have been dumped. The olive-green package lies crumpled on the rock fire ring.

"Yeah and no," Trey replies, managing to sound sulky and sarcastic at the same time.

Rick looks up and squints at me, deep lines fanning out from the corners of his eyes, like rays in a child's drawing of the sun. I remove the shoulder holster and pistol and hand them to him and explain what happened on the river. He nods to tell me that I did the smart thing, and Elise seconds him.

"Mama bear starts to look at you like that, you relocate. But you don't turn and run. That would trigger a chase response, and a grizz can outrun a racehorse. You back away from her, cooing like you're putting a baby to sleep."

Trey opens his mouth to say something, and fearing that it will be smart-alecky, I'm grateful when Elise checks him with an upraised hand.

"Now, sometimes a grizzly will charge anyway, sow or boar. You'll know a charge is coming when the bear clacks its jaws. It can be pretty loud, all those sharp teeth, and it's the most shit-your-skivvies sound you'll ever hear in the bush. To give yourself a chance that it isn't the last thing you'll ever hear, you fall on your belly, cover the back of your neck with your hands, and play dead. If you're lucky, the bear leaves you alone."

"And if it doesn't?" Trey asks.

"You'll probably die."

"Why not just shoot the damn thing first?"

"That assumes you have a gun with enough oompf to drop it right away. Take those .270s you and your dad have. . . ." She twitches her head at the yellow-and-green tent a few yards away, our tent. "They'll kill a grizz if you can shoot it right through the heart or the brain. Otherwise, you'd best be sure you've removed the scope and filed the front sight off."

Trey skews his face into a puzzled expression. Elise smiles—she has a toothpaste-commercial smile—and I grin, too, knowing what's coming.

"That way, it won't hurt so much when the bear grabs the gun and shoves the barrel up your ass."

Trey's laughter is welcome. Elise has brought out the good Trey, for the moment anyway. She talks like a Calamity Jane and looks like a supermodel: the dazzling smile, reddish-blond hair that falls in waves a little past her shoulders, hazel-green eyes, and the finely cut features of a WASP princess, though she attests to come from dirt-poor country stock. What she's doing with Rick is mystifying, a study in the perverseness of human sexual attraction. He's my age, twenty years older than she, and two inches shorter. Gray spatters his unkempt, dingy brown beard, and the teeth that show through it now and then are crooked and stained from his former habit of smoking a pack of unfiltered Camels a day.

Trey reaches into his canvas creel and, one by one, pulls out four fat grayling.

"I got these at least," he declares, lays them on the ground in a neat row, and waits to be praised as the camp's provider.

"We'll have a two-course meal, then," says Rick, who fetches a sheathed knife and a small cutting board from a canvas bag. "Fillet 'em, but not here. Nothing like fish guts and slime in camp to draw critters, so do it there."

He points at the lake a short distance away, where the float-plane delivered us yesterday afternoon. Trey looks at him as if he's been ordered to scrub a toilet.

"Something the matter?" asks Rick.

"Isn't that the guide's job?"

Rick clenches his jaw, then forces his lips to part, his teeth like chunks of almond. "I'm not your guide. This isn't a guided trip. It's just the four of us, and we all pitch in, right?"

"Meaning," I say, shamed by my son's spoiled-brat attitude, "filleting the fish is your goddamn job."

He says nothing. Words would be superfluous. Ill adept at disguising his feelings, he seldom needs to express them out loud.

Elise grabs the knife and cutting board. "C'mon, Trey. We'll get it done in two minutes."

When they're out of earshot, Rick says, "It's none of my business, but—"

"I'll apologize for him. We taught him manners, Cheryl and I did, but sometimes he's a thirteen-year-old in a twenty-year-old body. Been a handful since day one. Nothing like his older brother."

Gloving his hand, Rick removes the pot from the coals and covers it. "I meant there's something simmering between you two. It's damn near visible. Even an idiot like me can see it."

He and I go back a very long way, to high school in Manitou Falls, Michigan, where Rick, a skinny misfit, had been nicknamed "Nature-Nerd" because he spent most of his free time in the woods, collecting plants and bugs and taking pictures with an Instamatic of rabbits, raccoons, birds. I'd gone on a few of his expeditions and had been impressed by his skills and eventually became his friend, shielding him from bullies and taunts. We haven't seen each other in years, and although he no longer needs me to protect him from anything, our old bonds are like the strings in a fine piano—still in tune, even though it hasn't been played in decades.

Which is why I have no trouble being candid with him. Last April, near the end of his sophomore year, Trey had been expelled from UM for, as the police report phrased it, *posses-sion of a controlled substance with intent to distribute.* Hashish was the controlled substance. His partner, a girlfriend studying abroad for the semester, had mailed him a kilo of the stuff from Amsterdam.

"That proved the both of them flunked Drug Trafficking 101," I say.

Rick frowns, puzzled, then arches his eyebrows. "Oh, yeah. Dope is legal in Holland, so . . ."

"So a package mailed from there is likely to get special attention. Okay, the mailman delivered it to Trey's apartment—he was living off campus with a couple of his frat brothers. The mailman had him sign for it. The cops had set that up with the post office. Trey stashed it in the fridge. Five minutes later, narcs from the sheriff's department kicked down the door, confis-cated the dope, and off Trey went to the county jail in hand-cuffs." I pause for a moment, mentally composing an abridgment of the miserable tale. "First I heard about it was when he phoned me, begging me to bail him out. Somebody—a public defender or cop, I don't know—told him that because it was his first offense, the felony would be wiped from his record if he pled guilty and went to Narcotics Anonymous meetings once a week for a year. I sent him to college for a degree; now I had to cough up twenty-five hundred bucks to keep from acquiring a rap sheet. If I'd had *Star Trek* powers, I would have teleported from Lansing to Ann Arbor and strangled him with the phone cord."

Rick chuckles.

"I'm serious, Rick. I felt capable of killing him."

"So what did you do?"

"Waited twenty-four hours before wiring the money. I fig-ured a night behind bars might be a teaching moment. You want a lesson in humility, go to a strip-mall Western Union to wire bail money to your kid."

"That's a lesson I've never needed. What's so humbling about it?"

"You stand in line with trailer trash bailing out their relatives."

"Uh-huh." His narrow gray eyes fix on me. "So what's pissed you off is that Paul Egremont, PhD, professor of Russian lit, had to stand in line with the trailer trash."

He makes no attempt to scrub the bite from this remark. Back in high school, Rick had been the only child of what was called in those times a "broken home." He lived with his mother, a waitress, in a rented cottage near the ore-freighter docks on Lake Michigan. Two divey bars a block away in one direction, a strip joint in the other.

"The teaching moment—how's that worked out?" he asks.

"So far, no good. He still claims he's innocent, had no idea there was hash in the package. I ask him, 'What did you think was in it? Cookies? Fruitcake? Is that why you put in the fridge?'"

Rick, glancing over my shoulder, signals that the conversation is over. Trey and Elise are on their way back from the lake.

* * *

The air has teeth in the morning, whetted by a north wind. It's late summer back home, mid-autumn here; the tundra vegetation is changing color, bursts of burgundy and orange amid the green; the yellow leaves on the aspen that share space with spruce flutter like candle flames. We crawl reluctantly out of our sleeping bags, shiver ourselves warm, brew coffee, and cook instant oatmeal over the campfire.

Trey has gotten over his disappointment with losing the big char. He cracks jokes, volunteers to gather firewood and to fetch wash water for our mess gear. The good Trey again. Of course, that could change at any moment. His sharp, unpredictable swings from cheerful to sullen, civil to rude, are what make him so problematic. They keep me off-balance. He would be easier to deal with if he were a jerk all the time instead of half the time. He reminds me a little of Cheryl's youngest brother, Todd, also a moody character, affable one minute, offensive the next. What's more, like most self-centered people, Todd lacks self-awareness, doesn't realize when he's being obnoxious, and is shocked and perplexed when anyone—me, for instance—tells him so. He'd been a commercial real estate developer, a chiseler, a cheat, a crook who'd bought a sixteen-room house in Bloomfield Hills at thirty-two and at forty was sentenced to three years in federal prison for bank fraud. What upsets me most about Trey's abortive venture into crime, and his absence of remorse, is the possibility that he's inherited an outlaw gene from his uncle.

We break down the two smaller tents, stuff them into backpacks with our sleeping bags (in case we have to spike out), and start for a drainage where Rick had spotted sheep last week, on an aerial reconnaissance. From a distance, we must look like some sort of guerrilla band in our hunter's camouflage. Walking on tundra is like walking on a waterbed stuffed with bowling balls, the squishy tussocks rolling under your feet. Half an hour of it, carrying a pack with a rifle strapped to it, wears me out. I'm grateful when Rick, in the lead, finds a game trail that winds through the trees galleried along the river. Trampled by parades of moose and caribou, it feels solid as a sidewalk.

I'm bringing up the rear. Trey is in front of me, head and torso canted slightly forward, probably to ease the weight of his pack but possibly to give himself an uninterrupted view of Elise's ass, whose contours her baggy pants cannot completely hide. I'm not so old that I've lost all memory of what it's like to be his age—the perpetual roil of male hormones. I'm not totally past that even now, though it isn't Elise's backside that captures my attention but her copper-colored hair, flowing out from the back of her wool watch cap to flounce and bounce on her shoulders.

I don't know much about her. What I do know she revealed at an awkward moment at the hotel in Fairbanks, the day before we were to board the floatplane. I'd complained of a sore neck from the long, tedious flights from Detroit. Twelve or thirteen hours. She claimed to be a qualified masseuse and invited me to her and Rick's room for a rubdown. But Rick wasn't there; he was out running last-minute errands. She told me to take off my shirt and lie facedown on the bed. I did; then, straddling me, her knees pinning my ribs, she proceeded to dig her strong hands into the back of my neck, into my shoulders. I wondered, *Is this a tease? Is she up to something?* She must have known that her ministrations could be arousing—which they were—but she could not have been so reckless as to think of stealing a quickie with a married man whose son was in the room down the hall, not to mention the chance that her boyfriend might walk in at any minute. I squashed my own erotic thoughts by asking her about herself, as if I were a human-resources director interviewing an applicant.

She lived in Anchorage, where she met Rick. She'd been a student in the photography class he teaches at the local community college. In the past, she'd managed an inn, owned by her ex-husband, in a remote town named Eagle. The End of the Road Roadhouse. After the marriage broke up, she guided eco-tourists on hikes and rafting trips, then spent four years as an instructor at the Wilderness Leadership School.

"Alaska's the right place for me," she said in a chatty voice, as if we weren't alone on a bed in a hotel room, me bare to the waist. "That's because the twenty-first century is the wrong century for me. I've got skills that are of zero value in the modern world."

She enumerated them while I, with a rapid heartbeat, waited for Rick to suddenly return and make a scene. "I can gut and skin a caribou, smoke salmon strips, paddle a rubber raft through class-three rapids, find my way by the sun and stars, tie a diamond hitch to a packhorse. I shot a bear once, back when I was managing the roadhouse. I'd gone out for firewood and it came at me. A .300 Winchester Mag. Right here." She paused her massage to reach over my head and press a finger between my eyes. *Plus*, I'm a published author."

"What did you write?"

"Kind of a self-help book. *How to Wipe Your Ass Without Toilet Paper: Survival Tips for Cheechakos*. That's the title."

"Uh, kind of wordy, don't you think?"

She pounded my back, bottom to top, with the heels of her hands.

"But catchy, don't *you* think?"

"What's a cheechako?"

"You are. A tenderfoot."

"And you're what? An apprentice photographer?"

"You could say that. Okay, all done. How's the neck?"

"Loose," I answered as she dismounted and I stood to put my shirt back on. There was a mischievous twinkle in her greenish eyes. Easy to understand why Rick had fallen for her. My protective instincts rising to the surface, I hoped she wouldn't dump him after he'd taught her the tricks of his trade.

* * *

We come to a steep ridge. I'm slipping and sliding in the shale—imagine climbing the roof of a ski chalet that's five or six hundred feet high and covered with loose shingles. Rick's smoking habit—he quit only a couple of years ago—appears not to have affected his wind. With a camera and binoculars harnessed to his chest and twenty or thirty pounds on his back, he strides up as if the slope is as gentle as a pitcher's mound. Elise keeps pace with him, and Trey's young legs seem to devour the 60 percent grade. The others reach the crest when I'm barely halfway to it.

Ten minutes more and I'm there. Gasping. Below is a wide valley split by a nameless, almost waterless creek hemmed by stunted spruce that draw a winding dark-green line across the paler green of the tundra grasses. Lying flat behind a spotting scope, Rick glasses the ridge on the opposite side, twice as high as the one we've just climbed, topped by sheer limestone crags resembling ruined temples. Low shrubs speckle its slopes; otherwise, it's as rocky and gray and barren as a ridge on the moon. Right below the crags are what look like whitewashed rocks— Dall sheep. All ewes and lambs, Rick declares, except for one ram.

"Not shootable," he adds, then motions to Trey and me to have a look. "He's way off to the left and way down from the rest."

The 60-power scope brings the ram startlingly close. I can see his black snout and his eyes, and they seem to be staring right at me as he turns his head, crowned by brownish horns curved like fingernail moons.

"He's eating rocks," Trey says after I turn the scope over to him. "What's he eating rocks for?"

The question elicits Rick's pedantry. The valley was a sea-bed sixty million years ago, he begins. Fossilized corals and marine organisms are embedded in the shale, and the phosphorus and nitrates in those ancient skeletons leach out. The ram has left the safety of the high elevations because he needs those minerals in his diet. He isn't *eating* rocks; he's *licking* them.

"It's wonderful. Those rocks are graveyards for things that died when dinosaurs were roaming around," Rick goes on, rapturous. "And now they feed animals living today. It really is wonderful when you think about it."

"I suppose," Trey replies. "So why can't we shoot him?"

"What did I tell you the other day? The horns have to have a three-fourths to a full curl. That makes it legal. This ram isn't much more than a spikehorn."

Trey, shading his eyes with a palm, looks this way and that—a parody of a scout spying out the countryside. "Don't see any game wardens," he says, drawing a scowl from Rick. "Hey, kidding. I'm just kidding."

I'm not sure he is. Maybe the outlaw gene is speaking to him: *If you think you can get away with it, do it.*

Just then, Elise hisses for our attention. She's pointing at three caribou that have appeared in the valley, seemingly out of nowhere, a kind of caribou nuclear family—cow, calf, a splendid bull with antlers like branched lightning and a cape that falls like a silver apron over his forequarters. They are ambling over the open tundra, grazing on the move. The bull is without question a legitimate animal, and Trey quietly chambers a round and looks to Rick for permission to shoot. That pleases me— the restraint shows respect—but Rick shakes his head, whispering, "That's a five, six hundred shot and all downhill"—which pleases me further. The chances that Trey would wound the animal at such long range are great; so are the chances that he would miss entirely and hit the cow or calf.

Rick notices something. He grabs the spotting scope, squints through it for a few seconds, then signals Elise, who pulls from her backpack a lens that looks as long as a rocket launcher. Rick locks it into his Nikon—such is the stillness that the click sounds alarmingly loud—and rests it on a flat boulder.

"What is it?" I ask, in an undertone.

"Those willow bushes on the right . . ."

Raising my binoculars, I scan the willows clumped at the creekside but don't see anything at first; a moment later, I glimpse movement. It's faint—shadows drifting through the thicket.

"We're about to watch a nature documentary, and it won't be heartwarming," Rick murmurs.

A hunting pair emerges from the willows, crouched low in the tundra grass. Their cautious stalk, their absolute, unshakable concentration, remind me of my bird dogs approaching a covey of grouse or quail. The caribou are upwind and facing away, and that favors the wolves. They have moved only a few yards before they halt to study their prey. The tension in their long gray bodies is palpable, even at a distance. The arrest between equal and opposite urges—spring or hold. They hold for now, probably waiting for more space to open up between the calf and the adults. The calf is what they're after. A pack could easily bring down the cow or bull, but these two don't have any help. The bull would be especially dangerous; he's twice their size put together; his antlers, larger than the female's, are bone-tined pitchforks; a kick from him could cripple or kill.

Suddenly, all three caribou raise their heads. An eddy of wind carrying wolf-scent must have alerted them. They look toward the thicket, as if to verify the wind's warning, but before they can bolt, the wolves explode, legs stretched out to run them down. I sweep the binoculars to follow them and see the bull whirl and charge into the wolves' charge, hooking with his horns. He grazes the larger of the pair—an alpha male, I assume—knocking it flat. Its mate rushes the caribou from behind, and he spins to confront her as the male rolls to his feet and stands motionless for a few seconds, like a dazed boxer taking a standing eight count.

Now begins a spectacle Trey and I have never seen before, a lethal ballet strangely beautiful even as it's horrible. The she-wolf charges the bull, he lunges at her, antlers throwing lefts and rights, but she nimbly dodges one side to the other. Instantly, the male sprints at the caribou's haunches, forcing him to face the new threat. This goes on for ten or fifteen minutes, the wolves taking turns, one attacking from behind, the other from the front, the bull pirouetting round and round. Rick records the dance of death, his camera's burst shots making a rapid chirp. The wolves' intelligence and agile teamwork are awesome to behold. They harry the caribou like matadors in a bull ring until he's exhausted. His silvery breast heaves, his head droops, its swings grow feeble. He stands on splayed legs, nose halfway to the ground while the she-wolf paces back and forth in front of him. She darts in, twirls away, darts in again.

A diversion.

The male, stationed some twenty yards behind the bull, decides the time has come to end the choreography. He covers those twenty yards so fast I almost don't see him streak between the widespread hind legs and bite into the belly, ripping it open. Entrails, a slick mass, spill out like groceries from a bag. Incredibly, the caribou is still upright, staggering, stumbling, intestines trailing. Both wolves snap at them, eating him alive.

"Jesus! Jesus Christ!" Trey cries, shouldering his .270.

Elise pushes the barrel aside. "There's no saving him now," she says, adding, "Nothing up here dies easy," with a calm that comes off as indifference.

The bull at last topples over—dead, I hope. The male wolf leaps onto him, bites a chunk out of his hindquarters, and illustrates what it means to "wolf it down."

"I feel like shooting them myself," I say.

Rick shifts his look from the camera to me. "They don't do it for fun, y'know."

He points with two quick fingers. Far below, the she-wolf has fetched her brood from the thicket, four of them. Even through my 10-by-50s they look like mere blackish puffs, trotting behind her in a row. They tuck into the feast, gobbling up guts and organs, devouring the bull from the inside out while their parents, savaging the haunches, go at him from the outside in.

"It's like he sacrificed himself for the cow and calf," I say, finding it impossible not to anthropomorphize.

"That's a nice thought," Rick replies.

*   *   *

It's ten-thirty and only now grown dark. The wind has picked up; cold, sharp gusts slap the tent. Snugged down into my sleeping bag, I hope I won't have to get up in the middle of the night to piss. Probably I will. Roughing it isn't for middle-age men with prostatitis.

"That was a hell of a thing we had to watch today," Trey says, his voice muffled; he's buried his head in his sleeping bag to keep the chill off his face. "The way they tore him open. I was imagining what that felt like. Your guts spilled and you're alive to see a wolf chomping them."

This tenderness, this empathy for a fellow mammal, isn't like him.

"Why are you feeling sorry for the bull now? A few minutes before the wolves got him, you were all set to shoot him."

"Right. Shoot him. He would've been dead before he knew what hit him. I wouldn't have sliced him open with a knife and gutted him alive."

"If the wolves could shoot a rifle, they wouldn't have, either."

"Ha ha."

"Would you rather see the wolf pups starve? Killing and eating—that's the background music up here. Elise had it right, nothing dies easy."

"Her Hard-Bitten Bitch of the Far North act gets real old real quick. A bullet through the heart would have been a lot easier than getting eaten alive. Anyway, I thought we were on a hunting trip."

"We are."

Lying on my back, I can see my breath plume and condensation spreading a sheen over the tent's ceiling. It is a hunting trip, and to make it, I'd had to pull more strings than a puppeteer to exempt him from two N.A. meetings and allow him to leave the state. Besides his father, I am, in effect, his parole officer. He's been living at home since his expulsion, working days for a landscaper I know, playing video games at night in his room. Dinners with him are studies in family non-communication. Yes, it's a hunting trip, but its purpose is not, for me, to shoot anything. A quest, rather, to discover what's going on in Trey's heart, his mind, his soul. I want to know my son, hard as it is to know anyone, even ourselves.

"All we did today was hang with Rick while he took pictures," Trey grumbles. "Him and the hard-bitten bitch."

"Keep your voice down."

"It is down. They won't hear us anyhow. They're probably fucking in there."

"Trey! Dammit . . ." A picture of a naked Elise embracing me in a sleeping bag has composed itself in my brain. "Rick's on an assignment. This is a job for him. He invited me to come along, and I invited you. An experience like this—your old frat brothers would give up their iPhones for it. So quit complaining."

"They don't hunt. Most guys my age don't. I'm like that Indian in *The Last of the Mohicans*. That Indian with the weird name, Changachuk or whatever."

"Chingachgook. Uncas was the last of the Mohicans. Chingachgook was his father, kind of the second-to-last of the Mohicans."

"Hey! Homeschooling."

"Good night, Trey."

* * *

We scour that hard country for a Dall ram, hiking into drainages as innocent of human footprints as Mars. There is enough water in them to overtop our boots, and willow and aspen stick fires do not burn with sufficient heat to dry our socks. The temperature falls a little each day, and each day loses seven or eight minutes of light. We are being stalked by an ever-advancing night. On the third day of this, we trek more than five miles from base camp and are too tired to return to it (five miles in Alaska is equal to twenty anywhere else). Also, it has begun to snow, lightly, but snow all the same.

We spike out on a saddle in the mountains, from which we can see the base camp's supply tent, bright green and blue dots on the tundra fell below, and the pewter-colored river flowing past it, and the lake where the plane is to pick us up in another three days, unless weather prevents it from flying.

Glassing the landscape, I watch a bear digging in an alpine meadow. It rises onto its hind legs, then crashes back down to all fours, long-clawed forepaws furiously flinging dirt. It's the same blondish sow Trey and I had encountered on the river; her cubs gambol nearby. "She's excavating the meadow for parky squirrels," Rick lectures. "Parkys—so-called because Inuit line

their parkas with the squirrels' fur—live in underground bur-
rows, like prairie dogs." He tells us that they weigh about two
pounds each, a pretty meager reward for the effort she's putting
into its acquisition.

"Calories in don't come close to calories out," I remark.

"They're called barren-ground grizzlies for a reason," Rick
answers. "Out here, you grab what you can when you can. She's
got to feed her kids something."

This prompts Trey to remark that he isn't being fed too well.
A cup of instant oatmeal for breakfast, beef jerky and a protein
bar for lunch, freeze-dried noodles for dinner. He reckons his
ratio of calories out to calories in at three-to-one, making it clear
by the sulky glances he tosses at Rick and Elise that he blames
them for his privations.

To avoid overloading the floatplane and to make room
for their camera gear, two boxes of food had to be left behind
at the airstrip in Fairbanks. "Better that we lighten up with
that than with warm clothes," Rick said. "We can subsist off
the fish we catch and the game we shoot." He must have been
recalling his hardscrabble youth, when he kept his mother and
himself off welfare by filling the freezer with venison every
deer season. I'll admit that living off the land appealed to me at
first; it lent a survivalist tint to what otherwise would have
been a sporty adventure. I'll admit to this, too: young men
Trey's age had been leading patrols in Afghanistan while he
and his girlfriend hatched their drug-smuggling scheme; I
thought that a little hardship, a little suffering, might benefit
his character.

But so far we've caught few fish and have shot nothing, making this more of a character-building exercise than I'd bar-
gained for.

* * *

The gunshot wakes me from a dream that flees my brain the instant my eyes open. I free myself from the sleeping bag, crawl outside, and see Rick, Elise, and Trey trudging up the saddle, toward a dark form lying in the snow on the mountainside. A couple of inches fell during the night, but the morning sky is unblemished. By the time I lace up my boots, throw on a jacket, and walk over to the others, Rick has fetched a camera and is photographing Trey, striking the standard poses with the caribou he has killed. While I slept, they'd spotted the animal making its way down the mountain. Trey got his rifle and lay down in a shallow depression, Rick and Elise beside him, whispering to wait, wait, wait until the bull was in range.

"One shot, Dad!" Trey says, his face alight. The bull isn't large, its rack modest as caribou racks go; but it is Trey's first one, and Rick has smudged his forehead with its blood—the hunter's ancient rite of initiation. My father had done the same with me when I shot my first deer at age fifteen. "We saw him when he was way up there"—Trey gestures at the peak, white and sharp and curved, like a fang—"and when he turned broadside, I dropped him. One shot!"

The picture-taking over, Rick draws his knife and, kneeling beside the carcass, begins the messy labor of gutting, skinning, and quartering. We all pitch in, and it's done fairly quickly.

"What the hell is going on?" Elise chimes in. She squats down to scrub her hands in the snow. "The college-boy cheechako catches the most fish and shoots the only game."

Trey beams.

I'm guessing that the "Hard-Bitten Bitch of the Far North" has, with this compliment, redeemed herself in his eyes. A breeze lifts a wisp of his broom-colored hair. I forgive his silly boast, shake his hand, clasp his wrestler's shoulder, and for a moment see him at twelve, grinning after he's kicked the winning field goal in a Pop Warner league game. He leans toward me, then draws back, almost imperceptibly. He senses, accurately senses, a certain half-heartedness in my congratulations.

We pack out the quarters, carrying forty pounds more apiece than we carried in. Although it's all downhill, the trek to base camp takes three hours. We arrive worn out, then turn to the tedious work of boning and trimming. The meat is crammed into game bags, and those are strung up in the tallest tree we can find nearby, an aspen. It's only twenty feet high at most, but the bags should be out of a bear's reach. Rick has saved the backstrap, which he slices into strips that we spit on sharpened willow sticks and roast over the fire and eat with our hands. Dress us in furs and we'd look like some band of Neolithic hunter-gatherers. We're so hungry that the lean tenderloin doesn't fill the hollow in our bellies, so Rick fetches an onion and green pepper from a food container, chops them up, and mixes them with a mess of shoulder meat for a stew. I can't remember tasting anything quite so good. A shot of hip-flask whiskey in a tin cup, sipped as the late sun tints the mountaintops, finishes things off nicely.

* * *

At first light the next morning, sitting on a bed of glacial till, we glass a mountain whose slope is spotted with Dall sheep, once again ewes and lambs and a few adolescent rams. Rick, standing behind a tripod-mounted camera, his head shrouded in a black cloth, is taking landscape shots. His instrument is big and bulky and could have been used by Ansel Adams. A four-by-five Crown Graphic, he told me earlier, more than fifty years old. Despite its antiquity, no digital camera can come near it for capturing the sweep of wide, wild country.

The stillness is like none I've experienced in the Michigan woods. There, even when you can't hear a man-made sound, the air seems to carry echoes of chain saws, traffic on distant highways, the shouts and laughter of campers. This is a silence never broken by humanity's clatter; it is layered, dense, virgin, alien—a disquieting quiet, if you will. All the otherness of the natural world is in it—a world complete unto itself, independent of man's endeavors and conflicts, his plans, schemes, joys, griefs, his egoistic certainty that he is a child of God. Compared with it, the noise I've left behind—the chatter at faculty meetings, TV sound bites, campaign speeches, talk-radio yelps, the whole busy racket—has all the import of crickets chirping. The thick soundlessness almost makes me hallucinate; once, I think I hear voices, an indistinct murmuring, as of a distant crowd. It's probably nothing more than the wind playing tricks, but a part of me wonders if it's the mountains speaking, in a language beyond my understanding.

"I see it! My ram!" Trey cries, and yanks me out of my reflections. He lowers his binoculars and points. "Up there on that ridge! The ledge just under the ridge!"

Rick ducks out from under the hood and falls prone behind the spotting scope, trains it on the ledge.

"Good eyes, Trey. A full curl."

I find it through my field glasses. It's kneeling on all fours, its horns swirled like massive whelks. He's so beautiful I would just as soon leave him up there, in magisterial repose, but I cannot deny my son his moment.

A bluff sheers down to the river; beneath it is a gravel strip, like a sidewalk beneath a building. We file along it, using the bluff to mask our approach—Dalls have eyesight equal to a

10-power scope. So Rick says, and I have no reason to dispute him. The river on this stretch, below cascading terraces, is deep and jade green. Fallen spruce lay out on the surface—giant quilled brushes swaying in the current. Sweepers, they're called. Upstream of the trees, a boulder big as a garage juts out from the bluff, blocking our path. We climb up and around it, shale and scree crumbling underfoot. Acutely conscious that we're out of contact with civilization—Fort Yukon, the nearest human settlement, is a hundred fifty miles away—I take great care with each step.

Now we begin to scale the ridge, the ram several hundred feet above us. Rockslides lead up the slope, the rocks piled one atop the other, precariously balanced, too unstable to walk on. We climb the tundra between the slides, clinging to willow bushes, tufts of grass, anything we can grab. It seems to take ten minutes to go as many feet. The goal, Rick says, are two limestone plinths, split into a V, that rise at roughly the same altitude and less than a hundred yards from the ram, perched on the ledge. Trey is to position himself in the notch and use his backpack as a rifle rest.

"I've seen you shoot, and it should be an easy one for you," Rick says in a subdued voice. The praise delights Trey. "But we'd better be quick," he warns, motioning to the north, where lead-colored clouds have begun to tower.

But the terrain won't allow us to be quick. Besides the precipitous slope, impenetrable willow thickets force us onto a rockslide, on which each step must be measured and tested before taking the next. In no time, the squall blows in at forty miles an hour, driving before it dense flurries that swoop and swirl. The willow brakes thin out and we hop off the slide, but the wind is howling with such force we can't climb any farther.

All we can do is flatten ourselves against the ridge so we aren't blown off and wait for the squall to pass.

It doesn't. The snowflakes, whipping our faces, feel like hailstones.

Elise voices what I'm thinking: "This is fucking nuts!"

Rick agrees. "We'll try again tomorrow," he shouts, and starts to toboggan downhill on his butt.

"I can make it!" Trey yells, and scrambles on all fours in the opposite direction.

I am just able to grab him by an ankle, and I hold on with both hands.

"Goddammit! Use your head!"

"Goddamn you!" he hollers, looking back at me over his shoulder, a bright, wild, predatory glitter in his pale eyes.

He kicks free. A second later Rick calls out, "Look!" and jabs a finger at the ledge. The ram has abandoned it and is confidently picking its way, niche by niche, up what looks like a wall. Snow flurries and cloud obscure him for a minute; the next time we see him, he's standing profiled on the ridge top, as though to taunt us, and then he goes over and out of sight.

"Shit! Shit and son of bitch!" Trey cries out in frustration. He swats the air, I suppose in lieu of swatting me. "He was mine! I could have had him!"

I know what he's thinking: after he'd worked so hard, after he'd come so close, the ram's escape was unfair. Still, his tantrum is disproportionate to what was lost—a trophy, that's all; a pair of horns to hang on a wall.

"He wasn't yours," I say. "He never was."

Going down is as harrowing as going up, even more so what with the buffeting gusts, the slick footing. Reaching the bottom, we retrace our route along the gravel strand under the bluff. The squall at last passes beyond us, rolling southward with the river. The sky is clear, except for a few ragged clouds. Well overhead, two golden eagles, wings outspread, gyre on the thermals.

Trey grows impatient with our middle-age plodding and stomps out ahead, still hot with anger and disappointment.

Rick, Elise, and I catch up to him at the giant boulder. On this side, it slants gently to its domed top; it drops straight down on the side facing the river, which picks up speed as it sweeps past, forming a series of low, standing waves. In a fit of youthful bravado, or just to show off, Trey digs his fingers into a fissure a little above his head, pulls himself up, and then crawls over the huge rock while we do the sensible thing and climb around it.

The rounded top is wet from snowfall. He slips and falls into the river, a ten-to-twelve-foot plunge. He lands feetfirst, and for a slivered instant, he stands in water that comes almost to his neck; then the current scoops the sandy bottom from underfoot, gives him a shove, and carries him on his back into the jumbled sweepers ranked downstream. All this happens in two seconds, too fast for me to react until I see his arms lunge through the surface and seize the first tree in the row. How, in his heavy clothes, weighed down with a pack and rifle, he stayed afloat, I count as miraculous.

With Rick and Elise, I sprint down the shore to the root-tangled base of the fallen spruce. Trey is perhaps only fifteen feet from me, with one elbow hooked around the trunk, the other around a branch. He is struggling to haul himself onto the trunk and straddle it, but he can't overcome the weight pulling him down, the current sucking at his legs. What had begun as a mishap now threatens to become a catastrophe—his clothes insulate him, but in water that cold, he hasn't got more than ten minutes. If, that is, he doesn't drown first.

I step out onto the tree, with no thought but to reach him.

"Take this! Tie it around him!" Elise hands me a coil of line. For some reason—really for no reason whatever—I observe that it's a bright-yellow synthetic.

Walking the spruce trunk is as close as I've ever come to walking a tightwire. It bobs under my weight. I keep my balance by grasping the branches sticking up in the air. Standing over Trey, I make a loop with a slipknot and drop it to him. He is looking up at me, shock on his face. Shock from the fall, shock from the cold. It's ceramic white.

"Grab it, Trey. Grab it and put it over your wrists and I'll pull it tight."

"I can't move my hands, Dad." His fingers are almost blue. "I'm going to let go and—"

"No! Don't!" *My boy is going to die.* The words crash into my head. If he does let go, he'll sink and become trapped in the submerged branches. *My boy is going to die.* In such circumstances, the human mind tends to attribute powers of intent to unconscious nature. The river seems a malevolent force that wants to drown my son; the branches underwater, waving in the current, are green tentacles, groping for him. But of course the river is only a river, of course the branches are only witless branches; the one will go on flowing, the other go on with their swaying motions whether Trey lives or dies; and that absence of all regard strikes me as more abominable than any malign purpose. "Grab it! Grab the rope!" I cry again.

He attempts it, but his fingers are frozen into claws. Bending forward as far as I can without falling in myself, I slip the loop over his left wrist, then the right, and cinch it.

"Hang on, Trey. We've got you."

I make it to the shore. The three of us, in a tug-o'-war row, pull hard and haul him onto dry land. He lies facedown, trembling from a cold I mistake for fear, or joy at being rescued, or both.

"He's in second stage," says Elise, meaning second-stage hypothermia. "Get him to his feet, strip him to the waist. You, too, Paul. Strip to the waist, hug him, get your body heat into his core. *Now*."

Trey is unsteady on his feet and shuddering uncontrollably when I embrace him. It's as though I'm hugging a stone statue, his skin is so cold. When he speaks, what comes out is gibberish. Second stage. There is no stage after the third. I press my chest against his, lock my arms around his back, imagining myself not as a father but as a kind of mother—a mother, yes, connected to him by an invisible umbilical cord, pouring my body's warmth into his.

Elise pulls a paperback book from her pack, rips out a few pages, balls them up under a pile of twigs, and strikes a match.

"He's not out of the woods yet. Keep holding him, walk him around, until I get the fire going," she says. "One time, a guy we thought was okay went into his tent to lie down. He died right there."

I don't need to hear that. *Did we save him from drowning only to lose him to something so petty as a few degrees of body temperature?* All the pain of Cheryl's long labor—seven hours— all the anxieties of nursing him through childhood illnesses and making sure he did his homework and trying so hard and so often failing to keep him out of trouble and when he got into it, getting him out of it because we believed in him, was all that to be for nothing? Trey's head lolls against my shoulder. I kiss his chilled cheek and indulge the need to plead, picturing myself down on a supplicant's knees. *His mother will be devastated; I will be devastated. We love him, we love him, do you hear?*

Though I'm not religious, I am looking up as these words fly through my mind, looking up at the sky, against whose blank, annihilating blue the two eagles turn and turn without a sound. And in their silence I hear an answer.

Rick has broken off branches from a dry driftwood log and stacked them in a teepee. They catch, and in a minute or two a small bonfire blazes.

"How are you doing?" Elise asks Trey.

Nodding, he mumbles that he's all right. He's a bit groggy, but the shivering has abated. Placing her hands on his shoulders, she turns his back to the fire, holds him there for a while, then turns him again, and yet again, as if he's a roast. I notice then that the book she tore up for tinder is her own. *How to Wipe Your Ass Without Toilet Paper: Survival Tips for Cheechakos.*

"I was going to give it to you when we got back, signed by the author, too," she says, with the same playful twinkle bestowed after my massage. "But I've got lots of others. I'll mail one to you."

Rick has meanwhile piled rocks behind the fire and draped Trey's jacket, shirt, and undershirt over them.

"Better get your boots and socks, too," he tells Trey. "Better get everything off and dry. It's a hike back to camp."

Trey takes off his boots, removes his socks, and wrings them out before laying them on the rock pile, but he demurs about stripping his pants and long johns.

Elise hoots, covering her eyes with both hands. "Promise not to look. I'll bet your swim made you a little Mr. Grape Nuts, am I right?"

And we all laugh.

* * *

His "swim" took more out of him than any of us realized. He's listless and subdued, spending the rest of the morning in the tent. Recalling Elise's tale of the man who had seemed to recover from exposure only to die in his sleeping bag, I check in on Trey a couple of times.

Rick and Elise leave to take more photographs and return in midafternoon. We lunch on caribou steaks, seasoned with pepper and fried in butter. Rick shows Trey an image on his Nikon—it's the ram, which he captured with a 300-millimeter lens as it stood this morning on the ridgetop, facing the camera, great horns curled in a natural coronation. It looks as if it's posing for its portrait.

"I'll make a print, send it to you," he promises. "Way better than a wall hanger. You've got a story to tell."

Trey's glance rises from the view-screen and roams over our faces.

"Thanks . . . Y'know . . ."

"No problem. Not like I'll have to make prints in a darkroom like in the olden days."

"No . . . I mean . . . all of you . . . thanks for, y'know, saving my life."

Rick pauses to peel the backing off a piece of nicotine gum. "Sure," he says. "You can thank us by doing something serious with it."

* * *

The sun, not yet risen over the mountains, brushes high cirrus clouds with orange and peach. We break camp in preparation for the floatplane's arrival. We don't know when it will—could be an hour from now, or two, or five—but we need to be ready.

Rick humps his cameras, the tripod, and other paraphernalia to the lake, then returns for his backpack. Elise, kneeling on both knees, shoulders a duffel bag containing the big supply tent and stands, bent under the load, like some refugee fleeing with all her belongings.

Trey is fully recovered. "Give her a hand with all that," I tell him.

Back to his old self—not necessarily a good thing—he snaps at me: "Yo! She's a hard-ass, and I've got my own shit to carry."

"Goddammit . . ."

"Oh, no worries, Paul," she sings out, with a kind of caustic weariness. "I'm not used to gallantry anyway."

She strides off, Trey right behind her.

"Son of a bitch," I mutter to myself.

Rick grasps me by the biceps.

"What is it?"

He displays his yellow teeth. "Thought it would be like the movies, right?"

"Movies? What movies?"

"That he'd be different. Faced death and all that and all of a sudden he's changed, grown up."

"I suppose, yeah."

"It doesn't work that way. He'll be all right. Give it time."

"Well, listen to the parenting advice from a guy who's never had kids."

It's a cruel, stupid thing to say, which I regret immediately.

"No, I haven't," he replies serenely. "But I've been around the block more than once—more times, I'll bet, than the college prof."

We four sit in the alders at the lakeshore for a long time, speaking very little. My thoughts wander back to the wolves killing the bull caribou and what Elise said then, and to Trey's rescue and the eagles soundlessly whirling while I held him, terrified that he might die in my arms. A wind has come up, as it usually does by midmorning. Keen-eared, we listen for the drone of an approaching plane, but all I hear is the wind and the voices it seems to carry, those strange murmurings from the unpeopled mountains. I understand them now. I feel I can be their translator.

LOST

1.

In the early spring of 2014, tired of the bar-and-restaurant business after more than thirty years, Will Treadwell sold the Great Lakes Brew Pub. He had just turned sixty-four; it was time. Considering its location in a small town on the south shore of Lake Superior, he'd expected it to languish on the market for no less than a year; instead, it sold within weeks.

The buyers were Patrick and Vicky Scully, a couple from Traverse City, old enough to have acquired some capital and a decent credit rating, young enough to take a chance. They'd owned a tavern in Traverse but felt that the city had grown too upscale for their tastes—"Too hoity-toity," in Vicky's words.

Will was not prepared for the quickness of the sale. More than expecting the brew pub to linger, he'd wanted it to. A part of him did, anyway. He needed time to get used to the idea of retirement and to plan what to do with himself. Moving to a warmer climate or traveling was not to be considered. Madeline, eight years younger, had no desire to leave her counseling job at the clinic in Newberry.

When the time came, Will read a little, watched television a little, tended to house repairs that had gone neglected, exchanged occasional emails with his son, Alan, now a junior at Ferris State. Once or twice, he stopped in at his old place for lunch and to offer his advice to the new owners if they asked for it, which they didn't. Otherwise, he occupied himself by hiking along the lakeshore or in the woods with his new dog, a lively young English setter named Samantha. Still, he was left with the retiree's dilemma: too much free time and no idea how to spend it.

* * *

Idleness, seldom good for anyone, was particularly unhealthy for Willard Treadwell. It unlocked a certain door in his mind, making it easier for Dark Ones to enter. They'd intruded on his days and disturbed his sleep for a long time after he'd returned from Vietnam, until, for no identifiable reason, their irruptions ceased. But when a semi-trailer T-boned Janine's SUV at an intersection, killing her instantly, Will relapsed. Nightmares. Spells of frigid gloom relieved by outbursts of anger. He was living in Marquette at the time, working for a firm that built log homes from a kit, supplementing his income as a hunting guide on fall weekends, a part-time bartender in the off-season. All the while, he was struggling to raise Dakota, his and Janine's only child. His shaky psychological state, along with money problems, made him less than a model single father.

He met Madeline Croft in the early summer of 1980, when she was just twenty-two. She and some friends were celebrating their graduation from Northern Michigan in a Front Street pub where Will tended bar on Saturday nights and sometimes downed a beer or two after a week of fitting prefab logs together.

That's what he was doing on that Friday evening. A tall woman with the blackest hair he'd ever seen drew his glance, though she wasn't trying to attract his attention. Will did not stare directly at her but at her reflection in the back-bar mirror. Of the five women in her group, she was by no means the prettiest— her face with its coppery complexion was too full, too round, a pie plate of a face, and her blunt nose had a slight skew, as if it had been broken once. The long, pitchy hair, spilling down to the middle of her back, and her gray-blue eyes were what arrested him, the eyes especially. They flashed a strange mixture of defiance and sadness, suggesting that she'd taken some hard knocks but wasn't about to let them keep her down. There was a certain boldness in her manner, apparent in the way she stood at the bar, one foot mannishly on the rail, while her friends sat.

It became more apparent a little later. A trio of young men, college boys from Northern, one of whom was wearing a green sweatshirt with gold letters spelling "NMU Wildcats," came in and started to chat up the women. The pub was crowded and noisy, loud music on the jukebox, so Will couldn't follow what brought on an argument between the black-haired girl and the guy in the sweatshirt. He could sense a familiarity in it, like an exchange of words between ex-lovers. He, "Sweatshirt," called her "Pocahontas," to which she gave a sharp reply that Will didn't quite hear. The next thing, they propped their elbows on the bar and clasped hands. They were going to arm-wrestle. Sweatshirt was small, five-six or so, two or three inches shorter than his opponent, but his wide shoulders and muscular arms hinted that he was stronger than he appeared at first glance. One of his friends, grinning at the prospect of an arm-wrestling match between the sexes, laid a palm flat on the contestants' joined hands, then raised it and said, "Go!" In two seconds, Sweatshirt had her arm nearly flattened, when she did something with her wrist. Will, watching in the mirror, couldn't see what—some quick, twisty move that bent her opponent's fingers backward. He yanked his hand from hers, as though he'd touched a hot plate, and yelped in pain.

"Who taught you that, you sneaky bitch?" he cried out, rubbing the injured hand. "That black-belt gook?"

She nodded. "And I'll be getting mine pretty soon."

"Bitch, you broke my fucking fingers!"

"No, I didn't," she said in a level voice. "But I will if you call me Pocahontas or bitch one more time."

Will walked over and bought her a drink.

Their first year of marriage was one of unpleasant discoveries that came close to breaking it up. They rented a house near Northern's campus, where Maddie was studying for a master's in psychology. She found herself, only twenty-three years old, with a troublesome stepdaughter and a husband subject to mood swings as baffling as they were frightening, while he found himself wed to a woman with what they genteelly referred to as a "drinking problem," which his ups and downs aggravated. She knew they had something to do with the war, something to do with his upbringing in a rough Detroit neighborhood. On his part, Will thought his new wife was the recipient of double genetic bad luck, inheriting from her Ojibwa mother and Irish father her feisty temperament and fondness for booze.

But they, Will and Maddie, were reluctant—no, they refused—to admit they'd made a mistake. That's what saved the marriage; that, and a trip to Vieux Desert one weekend in the summer of 1982. A run-down bar, one of only two in town, was for sale. The Anchor Inn. Will made inquiries, contacted the VA to find out if he qualified for a small-business loan (he did), and the couple decided to move from the "big city" to a town with no stoplights and eight hundred people. Maddie quit drinking.

The irony that a recovering alcoholic was married to a saloon-keeper was not lost on her. She'd joined Vieux Desert's evangelical church and credited her renunciation of the bottle to her acceptance of Jesus as her savior. At first, in the fresh zeal of her conversion, she attempted to evangelize Will. If he took Christ into his bosom, those black holes he fell into would close up. Her preachiness got on his nerves. Vietnam, he told her, had robbed him of faith in God but deepened his belief in the devil. She retorted that he could not possibly believe in the father of all evil without believing in the source of all good. "Oh, yeah, I can," he answered, "and you would, too, if you'd been there."

Eventually, resigning herself, she climbed down from the pulpit. But Will did undergo another spontaneous remission that really wasn't all that spontaneous. Learning to run a bar and restaurant, managing employees and accounts, fixing up the place and the upstairs apartment where his family lived, absorbed all his mental energies. Physical energies, too—he did most of the repair and renovation work himself. He hired a new cook, expanded the menu from burgers and hot dogs to white-fish and pizza and ribs and steaks. He learned craft brewing, built an addition in which he installed stainless-steel tanks and copper kettles, and changed the establishment's name to the Great Lakes Brew Pub. In 1993, before her biological clock ran down, Maddie got pregnant. Alan was born the following year. Will bought twenty acres outside of Vieux Desert and built a house. He did some guiding in hunting season, as much to get outdoors as for the extra income to help pay off his VA loan. Every year, he packed a freezer with venison and game birds and tapped his sugar maples in the winter to make syrup; Maddie planted an herb and vegetable garden and taught herself how to can and put up preserves.

Dakota flew through her adolescence as a plane through the

sound barrier—a lot of turbulence (sulks, tantrums, fights with Maddie), a lot of shaking and shimmying (bad grades in high school, driver's license suspended in her senior year after three speeding tickets)—but the wings stayed on, she got into a community college, did well, and was admitted to Michigan State, graduating with an education degree as the century and the millennium turned.

* * *

Will was a happy man, which amazed him.

Then, four years before he retired, something bad happened—a crime that should have given the Dark Ones a chance to deal him another severe setback. But he didn't let that happen. He had suffered no lasting aftereffects, which encouraged him to believe that they'd been banished from his life for good and all.

* * *

The weather warms, the trees leaf out. With the arrival of summer vacationers and trout fishermen, Vieux Desert's three motels display No VACANCY signs; RVs and trailers crowd the campground outside town.

On the Friday of Fourth of July weekend, antsy to do something productive with the remaining hours of daylight, Will drives out to Bruce Skrydlowski's cabin to help him cut firewood. He's in an edgy, irritable mood, though he can't quite say why.

Skryd, as everyone calls him, lives off a logging road six miles east of town, on acreage he'd bought from a paper company. He's a high-strung man in his late fifties with big ears, a small nose, and graying black hair that resembles a pile of steel wool. His two-room cabin faces a small lake. It's no ramshackle hovel, like the deer camps scattered throughout the northwoods, but is pretty enough in its setting to go on the cover of *Field & Stream*. He'd cut, skidded, notched, and fitted the logs; installed the windows; dug a septic pit; put in plumbing; roofed the place; and wired it to a diesel generator; all on his own except for the roof. Will had lent a hand with that.

Skryd is a refugee from the Great Recession, swept from Flint northward to the Upper Peninsula by a tsunami of hard luck. He'd lost his job at a spark-plug factory—it emigrated to Mexico—then his house to foreclosure. Figuring that at fifty-plus, with nobody hiring anywhere, he had a better chance of winning Powerball than of landing another job, Skryd made no serious attempt to find one. He did just enough job-hunting to qualify for unemployment compensation. Fed up, his wife filed for divorce. "Good thing our kids was all grown up and gone, or I'da lost them, too," he once told Will.

He took half his savings (Mrs. Skrydlowski got the other half), packed his tools in a 1985 Dodge pickup, and drove to Vieux Desert to build his hermit cabin. He'd concluded, with considerable justification, that his life until then had been "built on the idea that if you gave a man eight hours' work for eight hours' pay and didn't piss it away, you'd be all right, which turned out to be total bullshit."

He's since become a cherished local character. The Marquette *Mining Journal* had discovered him; the reporter cast him as a self-sufficient Jeffersonian rustic who grew his own vegetables, ate whatever he could shoot or catch, and earned pocket money making driftwood carvings that were sold on consignment in U.P. tourist shops.

The carvings are of birds, mammals, fish, and are quite beautiful, but for all his varied talents, there is something a little off about Skryd. Maybe more than a little. He suffered from fugue states—fleeting bouts of amnesia (for which he'd been medically discharged from the Air Force back in the eighties).

Will had met him years ago, when they were both in their thirties. Skryd had come to the U.P. to go bird hunting, and someone had recommended Will to him as the man who could show him around. One day, as they were walking a logging road near Sawyer Air Force base, then a Cold War outpost, a huge unmarked cargo plane, black from nose to tail, flew low over the treetops with a startling roar. Skryd, who'd been an air-traffic controller in the Air Force, identified it as a C-141, "a CIA plane, that's why no markings," he said. "Delivers weapons to the Contras in Nicaragua."

Will thought about that, and after they'd tramped for another half hour, he asked, "Why would the CIA fly weapons from way the hell up here to way the hell down there? Wouldn't it be easier and cheaper to fly 'em out of someplace closer, like Texas?"

Skryd gave him a baffled look.

"The plane," Will said. "That big black plane."

"What plane? I didn't see any plane."

* * *

Now he parks his pickup alongside Skryd's vegetable garden, surrounded by a seven-foot deer fence, climbs out, and grabs a chain saw strapped to the bed panels with bungee cords.

"Hey! Glad to see you could make it!" Skryd exclaims, and throws an arm out toward a deck of beech and birch logs. "Take me two days to cut all this on my own. Let's get 'er done."

The beech is to be cut into small pieces for wood burning stoves, the birch into fireplace logs. Selling firewood is another way Skryd earns pocket money. The work needs to be done now, in July, so the wood can cure before it's sold. They spray themselves with insect repellent, clamp on earmuffs, and cut for an hour, tossing the pieces into piles, beech in one, birch in the other. Usually, Will enjoys hard, mindless physical labor, but he doesn't today. It's hot and muggy. His eyes burn from the mixed sweat and bug dope dripping into them, and as the repellent washes away, mosquitoes sing in his ears, drill his arms and forehead. When they have cut what should make a cord each, they stop to refuel the chain saws and give themselves a break. Skryd fetches two cold beers from his cabin.

"Bud Light, the redneck drink of choice," Will remarks, raising the can.

"So did running a brew pub make you a finicky conneysewer of fine beer? You can pour it out if it ain't to your taste."

"Take your pack off, Bruce. I was just making a joke. Didn't mean anything personal."

"Sure sounded like it was. I'm no redneck anyways."

"Didn't say you were."

"I'm an artist. A sculptor, like. But I work in wood, 'stead of marble or whatever."

"Okay, Mr. Arteest, let's get back to it."

Skryd pauses and, running his tongue around the inside of his mouth, studies the uncut logs. "Y'know, this'll go quicker if we cut the beech first," he says.

Will slaps two mosquitoes on his forearm, both gorged with blood. It feels good to smash them. He asks, "How will that speed things up?"

"You're cutting bolts and I'm cutting small pieces, so if we tackle mine first, it'll all go faster."

Will considers this proposal for about one second. "Look, if it takes two more hours to cut the stove pieces and one more hour to cut the bolts, then we've got three hours' work, right?"

"Sure."

"Then what's the difference which gets cut first?"

"What're you driving at?" Skryd asks, with a squint.

"I'm not driving at anything," answers Will, thinking, *The great artist is a fucking idiot.* "All I'm doing is pointing out the flaws in your thought process."

"My thought process is flawed? How's it flawed?"

An injured look clouds Skryd's face. It's almost a pout, and it excites in Will a malicious urge to smack some sense into him. Skryd is one of those people who unconsciously invite abuse; it's as if they wear a sign: KICK ME. Which doesn't mean that you are free to accept the invitation.

"I can't explain it any better than I already have," Will says, forcing a calm, if not exactly amiable, tone of voice. "You want to cut the beech first, then we'll do it your way, and when we're done, you'll see that it wasn't any faster than the other way."

"How's my thinking flawed, that's what I want to hear."

Screw this, Will thinks, gripping the chain saw's handle. "Know something? Doesn't surprise me you got canned from your job and your wife took a hike. This is a good place for you, out here all by yourself in the middle of the woods. A good place for a fucking loser."

Will isn't surprised when Skryd tells him to leave.

* * *

During the drive home, Will's irritability turns on himself and moves a little ways into remorse. *Why did I say that?* he thinks. *Pretty damn harsh and no reason for it.* He ought to turn back and apologize, but he drives on to the paved county highway, then on to a gravel road that brings him to his house.

Will's home is as much a product of his own labor as the cabin is of Skryd's and is quite a bit larger and more architecturally complex—L-shaped, two-storied, with dormers on the upper story and embraced by a wraparound porch. Four years ago, because of the incident with Lonnie Kidman, he'd considered selling it, but he couldn't bring himself to make the move; there was too much of himself in the place.

He parks in the yard, which backs up to a stand of red oak and sugar maple, and before he's slammed the truck door shut, Madeline is out on the porch. Dressed up—by local standards—in white jeans, a purple linen blouse, and open-toed shoes, she crosses her arms over her chest and tilts her head aside.

"I suppose you forgot," she says.

Will stands at the bottom of the steps, looking up at her.

"You're wearing your Mr. Magoo look. The party? We're supposed to be there in fifteen minutes."

Shit, he did forget that the Scullys, who have been renovating the bar for the past two months, are throwing a grand-opening party this weekend. A barbecue followed by Fourth of July fireworks on the town beach.

"I thought that was tomorrow night."

"Nooooo, tooo-night," Maddie sings out, with a scolding undertone in her voice. "Get yourself cleaned up."

* * *

From the outside, the Great Lakes Brew Pub is the same, except for a fresh coat of yellow paint on the cedar-shake shingles. But the only things Will recognizes inside are the long antique bar and back bar; otherwise, it looks like the kind of place where people in Timberland hiking boots and Columbia fleece will plop their trim asses on the chairs and barstools (which are also all new, replacing the ones with taped or torn vinyl cushions) and quaff imports. Gone are the age-darkened pine paneling, the mounted deer heads, the stuffed bobcats and coyotes, the collection of pikes, crosscut saws, and double-bit axes commemorating Vieux Desert's heritage as a logging town. Blond wood now covers the walls, and nailed to them are panoramic photos of autumn landscapes, loons in ponds, Great Lakes lighthouses. The Scullys fled Traverse City only to bring Traverse City to Vieux Desert, and the rehab makes Will feel as antiquated as the discarded logger's implements—a sort of living relic.

"They said they'd be in the back," Maddie says, meaning their friends Jim and Helen Magnuson, who own the hardware-cum-sporting goods store on Schoolcraft Street, the closest thing the town has to a main drag.

The larger room of the bar teems with tourists; the smaller one in the rear (an addition Will built years ago), where four round tables face the brewery's gleaming tanks and kettles, is less crowded. Two couples Will and Madeline don't know sit with the Magnusons at the table nearest the back door, through which the smell of grilling ribs drifts from the tiny yard behind the building. Will is famished; he'd eaten a skimpy lunch and worked it off cutting firewood.

Jim, who has a long, narrow face and the gregarious manner of a salesman, makes introductions. The couples are friends of his and Helen's, visiting from Ohio. Will forgets their names the second after he's heard them. He takes the open chair between them and feels hemmed in. He pours a beer from one of the pitchers on the table; Maddie, across from him and next to cheery Helen, orders a Diet Coke from the waitress—a new hire whom Will doesn't recognize.

"I was telling them that you built this place, made it into something," Jim says, canting his head toward his guests. "A run-down dive when you bought it . . . When was it, Will?"

"Eighty-two. August."

"Eighty-two, man, eighty-two. A run-down dive then, and now it's been featured in travel magazines."

"It's a nice place. Just *love* those photos on the walls," remarks one of the women. Her pert smile and practiced friendliness, with its undercurrent of fervor, cause Will to typecast her as an Amway saleswoman. "Where did you find them?"

"I didn't put them up, the new owners did," he answers, letting her know by the way he says it that he doesn't love the pictures or the gentrification the bar has undergone.

Platters of sizzling ribs in a tangy sauce, with sides of coleslaw and roasted red potatoes, are delivered, along with a fresh pitcher—"our summer ale," the waitress announces.

Will eats two or three ribs from his rack, then abruptly loses his appetite; his stomach seems to shrink down into a hard little ball. When the waitress comes by to clear the table, Jim asks what time the fireworks begin. "When it's good and dark," she answers, ten or so.

Jim checks his watch. "Two and a half hours. Can we all hold out till then?"

"Think I'll pass," says Will, glancing at Maddie.

"Oh, come on, honey. Live a little," she says.

"Worried you'll get a flashback?" Jim composes a jocular expression to show that he's making a quip, the sort of thing a friend can say to a friend without giving offense. Then, fixing a more serious look on his visitors: "Will is a war hero. He was in the Nam with the Marines."

Will detests that abbreviation, "the Nam," especially when uttered by someone who wasn't there, and he considers himself a survivor rather than a hero. People like Jim seem to think that the mere act of getting shot at elevates a man to the level of Achilles.

"Well, the Fourth is a good day to meet a vet," says the Amway woman's husband. Like her, he's in his early fifties, fair-haired, fair-skinned, a generic American. "Thank you for your service."

Another phrase Will dislikes. While it's a big improvement over the greetings he heard when he came home in 1970, it's become an empty, rote response, like "bless you" after someone sneezes. Every time he hears it, he's tempted to reply, *You're welcome. Whenever I can fight in a pointless war for you, let me know.*

The temptation is upon him now. He resists it.

"He's more than a war hero, he's kind of our town hero," Jim prattles on. "Remember those cop killings up here a few years back? It was all over the news. The psycho who murdered two Chicago cops who were up this way on a hunting trip?"

His friends shake their heads.

Will, fixing a look on Paul, also shakes his head, signaling him not to continue the story.

"Aw, c'mon, Will. Let me brag on you. Don't be humble." Jim returns to his guests. "Will was right next to them, in his truck, when the nutjob—his name was Lonnie Kidman—shot them dead with an assault rifle. Damn miracle Will wasn't . . ."

Maddie shoots him a censuring look. He's aware, everyone in town is aware, that Will never speaks about what happened then, that he avoids all reminders of it. But Jim is more than a little buzzed; he's captured his audience's attention and is unable to check himself.

"I've always said somebody was looking out for you, Will."

Will feels rather than sees four pairs of eyes turn toward him. He says nothing. No one was looking out for him. His survival then, as it had been during the war, was not providential but pure luck.

"Well, the psycho took off into the woods. Cops and blood-hounds trying to find him. Whole damn town was scared, let me tell you, like in the movies when an escaped convict is on the loose. Will sent Maddie and their boy to stay with us, because their place is outside town, and—"

"Maybe you shouldn't tell this story; you're making him uncomfortable," Helen admonishes her husband.

Will is not uncomfortable—he's panicked. But Jim rolls on, relating that Kidman carjacked a motorist at a highway rest stop and made his way to Will's house for a showdown. Jim's voice grows faint; it's as if wax is plugging Will's ears, and this produces a weird sensation that he's . . . He can't think of a word for it. Sinking, maybe. Sinking into himself.

"He broke in with that rifle. He broke in, but Will was ready for him. Dropped him with a shotgun, right there in his own house. *Put him down.*"

Mrs. Amway stares at Will, wide-eyed. "Do you mean you . . ." she begins, but doesn't finish.

"Shot him in the legs. Kneecapped him," Jim says, answering the question she didn't dare ask. "Kidman got life—too bad this state doesn't have the death penalty—and Will, this man sitting right here, let me tell you, if he ran for mayor of our little burg, he would've been elected for life."

Will has a feeling that he knows is crazy but cannot shake: that he's being stared at as if he were some sort of exotic creature. Why is Jim doing this? To impress his friends? Amuse them with a true-crime thriller? Will clutches the beer glass in both hands. A pressure builds inside him. He's afraid he's going to do something awful any second now—crush the glass, or toss its contents into Jim's face. What he must do is get out of here and collect himself, but he's trapped, a wall behind him, people on both sides.

"'Scuse me, gotta go," he murmurs to Mrs. Amway, nudging her shoulder with his.

She pulls her chair closer into the table; her husband does the same to give him room. Will rises and sidles between them and the wall. Everyone thinks he's going to the bathroom; instead, he flies out the back door into the yard, then jogs across Schoolcraft and down a staircase to the beach fronting Vieux Desert bay. It's empty at this hour, marked by the day's activities—footprints, a child's plastic pail, an attempt at a sandcastle. Drawing deep breaths of cool lake air, his fingers opening and closing as if squeezing rubber balls, he walks along the water's edge, where waves have smoothed and hardened the sand. The wind has calmed; the bay, barely rippled, is a great aquamarine plate, and the line between it and Superior's oceanic blue is as definite as one drawn on canvas. Far out, beyond the shoreline's curve, a sandstone cliff rises to form the point marking the bay's easternmost limit. Will doesn't notice how the lowering sun tints the sandstone gold, or the colors of the water, or the birch trees, white as plaster columns, leaning out from the point. He just keeps walking, blind to the beauty all around him.

* * *

For the rest of the summer, Will avoids Jim. He refuses to patronize the Magnusons' store. If he needs a tool or hardware of any sort, he drives to Munising, nearly fifty miles away. Maddie tells him that it's idiotic to burn a lot of gas just to show Jim how upset he is with him. Sure, he had been tactless to tell the story when Will so obviously didn't want perfect strangers to hear it, but he hadn't done so maliciously. "The guy thinks you're a hero; he's proud of you, proud to know you," Maddie said.

To Will, Jim's motives, his lack of malice, his tactlessness—none of that is relevant. What counts is the brute fact that he told the story, and the telling was like an incantation, conjuring up memories Will had buried. They barge into his brain at random times, without warning, without any discernible trigger—Kidman firing the AR-15, shattering the windshield of Will's truck. Lewis, the black cop, crying out, *Don't shoot me anymore,* the white cop, Walsh, already dead. Kidman kicking the back door open in Will's house the next day. Will crouched in the hall, waiting for him, a 12-gauge shotgun in his shoulder. The shotgun's twin blasts, Kidman tumbling backward, knees and legs flayed.

He relives these moments. No matter where he is—on a walk, driving somewhere, watching a ball game on TV—he is there in body only; in all other respects, he's lost in the past as the episode unfolds before him, scene by scene. Their vividness reproduces the sensations he felt then: the sharp spike in his pulse rate, the sudden rush of blood from his face, the cold prickling in his forearms and across the back of his neck.

There is one moment that makes him cringe—after Kidman, about to poach on Will's bear bait, refused to leave, and Will burst out, "Get your skinny ass out of here . . . you scum-licking little shitbird." That was when Kidman grabbed the rifle and started shooting.

Will had known Kidman was a violent hothead; he should have been more in command of his own temper, should have known better than to use language like that. Part of him wonders if he incited the killer, as if he, Will, had been an unwitting accomplice.

Sometimes he reimagines this scene with a happy ending. He orders Kidman to leave, as before, but with no profanity, no provocative insult, his words firm, his tone calm. His bloody impulses overcome by Will's self-mastery, Kidman gets in the truck and drives off.

Pleasant as it is, this version has an unwanted side effect— it always spurs a downward spiral in Will's mental state. By showing what he could have done—no, *should* have done—it leads him to reproach himself for what he did do; and the self-reproach, in its turn, brings on morbid examinations of other things he should have done but failed to do, mistakes he's made and every stupid or cruel word to come out of his mouth, including the ones he'd spoken to Bruce Skrydlowski that day. Minor transgressions are magnified into cardinal sins, stumbles into falls. These retrospectives make him feel worthless, but then, willy-nilly, his brain flips into spells of paranoid rage at people he imagines have wronged him or want to. Jim Magnuson, he thinks, intended to upset him, even though his rational mind tells him that wasn't so.

* * *

Autumn arrives. Few places equal the Upper Peninsula in beauty in that season; none exceed it. Aspen leaves flutter like tongues of golden flame; tamaracks yellow; hardwoods form islands of color in the great green expanses of pine and spruce. But Will sees none of it, only grays and blacks.

Now and then he catches himself staring at the window Kidman's bullets had shattered, or at the wall they had gouged, or at the hallway floor his blood had stained. Will replaced the window, patched the drywall, removed the stains with a belt sander and refinished the oak planks. The spot is still visible—a square lighter by a tone than the surrounding floor—and that's enough to flip the switch in his memory.

Maddie is patient with him, with his simmering silences, his flares of anger, usually over some triviality or over nothing at all. She tells him one day that she's going shopping in Marquette and to see a movie with a friend; he replies, "Why is it you're going with her but it's always no when I ask you to see a movie?"

She reminds him that he hasn't asked her to the movies since she can't remember when, the moderateness in her voice kindling his temper further. He stomps out of the house, slamming the door behind him. Spasms of guilt inevitably follow these fits, and the guilt generates more brooding, which generates the next outburst. He is ensnared in endless repetitions, a kind of feedback loop, like a drunk who drinks to forget whatever it is that makes him drink.

Maddie's tolerance, of course, is not limitless. One Saturday morning, Will kicks Samantha hard enough that he fears he's broken her ribs or damaged an internal organ. The setter has a habit of begging for food or for a biscuit by prancing in circles around him, whining desperately. The whines and her claws' rapid clicking on the hardwood floor always annoy him; on this morning, she spins in front of him as he carries a cup of coffee to the breakfast table and trips him, spilling the coffee. "You dumb bitch!" he yells, and as automatic as an eye-blink, his booted foot lashes out and catches her side. She tumbles over with a piercing yowl.

Maddie is very fond of the dog. She embraces Samantha, pulling her away from Will, like a mother shielding a child from an abusive father.

"You asshole! What the hell is wrong with you?" she cries, and kneads the dog's side and stomach to see if she's been seriously hurt. Apparently not—the pressure of her hand doesn't elicit a flinch or whimper.

Will sits down, disgusted with his loss of control. Maddie, recovering from her own anger, takes her chair. They poke at their breakfasts without speaking until she says, "You're scaring me, Will. Who are you going to kick next? Me?"

"I'd never do that," he replies, shocked that she would think him capable of harming her.

"What's happening to you?"

Every day, five days a week, she has to deal with messed-up people, more than ever now that the opioid epidemic has spread even to this isolated corner of the country. She would like her home to be a refuge. She's his wife and lover, she says, not his counselor, but she needs to hear what's eating at him. *Tell me, Will, tell me, please.*

To his own surprise, he does. To his surprise because he's a former Marine, because he doesn't come from people who readily confide their troubles to others—no, not even to their spouses or closest friends. To do so is a sign of weakness. Maddie listens thoughtfully, without interrupting, exactly as she does when her clients confess their falls from sobriety, their struggles with booze or pills or meth, all their secret and not-so-secret sorrows.

The cause of Will's is plain, she says when he's done: he has never confronted the demons conjured up by the incident with Lonnie Kidman; running his business, being a father to their son, taking care of things around the house, merely put them into suspended animation. Now that he has little to occupy him, little that requires all his faculties, they've awakened and come at him with redoubled fury.

"I've wanted to tell you that for weeks, but I've kept my mouth shut," she adds. "Hoped you'd work it out on your own."

Her clinical analysis rubs a raw nerve. Just what does she recommend he do? he snaps back. Find a job, at sixty-four? Community service? How about woodworking?

Maddie shakes her head, dismissing his scorn.

"You need to see somebody," she answers sharply. "There's the VA in Iron River. I've referred a couple of Afghan vets to them. Maybe they can help."

He retreats into a silence.

"Yeah, I knew you'd react that way." There are notes of resignation and disappointment in her words. "It's what you told me when we were first married. That time I fell on the floor at that dance club in Marquette. If I didn't straighten up and fly right, you said, then everything was off. You remember?"

"Sure."

"So I did. I've been going to those damn meetings every week for over thirty years. I don't see why you can't make an effort."

"For what? To hear that it's post-traumatic stress and get fed Elavil or amitriptyline or whatever?"

She rests her chin on her knuckles joined above perched elbows. Her eyes fasten on him. "Well, you've got to do something. I'm not going to go through what we did those first couple of years we were married. Not again. I'm not going to live like I have been the past couple of months."

Maddie inherited her hair from her mother, the straight hair that looks spun from charcoal, and the arctic gray-blue eyes from her father. The contrast has always captivated Will, as it does now. But her threat tampers with his captivation. He cannot imagine a life without her; the possibility of losing her rises in him as terror of the night rises in a child.

2.

The next morning, while Maddie is at church, Will writes down every instance he can remember when he's said or done something offensive and to whom. Some of those people are gone, dead or moved away, but he intends to apologize to as many as he can. His thought is that making amends will aid in his own rehabilitation; it will improve his opinion of himself, giving him the mental strength to wrestle the Dark Ones to the mat. It is a less-than-logical idea, but Maddie pleaded that he do something, so this is what he will do. He decides to begin with Bruce Skrydlowski. It's been about ten weeks since he called him a fucking loser; Skryd, who couldn't remember the huge black airplane half an hour after seeing it, has probably forgotten. Nevertheless, Will is determined.

Skryd's thirty-year-old pickup is not at the cabin. The generator thumps in a shed outside; a light is on inside. It's not a good idea to leave a house with a generator running. Maybe Skryd wants any would-be burglar to think someone's at home. Not that there's much threat of a burglar this far into the boondocks. More likely, he plans to be away only a short time. Will believes that is the explanation when he tries the door and it swings open. The morning is dull and overcast; it's dim inside, except for a low-watt desk lamp and a hazy shaft falling through the skylight onto the small pinewood dining table, across which a topographic map is spread. A Post-it note is attached to the doorjamb: *Roseanne—Out hunting. Back this aft. Make yrself at home. Leftovers in fridge.*

Does the eccentric recluse have a girlfriend? That doesn't seem likely. Will steps inside to look at the map. On a vast smear of nearly trackless green, a black circle has been inked between a lake and the Big Two-Hearted, the river Ernest Hemingway made famous; complicated directions are written in the left-hand margin: *H-44/ S. 5 mi. jeep trail on left. ESE 1.5 mi. Dead end. E. 1/2 mi. Beaver ponds. E.+ 1/2 mi. Old clear-cut.* Why Skryd made such detailed notes, only to leave them here with the map, is mystifying. That area is one of the wildest and most remote in the county. Right then Will's less-than-logical plan dips further into illogic. He swipes the map and drives home.

Maddie isn't there when he arrives. He feels a stab of panic at her absence, then he remembers that the church holds a social hour after services. The saved celebrating their salvation over coffee and stale sweet rolls. He calls her cell, gets her voicemail, and leaves a message that he's gone hunting with Skryd and will be home in a few hours. He collects his gear, shotgun, and Samantha—yipping ecstatically—and is out the door.

The county road, H-44, is paved as it runs eastward from Vieux Desert, skirting Lake Superior for some twenty miles before it turns to dirt and hooks due south for thirty more to its intersection with a state highway. At the turn, Will zeros his trip odometer, then heads south, at first through pine barrens, later through mixed popple and spruce, and crosses a wooden bridge over the brandy-brown Two-Hearted. The odometer reads exactly five miles, but he doesn't spot a jeep trail on the left side. After driving on for another half mile without success, he stops to study the map, which doesn't show any sort of trail joining the road. That's not unusual—not every track in these big woods has been plotted. He turns around and has back-tracked two or three hundred yards when he glimpses, now on his right, an opening in the wall of trees.

The jeep trail—two ruts divided by a grassy strip—is so narrow that Will has to pull in the side-view mirrors to avoid hitting low-hanging branches. And it's so rough that covering the one and a half miles to its end, in a clearing matted with bracken fern, consumes almost twenty minutes. He could have walked it faster.

The old brown-over-cream Dodge is not there as he'd expected. Now that Will thinks about it, he hadn't seen any fresh tire tracks on the way in. Skryd has gone hunting somewhere else. His absence ought not be cause for dejection, but there's been nothing ordinary about Will's emotions lately. His idea had been to run into Skryd accidentally on purpose; they would hunt together, as they had in years past, and at an opportune moment, he, Will, would ask Skryd's forgiveness, whether or not the absentminded hermit remembered the insult. Feeling as gray as the sky, Will reflects on the idiocy of this scheme. Did he really think he could engineer a chance meeting in this wilderness? Skryd would have needed to be wearing a tracking collar.

The thought of going home to sit around idle all day oppresses him. But something can be salvaged from this foray. The release of motion. If he can keep moving, he can stay ahead of the Dark Ones, for now anyway. Satchel Paige's droll advice comes to mind: *Don't look back—the bastards may be gaining on you.*

Samantha, leashed to a spare tire in the truck bed, is straining to jump out and hunt. *Keep moving,* Will commands himself. *Walk it off.* Ever since boyhood, when his father took him out of Detroit's mean streets on hunting or fishing trips, being in the woods has seldom failed to buoy his spirits. He climbs out of the cab with his shotgun, drops the tailgate, and clips a leather bell collar to Samantha's neck. She licks his face. In the way of dogs, she's forgotten and forgiven the kick he gave her yesterday. Will checks the compass hung pendant-like on a lanyard around his neck. East for half a mile, the map directions say. Samantha leaps from the truck and sprints off into the shadowed forest. He follows her. *Keep moving; don't look back; walk it off.*

They are in hardwoods, the ground matted with orange and yellow leaves. Will shoots a compass bearing at a black-eyed knot bulging from the smooth gray trunk of an old beech tree.

When he comes to it, he takes another bearing on a prominent tree farther on. He doesn't carry a GPS, partly because he dislikes depending on an instrument that requires batteries, partly because he's proud of his reputation as a woodsman's woodsman who doesn't need high-tech devices to find his way. On clear days, he can navigate by the sun alone. The sun today is a pallid, diffuse wafer, barely visible through the thick overcast, so he relies on the compass.

Samantha is out ahead of him somewhere. He can tell where only by the erratic jingling of her bell. She's what's known to setter aficionados as a "blue belton," although her ticking is black rather than blue. A precocious dog who hunts, at two, like a veteran of five or six. She reappears, quick-stepping, zigzagging, nose to the ground, keen for the scent of wild birds. She was bred for this. It's the full expression of her being. *What's mine?* he asks himself, pressing farther into the woods. *Keep moving; don't look back; walk it off.*

Samantha stops suddenly, striking a solid point, long, feathered tail curved at the tip like a fishhook. Poised, alert, she pulls Will out of his own head and puts him in the moment. He takes a step or two toward her. A grouse pair burst from under a baby spruce, zero to thirty-five in one second, and fly out of sight before he can shoulder his gun.

"Nice work, Sam," he says, rewarding her with a head rub. "Go ahead. Hunt 'em up."

And she's off again. He senses the joy she feels in running through rough country, and somehow she transmits a measure of it to him.

Skryd's directions—assuming it was he who wrote them— are inaccurate. It's not half a mile to the beaver pond but twice that, at least. Looking down from the hardwood ridge, Will sees that there are three ponds: peninsulas of hard ground, choked

with tag alders, spread between the ponds like long green fingers. He crosses the nearest pond by way of the beaver dam and
plunges into the alders. They remind him, in their tangled den-
sity, of the liana and mimosa vines in Vietnam. Samantha flies
a woodcock. He hears its high, piping whistle but never sees it.

He thrashes forward and climbs a gentle rise into a spruce
and birch woods, relieved to be out of the alder jungle. Samantha trees a grouse. Will spots it perched on a spruce branch some
twenty feet above, takes aim, and fires. The bird drops like a lead
ball, feathers twirling in the wake of its fall. Then he sees another
in a neighboring spruce and kills it. The dog retrieves both, and
the weight of the birds in the game pocket in the back of his vest
feels good.

Once again, the directions are off the mark. Half an hour's
hike, representing a distance of a mile or more, brings Will to
the destination scrawled in the map's margin—the clear-cut.
Stretching across an oblong basin below the pine and birch
woods, it must cover an entire section—that is, a square mile.
Whatever trees had grown there had been logged off at different times. Will discerns this by the height of the aspen that have
sprouted up in their place. The fifteen-to-twenty-footers are about
ten years old, the shorter ones anywhere from two to five.
Grouse will be in the older aspen, the cover thick enough to
offer concealment from hawks but not so thick as to block flight
from terrestrial predators. Pine martens. Fox. Coyotes.

The birds, however, are not where they're supposed to be;
they are where they're not supposed to be. He and Samantha
cross the clear-cut without a flush and are skirting a stand of
mature red pine, an eco-desert, where, to Will's amazement,
they fly a bird. He downs it on the wing. A hundred yards farther in, a second grouse takes off, crossing right to left, a brownish blur against the steel-colored sky. Will's shot produces a

puff of feathers, but the bird doesn't tumble; it glides downward as if on an invisible inclined plane. He marks its long, angled fall and heads in its direction. He never leaves a wounded bird in the bush, not if it's humanly possible to find it. Ten minutes later, Samantha's run slows to a quick but methodical walk, her nose down. The grouse, either wing- or tail-shot, is running. Her stalk ends at a clump of young pine. She pauses, then darts in and emerges with the bird in her jaws and presents it, still living, to Will. Taking it in hand, feeling its heart beat against the tips of his fingers, he sees its reddish eye staring up at him and the light go out of it when he breaks its neck with a quick, hard twist. The heartbeat stills. He shoots only what he can eat, but he hates moments like this; the grouse, after all, was a free, wild creature, not some factory-farm chicken bred for slaughter.

He has four, enough for two meals for Maddie and him. With the sun all but completely hidden, he takes a westerly bearing with his compass and starts back to where he left the truck. After bushwhacking a quarter of an hour, he realizes that something is wrong—he should be in the overgrown clear-cut by now. He must have lost direction, chasing the wounded bird. He pauses to take stock. The long axis of the oblong-shaped cut runs north to south; the older trees are at the northern end, where he'd crossed into the red-pine forest. If, pursuing the injured grouse, he'd veered north, backtracking would have taken him past its northern boundary. That explains why he missed it. The damn thing is close to a mile wide, so if he walks south from here, he should find it.

Which he does. His confidence renewed, he continues south through the aspen, guesstimating at what point he should turn west again toward the beaver ponds. Samantha slows him down. In her mind, they are still hunting. She slams onto a point, a woodcock towers, and the dog bounds off again. In minutes,

Will can no longer hear the bell. It's usually audible at seventy-five to a hundred yards; therefore, she's either on another point or out of hearing range. It turns out to be both. When he locates her at last, she's frozen on a slash pile in the younger aspen, ten-foot trees packed so closely together that he has to turn sideways to pass between them. A woodcock whistles skyward.

He doesn't bother shooting. To stop Samantha from hunting, he leashes her and leads her back into the older part of the cut, where there is more room between the trees and he can make better time. Less than three hours of daylight are left, and he reckons he has at least three miles to go. If he can maintain a good clip, say two miles an hour, he should make it before dusk. Walking Samantha on lead slows him down—she wraps the leash around tree trunks or catches it in underbrush, forcing him to disentangle her. He removes the leash and proceeds out of the cut into big trees, figuring to reach the beaver ponds in an hour.

That isn't what happens; skirting windfalls and deadfalls shunts him off course no matter how hard he tries to stay on. He comes to a stream, most likely the one the beavers dammed to form the ponds. Are the ponds upstream or down? The latter, he thinks, though he isn't as certain as he'd like to be. Following the stream isn't an option—its meandering bends and bows will add distance, and the tag alders strangling both banks are all but impenetrable. A hardwood ridge rises on the opposite side, probably an extension of the same ridge he'd traversed from his truck. At this point he realizes he can't find it by direct backtracking, but he does know that the county road, H-44, scribes a straight north–south line for miles. All he has to do to reach it is go west as accurately as he can. Once on the road, he'll hike to its junction with the jeep trail, then take that to its end in the bracken-covered clearing.

That's his new plan. He bashes through the alders, fords the stream—it's shallow and no more than six feet wide—and scrambles up the opposite bank into the oaks and beech and maples. Paying close attention to his compass bearings, he sets as fast a pace as the woods allow. The old-growth trees, spaced wide apart, are like a park compared with what he'd gone through earlier. Will is feeling much better than he did this morning. The day's exertions, solving his navigational problems, watching Samantha work, have combined into a kind of medicinal cocktail, purging the toxins from his brain; he hopes the remission is permanent, though he knows better.

But the day's exertions have also taxed his sixty-four-year-old body. He's dragging his feet a little while he squints at his compass in the fading light. He trips over a tree root—partly hidden under a pile of leaves—and pitches forward, his gun flying from his hands as his arms windmill in a futile attempt to keep from falling. At the last second, he throws one arm across his chest to execute a kind of shoulder roll, which spares him from smashing his face against a rock the size of a medicine ball but twists his knee as he goes down, tumbling over something hard, another rock or root.

He pushes himself onto all fours, catches his breath, and stands; but when he takes a step, pain shoots through his right knee, and it buckles. Bending down to massage it, he notices another misfortune: the compass hanging from his neck was smashed in the fall, the dial cracked in two, the needle bent.

"Son of a bitch!" he yells into the silent woods, then, with his good leg, kicks the root, as though some malignant spirit had placed it there for the express purpose of tripping and crippling him.

Knee throbbing, he retrieves the shotgun, then looks up through the trees, seeking the brightest part of the skies. That will be west—maybe. It could be nothing more than a thinning in the clouds and thus a deception. Nevertheless, he hobbles toward that band of shimmering gray; then his knee betrays him, and he trips again, nearly impaling himself on a branch protruding from a fallen log. He unloads the gun, repurposes it as a crutch. A few limping yards later, he's convinced that he's not going to make it out of here, not today. He's hurt and he's lost. Panic flashes through him, and he yells again, "Son of a bitch!"

He calms himself and says, mostly to hear the sound of his own voice, "Hey, Sam! We'll be spending the night right here."

A pine grove stands nearby, half a dozen trees, give or take, tightly bunched in a semicircle. Despite his disbelief in providence, he regards the presence of this conifer island in a hardwood sea as heaven-sent. The pines form a natural tent that will shelter him from a wind, should one spring up, and offer some protection from a rain, should one fall.

Will carries basic survival gear in a jacket pocket—headlamp, waterproof matches, a pocket saw. For the next half hour, as late afternoon matures into twilight, he gathers firewood, picking up oak and beech twigs for kindling, cutting branches from blowdowns with the saw. The task is harder, and takes longer, than it would if his knee were fully functional. The pain is bearable but occasionally sharp enough to force him to pause until it subsides.

He spots a paper birch not far from his campsite, another providential find—the bark makes excellent tinder. Peeling off a roll from the trunk, he remembers his mother-in-law's tales about the Ojibwa shamans of the Midewewin, the Grand Medicine Society, and how in centuries past they kept birchbark scrolls on which remedies to various diseases had been written in pictographs.

Inside the semicircle of pines, he builds a teepee of kindling over the bark and lights it. When the kindling catches, he lays on larger pieces, and the fire leaps into a cheery blaze. Next, he saws and breaks off pine boughs and piles them on the ground to make a bed for himself. Not very comfortable, but it will provide some insulation from the cold in the soil. All this gives him a feeling of competency, though he doesn't suppose he'll be asked to host a survivalist reality-TV show anytime soon.

In the woods, under clouded skies with no moon shining, the darkness is impenetrable. Strapping on his headlamp, Will lays out the four grouse, cuts off their heads and wings and feet, guts and skins them, and feeds the entrails to Samantha. She doesn't eat so much as inhale them. When the fire has burned down to coals, he whittles each end of a long stick to a point, drives it firmly into the ground at a slant, braces it with a rock, and spits one of the grouse over the other end, so that the bird hangs about half a foot over the coals. Dripping fat raises tiny flames, and the smell of the roasting meat is drool-inducing. It takes a long time to cook through. He removes the grouse from the fire and lays it on the pine boughs to cool. Once it has, holding it in both hands, he bites into the breast. Juices dribble down his chin. He imagines that he must look like a Neanderthal, devouring his kill.

Samantha drains the collapsible dog dish into which Will has poured half the water bottle that's ridden all day in his game pocket and is plastered with grouse feathers. He treats his companion to the grouse thighs and himself to a swig of bourbon from his hip flask. He is circumspect about drinking at home, to avoid tempting Maddie. The wreckage she sees every day at the clinic serves as a kind of aversion therapy at least as effective as the A.A. meetings—but he limits himself to one glass of wine at dinner and keeps his whiskey in a locked drawer to which he holds the only key.

He now has time to worry about her. She must be worried about him. She must have called his cell several times. It's in the truck's glove compartment. No point in carrying an expensive iPhone on his person and risking losing or breaking it—out here, far from any cell tower, it's as useless a means of communication as two tin cans connected by a string. Will she notify the local volunteer rescue squad? What can she tell them? The message he left—*Gone hunting with Skryd*—might as well have been no message at all.

The night's chill descends. Gritting his teeth, he stands and drags a beech log six feet long and as many inches thick and drops one end into the coals. It soon catches; bright, welcome flames lick away the darkness surrounding his campsite. He buttons his jacket collar and scuttles closer to the fire, trying to draw heat into his body so he can sleep. The burning section of log flickers down to embers. He shoves the next eighteen, twenty inches of it into the fire. The bad knee has stiffened, feels like a rusted hinge. If it's blown, he might not be able to walk out in the morning. He leans against a tree trunk and takes another pull from the hip flask, longer than the first, both to dull the throbbing and make himself drunk enough to sleep.

"Y'know, Sammy girl, was a time when I could sleep anywhere anytime on anything, kind of like you." Samantha crawls onto his lap, snuggles up to him as if she's a puppy instead of a fifty-five-pound dog. "Once, on a patrol, I conked out on the floor of a bombed-out pagoda. Had a hole in the roof an elephant could have flown through, if elephants could fly. Monsoon season, rained all night, three, four inches of water on that floor, and I slept right through it."

He rubs under her ears, as much to show affection as to feel her body heat in his hands. Her trust in him moves him, arouses a flashing shame.

"Sorry for what I did yesterday. We've got to stick together and get through this, okay?"

He lies down on the pine boughs, curling into the fetal position, and falls into a shallow sleep disordered by weird dreams. At some post-midnight hour, he is startled awake by Samantha's growl. In a state of bristling vigilance, she's up on all fours, facing out past the fire's embers.

Will, his nose and ears tingling from cold, whispers, "What is it, girl?"

A low rumble in her chest answers him. He stares into the darkness but can make out nothing, not so much as the silhouette of a tree. It's as if he's looking at a solid black wall. Then he hears them. One starts off with a long, high-pitched howl, drawing a chorus from the others. They sound like a madhouse glee club, their individual cries merging into a single note, rising until it mimics an air-raid siren's moan, before it shatters into a series of yelps and demented cackles. The pack is not too far away, maybe a quarter mile. Will knows that wolves do not attack people—one good whiff of human scent and they'll be gone. But that baying choir bypasses his frontal lobe, penetrating straight through to the paleo brain, where primeval terrors reside. The hairs on his arms and on the back of his neck rise; there is a fluttering in his chest, as if a small bird is trapped in his rib cage—the same sensations he felt when Lonnie Kidman, in a half crouch, waving the AR-15 like a wand, stepped into the hallway, at the other end of which Will waited with a shouldered 12-gauge.

Will had meant to kill him, but in the instant before he fired, it came to him as a certainty that Kidman sought what in his deranged little mind would be a glorious death in a gunfight.

To deny him, to ensure that the little psychopath would suffer a lifetime in prison, Will dropped his aim to Kidman's knees and pulled the trigger.

The wolves have ceased their racket. The quiet is disturbing. He imagines they are stalking him. He pictures their yellow eyes, glowing with intent to tear him and Samantha to shreds. They become for him the incarnation of all that is savage, dangerous, and unpredictable in wild nature—and in people. When the lupine sing-along recommences, he wraps one arm around Samantha's neck, grasping her collar to hold her steady. With his free hand, he grips his shotgun, bracing the stock against the ground. The gun is a side-by-side with two triggers, one behind the other. He yanks the front trigger as hard as he can, and the weapon doubles—that is, fires both barrels at once. The recoil nearly tears it from his hand. The blast echoes, and the wolves instantly stop howling. In a moment, he feels the tension pass from Samantha's body; she flops onto her belly. The pack has fled.

"That settled their hash, Sammy girl," he says, aware that he sounds more confident than in fact he is. He reloads and lies down again, the gun within easy reach.

3.

Dawn breaks silent and cold. No birds sing; no breeze stirs the trees or the leaves on the ground. The sky is a vast arch of lead-colored crepe, rent here and there to allow a little light to pass through. Will's knee as he stands to rebuild the fire launches rockets of pain down to his ankle, up through his thigh. As he wonders if he's torn the meniscus, he considers his options. Surely, Maddie has called the search-and-rescue squad by now. Maybe the sensible thing would be to stay put, piling dead leaves and green wood on the fire to create smoke and make it easier for a plane or helicopter to spot him. But what information could Maddie have given? She has no idea where he'd gone, so they'll have no idea where to look for him. There is also the matter of his pride. He doesn't want anyone to rescue him; he wants to rescue himself. He will walk out, exhausted as he is. Christ, he can't be much more than a mile from the road. He hobbles over to a blowdown, saws off a stout forked branch with the pocket saw, cuts the forks down to size and the stick to the correct length. It's a cartoon of a crutch but more effective than his shotgun.

He must maintain as straight a westerly course as possible. He remembers that his Ojibwa friend, Johnny Bugg, performs a ritual every morning, facing each of the four cardinal directions to spiritually center himself. Will tries it now, not for any religious purposes but to imprint a compass in his brain. Looking first to where the clouds are reddening, he turns slowly leftward, north to west to south and back again to east. Making one more half circle, he faces in the direction opposite the sunrise, telling himself, *West, this way is west,* and pushes off on his makeshift crutch.

To keep track of distance traveled, he counts each time his left foot strikes the ground. That equals a pace—five feet, give or take. The concentration this requires takes his mind off his knee. The pain often makes him dizzy and he has to stop to regain his balance. Or to whistle for Samantha, who, oblivious to their predicament, once again thinks she's hunting and sprints away on long casts. At last, he spies an opening in the woods not far ahead. It's got to be the county road.

It isn't but rather two broad, dried-up cranberry bogs linked by an isthmus, where an enormous old pine has fallen. Will checks his watch, gazes up to find the blanched eye of the sun, and disappointment at not arriving at the road clots into dismay—in an hour and a half, he's come just three hundred eighty paces, little better than one-third of a mile, and he has somehow drifted off to the south. The compass in his head, it seems, isn't much of an improvement over the broken one in his pocket.

As Will reorients himself, Samantha trots across the first, and widest, bog to the isthmus. She stops suddenly a few yards from the dead pine's exposed roots. Mortared with packed dirt and rock, they resemble the twisted spokes in a giant wheel. It leans out over the pit where the tree once stood, forming what looks like a cave's mouth. Samantha stands utterly still. Her tail is not extended, as it would be if she were pointing a bird. Instead, it's bent between her legs. *Porcupine,* he thinks. A porcupine is lurking in the pit. A creature Samantha has learned to fear: a few months ago, she was quilled and nearly blinded in one eye.

Will crosses the bog and limps up the isthmus to her. Tremors ripple through her flanks; otherwise, she's as motionless as a painted dog—literally petrified. He's about to pull her away by the collar when he catches a smell familiar to him, a strong, greasy stench like rancid bacon fat, and in the same moment sees a pair of eyes peering out from the darkness of the cavelike opening. A bear that's found its den. The dirt scattered around the entrance indicates that it's been making home improvements before settling in for the winter.

Will doesn't have time to be scared. Dropping the crutch, he snatches Samantha's collar and tugs her as he backs off. She resists, surprisingly strong for her size. Possibly she's too terrified to move—she's a sweet-natured bird dog, not some bear-hunting redbone or bluetick hound. But then, with a quick, twisting movement, she breaks his grip, yanking him off his feet, and bolts into the woods. This comes in reaction to the bear's emergence from its den. It makes neither menacing sounds nor aggressive moves—merely stands with a stupid look on its face, which is as black as a tire and almost as wide. Or so it appears to Will, down on his butt, cradling his 20-gauge. What happens next happens in less than ten seconds, but there is a time dilation, as in a dream, that stretches those seconds into long minutes. The bear heaves itself onto its hind legs, its fur rippling like charred grass in a breeze. It's no more than five yards away, roughly the distance at which he shot Lonnie Kidman. And for a microsecond, Kidman's image superimposes itself in the space between Will and the bear. He raises the shotgun as the animal regards him, its barrel-top head cocked aside, its bewildered expression replaced by one of wary curiosity, such as a man might bestow on a stranger at his door. And Will, recalling his mother-in-law's stories about the bear spirit's healing powers, experiences something he never has before—a sense of communion with the wild beast towering over him. He lowers the gun and says in a subdued tone, "Hey, bear. Don't mean you any harm. Hey, bear . . ." It grunts, drops back to four legs, and the last he sees of it is its broad rump as it crawls back into the den.

Will retrieves his crutch and heads in the direction of Samantha's flight, whistling and calling to her. Within a short time, a curious feeling takes possession of him, one for which he has no words. The woods that the wolf howls had imbued with intentional threat have shed their menace. He's still lost in them, yet he doesn't feel lost. He can't describe the feeling any better than that.

He stumbles on, more worried about Samantha's safety than his own. He spots fresh paw prints in the soft loam, follows them for a while, loses them in drifts of fallen leaves, then, quite by chance, crosses them again. They no longer zigzag but run straight, leading Will through some hemlocks, down into a culvert, the crossing of which tests his tolerance for pain, and, to his astonishment, out onto the county road.

His relief at finding it at last is alloyed with anxiety. Where the hell is Samantha? Her prints lead south over what appear to be recent tire tracks, the treads' imprint sharp and distinct. She was chasing a car or truck. He follows her trail, which ends fifty yards farther on. There are boot prints in the beige dirt, a woman's or boy's from the size of them. The tire tracks continue southward. Someone has picked her up. Will fervently hopes that whoever has found her won't steal her but will call his home number, etched with her name into the brass plate on her collar.

Right then he notices a dust cloud rising about a quarter of a mile down the ruler-straight road. A pickup truck emerges from the dust, its horn blaring. He recognizes the old brown-and-cream Dodge and, standing in the middle of the road, waves his crutch, like some disabled hitchhiker hailing a ride.

The Dodge swerves to the side and stops and Skryd rolls down the window.

"Well, son of a bitch, we were getting ready to call the sheriff and the bloodhounds."

Maddie sits in the passenger seat; Samantha is chained in the back.

"Been driving up and down for the last hour, honking, calling for you, for the dog. She must've heard us, because she popped outta the trees and started to give chase." Skryd gestures at the crutch. "What'd you do? Shoot yourself?"

Will doesn't answer. Skryd gets out, opens the passenger door like a chauffeur, and helps him inside. Maddie, arms folded across her abdomen, slides over to the middle of the seat, grudgingly, as if she's not sure she wants to make room for him. Down vest, flannel shirt, hiking boots, fanny pack—she's dressed for the boondocks.

"Glad to see you," she says in a voice that could freeze meat.

"Not half as glad as I am to see you."

"So if you didn't shoot yourself, what did you do?"

He tells her, then asks how they knew where to look for him.

"Oh, that's quite the saga. You're aware that Mr. Skrydlowski and I hardly know each other? That I was completely in the dark about where to find him? Or how to get in touch with him? And you leave that message, like I'm supposed to know?"

"Okay, I should've—"

"Woulda. Coulda. Shoulda," she interrupts bitterly. "When you didn't show up by nightfall, I called the Magnusons. Where the hell do I find this Skryd guy? Jim didn't have a number for him but knew where he lived, and he and Helen drove me out to his place. And there he was with his daughter but no you—"

"Roseanne," Skryd interjects. He puts the pickup in gear and heads up the road to the junction with the jeep trail.

"Mr. Skrydlowski—Bruce, my new best friend forever—hadn't seen you all day," Maddie resumes. "I was frantic. I phoned our local search-and-rescue guys, and they said there was nothing they could do at night. Nothing they could do in daylight, for that matter. Because you could have been anywhere inside of a zillion square miles. They said I should call the state police. They have helicopters. They also charge for that service. Thousands, Will. *Thousands.*"

She falls silent. Will remembers an old word. "Dungeon." No, "dudgeon." "High dudgeon." That's what Maddie is in. They are bouncing up the jeep trail now, the Dodge's worn shocks slamming them against each other.

"Woke up this morning and remembered the map," Skryd says, picking up the "saga," as Maddie had termed it. "Remembered I'd left it on the table but it was gone. Roseanne said she didn't see it or put it away. So I figured that you must've let yourself in and helped yourself to it and went on out. Seemed like a real-long long shot, but I called your wife, and here we are." He pauses, runs fingers nervously through his wiry hair. "So how come you did that? Came out and took the map and told your wife that we were gone hunting together?"

"I came out to . . ." Will hesitates, unsure how to explain his cockeyed plan to pretend to run into Skryd. "I was going to apologize."

"What for?"

"For what I said. When we were cutting firewood this July."

Skryd muses for a few moments. "I remember you said my thinking was flawed."

"That and more."

"Well, I guess my thinking wasn't flawed this time around."

They arrive at the clearing and Will's truck, a sight as welcoming as lighted windows in a dark woods. Will climbs out, wincing.

"Thanks, Bruce," he says. "You're not what I said you were, and I'm sorry for saying it."

"Forget what that was."

Maddie takes the wheel and, with Samantha nestled in the back seat, follows Skryd out to the county road. Will watches the trees pass by and struggles to think of a word for the feeling that came over him after his adventure with the bear. A sense that he was not separated from his surroundings, or from himself. Oneness. That will have to do. Oneness.

"Since I'm in apologizing mode, I'll apologize to you, too," he says.

"No 'I'm sorry's, please," she replies. "I want you to promise you won't do this to me again. You're sixty-four years old."

"Any chance you stole some OxyContin from the clinic?"

"Hell, no. I've got Advil in there." She points to her fanny pack, on the seat between them. He swallows two with a long pull from the water bottle, realizing that he has a raging thirst.

"Okay. Promise."

She doesn't say anything for a full thirty seconds as they cruise along the Lake Superior shore. With its teal-green near-shore shallows shading to the royal blue of the deep water, the lake is as lovely as a tropical sea.

"Know what Helen said to me last night?" Maddie says finally.

"Not a clue."

"Coldest cold comfort I've ever got. Subzero."

"What, Maddie?"

"She said, 'Nobody knows the woods better than Will Treadwell, so he couldn't have gotten lost; he must have had a heart attack.'"

Will laughs a deep, sputtering laugh. He laughs long and hard.

"There's something I haven't heard from you in a while," Maddie says.

THE GUEST

Lisa Williams bought the century-old Victorian on Schoolcraft Street and converted it to a bed-and-breakfast two and a half years after her husband, Bill Erickson, died in a hunting accident. At least, that's what she'd been told. An accident. The house was the largest in Vieux Desert and at one time would have been considered stately, if not quite a mansion: a corner turret, a commodious porch dripping gingerbread, and five bedrooms. A detached cottage and an expansive yard with a gazebo were thrown into the bargain. And a bargain it was, the asking price so low that Lisa suspected the realtor was hiding something—fatal flaws in the wiring, the plumbing, the roof. Lisa, a neophyte in real-estate transactions, feared she might be taken advantage of and overcompensated for her inexperience by pretending to be a wily buyer. As she toured the interior with the agent, Jake D'Agostino, she tapped the walls, flushed toilets, turned faucets on and off, cast an appraising eye at the ceilings, the molding, the light fixtures, without the vaguest idea what she was looking for.

When the walk-through was finished, they went outside to the porch and D'Agostino asked, "Well, what do you think?"

She put on a skeptical expression and answered, "So, Jake, tell me what you're not telling me."

He answered with a puzzled squint.

"A place this size for so little—there's got to be a hitch."

D'Agostino smirked—a good-natured smirk—and said this was the first time he'd heard a buyer complain that the price was too low.

"Converting it would cost me," she said to explain herself. "I wouldn't want to sink money into it and then find out I've got to spend a fortune repairing the roof or whatever."

He threw out his arms, as if to show how open and above-board he was being with her. Sure, the place needed a little TLC—it had been vacant for a year, and a rooming house for a decade before that, but the infrastructure was sound. If Lisa needed to know why it was on the market for half its worth, it was because the owner was anxious to get it off her hands. She lived in Chicago; she was seventy years old—the granddaughter of the man who'd built the house back in 1910.

"There'd be a full inspection before closing," he added. "And if it turns up something that needs fixing, it would be her responsibility to fix it."

Lisa tried to think of something to say, a few words to make her sound canny and savvy, but nothing came to her.

He took advantage of her silence to apply a little sales pressure.

"Y'know, the fact that it was a rooming house would lower your conversion costs. Lower, I mean, than if it was still a single family home."

"I know that. It's why I asked to see it."

"Sure. This town's never had a B-and-B, but I'd bet the right person could make a go of one. We're a resort town now, sort of. Beaches in the summer, and the national lakeshore right nearby. Snowmobilers in the winter, leaf peepers—we get a lot of them in the fall. And then there's the outdoorsy types—hikers, hunters, fishermen."

"You don't need to sell me," she said, with some impatience.

"So, you're ready to make an offer?"

"I need to sell our place—I mean my place—first. Down in Manitou Falls. There's a sale pending, but you never know. The realtor there told me things can fall through right up to the last minute."

"Right he is, and—"

"She," Lisa said.

"Right she is and right you are. You never know." D'Agostino's face brightened. "Just to be clear, are you saying that you'll accept the offer, contingent on the sale of your house?"

"Yes."

That word, like the "yes" she'd spoken to Bill when he'd proposed to her, produced an anxious thrill, a happy terror. She was about to change her whole life, leave a career that paid well, that provided status, a sense of self-worth, and some excitement—she had been doing marketing and PR for the Northern Suns for over ten years; leave a midsize town with direct air connections to Chicago and Detroit for a small town, a very small town, with no connections to anywhere; leave a house where she'd been happy once but that now held only the memory of happiness. She would be leaving all that for the uncertainties of striking out on her own, in a place where she knew no one.

* * *

The accident, as she still preferred to think of it, occurred in mid-October 2004, on the last day of Bill's annual hunting trip with Tom Muhlen and Paul Egremont, his oldest friends, buddies since high school, football teammates.

He'd taken out two term life-insurance policies the previous May, one naming Lisa as beneficiary, the other his daughters. The policies contained the standard clauses allowing the insurance company to deny claims if the insured committed suicide. Given Bill's history of treatment for alcoholism and depression, the company conducted an investigation. A detective interviewed Tom and Paul, who had been with Bill and swore his death had been accidental: he'd been carrying some sort of obsolete shotgun that lacked a standard safety; he stepped into a hole, or tripped, or something, and the gun discharged right into his chest. The same account they'd given Lisa. They were very convincing. They convinced her. They convinced the investigator, and in a few weeks, she became a rich widow.

Later, after she'd recovered sufficient presence of mind to think things through, she wondered if she'd been convinced because she wanted to be. Bill had been in a bad way earlier in the year, worried, gloomy, incommunicative, sleepless. Too proud to admit that there was anything the matter with him— psychologically, that is—he'd stopped taking his Zoloft. Lisa began to spike his morning orange juice with the drug, and his mood ticked upward. He was cheerful the whole time between May and October, made love to her again—he hadn't touched her for weeks—talked about taking a vacation in the Caribbean. This dramatic change, she believed then, had been the happy effect of the Zoloft. But might it have been something else? Might it have been that he'd made a decision, after the insurance policies were approved? She'd read somewhere that depressives sometimes rose out of their melancholy once they'd resolved to end their pain by the appalling act of ending their lives. Yet it seemed far-fetched that Bill had been putting on an act, sustaining it for five months, all the while conspiring with himself, plotting his own death.

One day, her casino job took her down to Lansing to observe the legislature debate a gambling issue. The trip gave her a chance to talk to Tom and Paul—Tom was the Ingham County prosecutor, Paul a professor at Michigan State. She invited them to dinner at the State Room, where she asked them to go through the whole thing again. She listened for inconsistencies, hoping not to hear any. Tom was as persuasive as he'd been the first time. He was a courtroom lawyer; persuasion was in his DNA. Paul, the academic, left virtually all the talking to him. The little Paul had to say was evasive. He couldn't maintain eye contact with her when she asked, "And you heard Bill say before . . . before it happened, you heard him say he'd had the best time of his life?"

Paul sighed and answered, "Lisa, let it go. Why are you—"

"Best day," Tom interrupted, force in his voice, as if he were raising an objection at a trial. "Just to be accurate, he said it was the best *day* in his life."

The thought leapt into her mind fully formed, like a revelation. *Because he knew it would be the last one.* There was no way to prove it, yet she was sure it was true. The man she'd loved and lived with for almost eight years had deceived her, had taken himself from her thinking that a hefty insurance settlement would somehow ease the hurt. Rage combined with her sorrow to create an entirely distinct emotional compound, a kind of acid that ate at her heart. She might be at work, or grocery shopping, or washing dishes, and it would bubble up in her breast.

She would start to cry and, in the middle of her sobbing, suddenly feel like kicking something or someone. Once, while cooking dinner, she flung a kitchen knife at the photograph that hung above the fireplace, the one showing him in his Navy flight suit with the medals from Desert Storm.

* * *

A few months after she closes on the Victorian, after obtaining the required permits and licenses, after depleting three-fourths of the settlement money on decorating the rooms, updating the kitchen, buying bed linens, mattresses, and china, after taking out ads in travel magazines, setting up a website, hiring a housekeeper, and giving the North Coast Inn a shakedown cruise by inviting her brother, sister-in-law, and parents to stay for a long weekend, Lisa opens her doors for business, on time for the summer tourist season. It is a success. From Memorial Day to Labor Day, she is fully booked for every weekend but three; weekdays, at least one of the five rooms is occupied. She nets enough to hire a college girl as an assistant for the summer, and she enjoys meeting guests who come from all over, some from as far away as the East Coast and, on a couple of occasions, adventurous travelers from Europe. The B&B is written up in a magazine, *Michigan Highways,* a copy of which she sends to her mother, who had been opposed to Lisa's venture from the beginning. "You should invest that insurance money in something sensible, Lisa Mae." Gladys Williams always invoked the middle name when chiding her daughter. "You're quitting a good job, a darn fine job, to be an innkeeper in the middle of nowhere." "Innkeeper"—the word summoned images of a crabbed old man in a roadside dump.

Business falls off sharply after Labor Day—drops to zero, as a matter of fact. For a while, Lisa keeps occupied with finding handymen to make minor repairs, with household tasks like scrubbing scuff marks off baseboards, but when all that has been taken care of, she has nothing to do but check her email and voicemail for reservation requests. She has made friends—Lisa makes friends easily—but most are shallow acquaintanceships. The one exception is Aileen Earhart. Like Lisa, Aileen grew up on a farm and is tall, dark-haired, and sturdily built. Intelligent and witty, she is also madly energetic, owner of the Bayview Diner with her husband, Alex, as well as a published author of young-adult books. Awake before dawn, she writes for a couple of hours while she bakes muffins and scones for sale, then is off to the diner, where she waits tables and works the register while Alex cooks. At night, she retires to her room and writes for another hour or two before, finally, going to bed.

Aileen assures Lisa that things will pick up later, when snow begins to fall, drawing snowmobilers and cross-country skiers. Right now it's hunting season, and hunters tend to prefer motels or to hole up in their backwoods camps. Lisa envies her friend's enterprise and criticizes herself. *There must be something you can do to bring people in. Entrepreneurs are expected to grow whatever business they're in.* That phrase—"grow the business"— is a bit laughable, as if a restaurant or a factory or a B&B were a vegetable garden.

Loneliness grips her, especially at night, after she locks up the inn and retires to the cottage out back, which she's converted into an apartment for herself. Bill's ghost, banished during the busy summer, returns from exile to resume his haunting. He comes in, dragging the chains of anger and sorrow. Desire, too. He was a handsome man, the best-looking man she'd ever seen, six feet three, with platinum hair and translucent blue eyes.

* * *

A guest arrives early in October, a tall man (though not as tall as Bill), thin but not skinny—thin in the way a whip is thin. He's a walk-in. The first thing he asks, even before inquiring if she has a vacancy, is if her establishment is pet-friendly. Two rooms are, she answers, number one downstairs and number four up. What kind of pet does he have? A dog, a German short-hair that doesn't shed much.

"You're here for the bird hunting?"

He seems impressed that she knows a shorthair is a hunt-ing dog. "Yup. Every fall for the last, oh, it's got to be ten years now," the man volunteers. "I usually stay at the Lakeview"—waving in the general direction of the rental cabins that occupy a hill overlooking Vieux Desert—"but I saw your sign and thought I'd try something different. So is one of those rooms available?"

He speaks in a newscaster's voice, sonorous and authorita-tive. His looks are likewise authoritative, even a bit grave, his face gaunt and craggy—"Lincolnesque" would be the word—his hair thick and straight, the lead-gray color of Lake Superior on a cloudy day.

"You can have either one," Lisa replies brightly. "The down-stairs is bigger, but upstairs is less expensive. Either way, I don't think you'll be disappointed."

The man cants his head slightly to one side and offers a small smile. "I'm sure I won't be," he says, his eyes—they're a frosty blue—finding hers. "Eeney, meeney, miney, mo—I'll take down-stairs."

They move from the front hall into the tiny office—before renovations it had been a storage room—where Lisa sits at her desk and he presents his credit card without asking what the rate will be. She states it—one hundred ten a night plus a twenty-five-dollar pet fee.

"Not a problem, not a problem," he declares, as if she'd thought it might be. She scans the card, an American Express Corporate Platinum, and notices his unusual name: Gaetan Clyne.

"I'll be here the week," he says. "Maybe longer. I'll let you know ahead of time if it is."

She escorts him outside to show him where to park—on the gravel strip behind the backyard—and returns to the office, excitedly doing arithmetic in her head. Seven times one thirty-five equals . . . nine forty-five.

Clyne comes back inside, a cased gun and a duffel slung over his shoulders, a dog bed tucked under one arm, his free hand holding the German shorthair by its leash.

"My gosh, let me help you," Lisa says.

Taking the bed, she leads him to the room, which had been the master bedroom when the house was occupied by its original owners. The furnishings and decor lean toward Early American simplicity, a kind of Shaker look, rather than the luxurious. She's done all five rooms along the same lines—no canopied four-posters or faux-antique dressers or toilets with wall-mounted wooden tanks and brass pull chains, as she'd seen in B&B trade magazines that made a fetish of nostalgia.

"Perfect," Clyne pronounces, propping the gun in a corner. He shrugs the duffel off his shoulder and jerks the leash, as if the dog were a puppet on a string. "This is Klaus. Klaus, say hello to our host, Ms. . . ." He questions her with a glance.

"Lisa. Lisa Williams."

"Klaus, say hi to Ms. Williams."

Klaus nuzzles Lisa's crotch. She steps back, gently pushing his nose aside.

Clyne apologizes and says, "He gets a little too friendly sometimes."

"That's okay. I'm used to dogs. My husband is a bird hunter. He had English pointers."

"Good breed. Terrific at field trials. A little too rangy for me. What does your husband have now?"

Lisa flushes, realizing that she'd referred to Bill in the present tense. Lowering her gaze, she shakes her head emphatically to discourage further inquiries. She doesn't want to tell this stranger that she sold her husband's last dog, Rory, because her husband was dead.

"I lock up after seven," she says as she gives Clyne two keys, one for the front door, one for his room. "You can let yourself in. If anything comes up, I'm in the cottage in the back." She pauses, smooths the front of her trousers with her hands. An awkward feeling that she cannot account for creeps into her. "All right, then. That's settled. What time would you like breakfast? It's between seven and ten."

"Good thing I'm not hunting ducks. I'd have to be out of here by four. I'd starve. How about eight?"

Another smile, broader than the one earlier, multiplies the fissures in his face. They make him look older than his age, which she guesses to be mid to late forties. Lisa returns the smile and goes into the kitchen to consult a cookbook, *Best Recipes from American Country Inns*. She thumbs through the index, looking for something special. Here it is—*Puffed Apple Pancakes*. She intends to make Clyne's stay memorable. A five-star customer review for this time of year on the website could be exactly what she needs to avoid seasonal lulls in the future.

* * *

Awake at six, washed up and dressed half an hour later, she steps out of the cottage into the sharp morning air, pausing to admire the red-orange brushstrokes streaking the eastern sky. "Morning nautical twilight." Bill had familiarized her with the term the first time they'd watched dawn break from the deck of their new house on Lake Michigan. He'd been a sailor well before joining the Navy, crewing on his father's sloop in the Mackinaw Race. MNT, he'd explained, occurred when the sun's center was six to twelve degrees below the horizon, making it light enough to see the horizon, dark enough to see the brighter stars, allowing mariners to use their sextants to fix the stars in relation to the horizon and thus to navigate at sea. She recalls that lecture almost word for word—he loved to lecture about sailing and guns and gundogs and the techniques of landing fighter planes on carrier decks. He has invaded her thoughts once again.

In the kitchen, where pots and pans hang from hooks, like ornaments, she fires up the oven, then makes coffee, which she places on a sideboard in the dining room.

Returning to the kitchen, she whips up the pancake batter, pours it into a cast-iron skillet, lays apple slices on top, and slides the skillet into the oven. It's done twenty minutes later, and it looks pretty close to the one in the cookbook photograph, the apples nicely browned, the batter risen so that it resembles a pie. After sprinkling on some powdered sugar and cinnamon, she takes a picture of the creation with her phone and posts the photo on her website. She tries to come up with a clever caption but draws a blank.

She hears Clyne's door open and close, his feet clomping on the pine-board floors as he enters the dining room. *Shit.* She forgot to set the table. Her breath catches for a sliver of a moment when she sees him at the sideboard, pouring a mug of coffee, his back to her. The rangy, athletic frame, the hunting clothes—tan brush pants, khaki shirt with blaze-orange patches on the sleeves—it's Bill she sees in that instant. The image, a near hallucination, dissolves, and Lisa composes herself.

"You're early," she says with a chipper lilt.

He turns around, the mug raised to his lips, and gazes briefly at her over the rim. "Hey! Good morning! Yeah. Early. You know what they say—sleep is but a slice of death."

She's never heard that aphorism, finds it weird. She motions at the sideboard, which he's blocking. "I need to get in there."

Clyne moves aside, but not very far, half a foot, so that when she bends slightly to retrieve a napkin and flatware from a drawer, her shoulder presses against his arm. He doesn't pull away to give her more room. This touching doesn't feel quite right. Too familiar, damn near intimate. A low current of apprehensiveness flows through her. Alone in this big house with a strange man. He could be a serial rapist for all she knows, a thought she immediately dismisses as melodramatic, the result of watching a true-crime show last night.

She sets his place, then brings out the pancake on a tray and announces with a ceremonious flourish, "First breakfast to my first guest of the—"

He interrupts, riffing on the once-common practice for merchants to frame their first dollar and hang it on a wall.

She laughs a bit nervously. "You have a beau—" She blocks the word "beautiful." "A rich voice, like you're in broadcasting?"

Clyne twirls an index finger and points it at her. "Bingo. Radio commercials, some TV, voice-overs mostly. Ever see that one for Dodge pickups? 'This is only the beginning,'" he recites, his already resonant tone dropping half an octave to a man's-man rumble. "'Guts. Glory. Ram.'"

"That's you?"

"Nope. It's Sam Elliott. The actor? But I did an audition for that gig. Which reminds me . . ."

He pushes away from the table, goes to his room, and comes out with a manila folder, which he hands to her. Inside is an eight-by-ten black-and-white of his Mount Rushmore face, turned a little aside while he fixes an intense stare on the camera. He looks striking. *Accolade Talent Agency* is stamped on the bottom margin.

"It's yours. I've got lots more." Then, replying to the question on her face: "You could hang it on a wall instead of your first dollar." He spreads his hands, as if unfurling a banner. *"Gaetan Clyne—First Guest."*

Was he serious?

"I'm afraid you misunderstood. You're my first guest of the fall. I've been open since May."

He blushes at his vanity.

"Better eat before it gets cold."

Deciding to put off cleaning until he's gone for the day, Lisa crosses the backyard to the cottage and tucks the photo in a dresser drawer. She makes her bed, tidies up, and is relieved when she sees him, through a rear window, load his dog and gun into his truck—a Dodge Ram—and drive away. That low-wattage current coursing through her the brief time they spent talking stays with her. Although she's unable to identify the sensation, she does know now that it's not fear or apprehension. It's something else.

* * *

With no one around but the two of them, the situation feels oddly domestic, as if they're playing house. She serves him breakfast every morning at eight and on two occasions eats with him. They exchange small talk—she loves listening to him, no matter how banal the conversation. Then he goes off with Klaus, returning in the early evening.

On the second-to-last day of his stay, he tells her that he's decided to extend for three more days; the hunting has been better than he's seen in years. The grouse and woodcock he's shot are in freezer bags in the refrigerator, heads and claws cut off but still dressed in their feathers. Refrigerating game birds unplucked, he mentions, has the same effect as hanging them: it ages the meat, bringing out its full flavor. She knows this, she responds. Her husband used the same method. Clyne, probably noticing that she did not say "ex-husband," gives her an inquiring look.

"He died three years ago this month," she answers, managing to state the fact with no show of emotion.

"I'm sorry to hear that," says Clyne, and manages to sound as if he really is. "You're young to be a . . ."

"It was an accident. I'm thirty-eight, by the way."

She's at ease with him now. They have developed something of a personal relationship in the past week, and these disclosures, sketchy as they are, deepen it. She's delighted that he'll be staying longer. It softens her disappointment with the slow business. That is what she tells herself.

But with only one person to tend to, she doesn't have a lot to occupy her time. The next morning, Clyne's seventh, she inspects his room after the housekeeper, Gayle, tidies it up. She checks her voicemail and email for reservation requests (there are none), inventories the pantry and linen closets, and, following a lunch of tuna salad on whole wheat, changes into sneakers and sweats and goes out for her thrice-weekly run on the beach. She's a woman whom ads and commercials would diplomatically describe as "full-figured." Her height—five-ten—

permits her to wear her weight well; still, since she quit smoking, she's struggled to stay at size fourteen.

She drives a few miles to a campground on the national lakeshore, noticing as she passes through a brilliant gold tunnel of birch and oak that the fall colors are at peak. If the people Jake D'Agostino called leaf peepers are to come, they had better come quickly.

The beach on which she jogs is called "Twelvemile" for unknown reasons—it's a lot longer, stretching westward from the mouth of the Windigo River to the painted rocks near Marquette. It's deserted for as far as the eye can reach, fringed by wooded bluffs on one side, white breakers on the other. Seagulls hover above the waves, two quarreling over possession of a crab. She jogs two miles to a lighthouse, then back toward the campground. Approaching two big driftwood logs she'd dodged on the first leg, she breaks into a sprint and leaps over them. She ran hurdles in high school, twenty years and thirty pounds ago, and is pleased that not all of her teenage agility has left her.

The drive and the run consume about two hours. Showered, changed, she again checks for reservations and is thrilled to discover that a mother and daughter have booked a long weekend through an online travel agency. It's not quite three in the afternoon, and the rest of the day yawns before her, a void she can't think how to fill with useful activity. She tries reading for a while, but she couldn't call that useful unless she was reading the painfully dull publications put out by the hospitality industry. The listless afternoon drifts into dusk, dusk into night.

* * *

She looks in on Clyne as he reads in the library, an extravagant term for the room (it had been a sitting room before her renovations) that has only one bookcase, half empty, the other half taken up by paperback thrillers, with a few serious hardcovers thrown in. Clyne is seated in one of the club chairs Lisa bought online, reading under a floor lamp with a fake Tiffany shade. A log crackles in the fireplace; a glass of whiskey sits on the lamp's end table.

"All you need is Klaus at your feet," says Lisa, standing in the archway between the library and the dining room. He removes his reading glasses and lays the book in his lap. Alice Munro's *Runaway,* an odd choice for the deep-voiced sportsman but one that speaks in his favor.

"Excuse the interruption," she continues. "What would you like for breakfast? Bacon and cheese omelet or a redo of the apple pancakes? Or something else? I made up the menu for the week, but now the week's up."

"Oh, surprise me. I like surprises."

"All right, then. A surprise it'll be."

"Hold on," he says—commands, really—as she turns to leave. "Would you dine with me tomorrow night?" He delivers the line, which sounds like one from a Jane Austen novel, in a half-joking way, as if to show that a refusal won't disappoint him.

She laughs. Is her guest asking her on a date?

"What do you have in mind? You can't dine in this town. Eat, sure, but not *dine.* The only decent places are in Marquette, and that's a two-hour drive."

"Right here is what I have in mind. The birds in the fridge. I'll do the cooking." There is an audacity in his gaze and a directness that makes her think of those optometrist's instruments, the ones whose light penetrates to the backs of your eyeballs. "You were married to a hunter, so I figure you don't object to eating wild game."

"No." Lisa is a bit flummoxed. "Well, okay. Dinner. Why not? What will you need?"

Apples, he tells her. Also brandy, wild rice, green beans, and mushrooms, preferably porcini. She has everything in stock except the porcini, which she doubts can be bought at the local IGA. Will ordinary mushrooms do?

Clyne nods. "You said you lock up at seven. So let's make it for seven-thirty."

* * *

The next afternoon, after he returns from hunting, he takes four grouse and a woodcock from the refrigerator and plucks them in the backyard over a trash can, so feathers won't make a mess in the kitchen. Watching him through the cottage window, she recalls the autumn days when Bill performed the same task, the sun on his bright-blond head. In the evening, wishing to pitch in, she throws a salad together and volunteers to help with the prep work. He assigns her to chop the apples, sliver the mushrooms, trim the green beans. They have donned aprons because Clyne, who appears to have a sense of occasion, has asked that they dress for dinner, that being understood as any improvement over jeans and hiking boots. He's wearing khaki slacks, a tattersall shirt, and a corduroy jacket with suede elbow patches; Lisa is in a knee-length black dress and ankle-strap low heels retrieved from the cedar chest where she's stowed the clothes from her former life. The dress, which she'd last worn to an industry conference in Las Vegas, is a little snug in the waist and hips, but with her makeup on and her hair brushed to a sheen, she's confident in her looks.

Clyne's movements in the kitchen are smooth, economical, not a wasted step. Lisa is impressed.

"You must do the cooking at home," she remarks, not without ulterior motive. He isn't wearing a ring, but that is not unimpeachable evidence.

"I took courses at the CIA," he replies, fixated on the grouse he's browning in a skillet. "Not *the* CIA—"

"I know. The Culinary Institute of America."

Then he banishes her from the kitchen with an imperious wave, leaving her end-run inquiry unanswered.

Within the hour, they are at the table. The overhead light, on a dimmer switch, is turned low; two candles burn in brass holders. The rice casserole steams, and the golden-brown birds, with green beans on one side, gobs of red-currant jelly quivering on another, are a cookbook photograph. Clyne fills her wineglass from a bottle he's supplied. *2004 Frescobaldi Mormoreto,* the label reads.

She's never heard of *Frescobaldi* or *Mormoretoi,* but the wine is like none she's drunk before. Where did he get it?

"A wine shop in Chicago," he answers. "I always stock up before heading into the boondocks."

Chicago. Lisa remembers from the guest book he signed that he's from a suburb. Barrington. She slices off a piece of grouse breast, savors it.

"Heavenly. Gaetan Clyne must have been on the CIA honor roll."

"It's the bird. If you don't overcook it, the ruffed grouse is the el supremo of game birds. Beats the hell out of pheasant. It was Gaetano, originally. Still is on my birth certificate."

"So you're Italian? Clyne doesn't sound—"

"Italian on my mother's side," he interrupts. "She was from Florence." He spears an apple slice from the bird's cavity, then mashes it on a piece of meat with his knife. She observes that he uses his utensils in the continental fashion, fork in the left hand, knife in the right. "But I was born in Rome, back in the *La Dolce Vita* days."

Lisa refrains from asking when that was, but the question

must show on her face, because he adds, "The early sixties. Sixty-one."

So that would make him . . . forty-six.

"My father was in the foreign service, political officer at the U.S. Embassy, and my mother was working there, in Rome, for UNESCO when they met. She insisted on balancing my Anglo surname with an Italian first name. Lobbied hard for Marcaurelio, but the old man balked at that and they eventually settled on Gaetano. I had it legally changed to Gaetan after I went to college. She's never forgiven me."

Interrupting himself, he picks up his grouse with both hands and rips off a chunk with his teeth, as if he's in some Elizabethan banquet hall.

"Best way to eat these exquisite little buggers," he says, noticing her reaction. "Tastes better, too. Try it. Don't be shy."

She does, delicately wiping her mouth with her napkin afterward. If there's been any enhancement in the taste, she hasn't noticed it. The taste doesn't need improving in any case.

"To put the cherry on the gelato, I was baptized in Saint Peter's," he says, resuming the saga of his entry into the world. "And the Marchese and Marchesa Frescobaldi were my godparents." He delivers the last sentence with a clear note of self-mockery, as if aware of just how ridiculously pretentious he would sound without it. "My mother's family knew the Frescobaldis, and she never let anyone forget it. She can be a helluva snob."

"So, this wine? It's a present from your godparents?"

"Oh, hell no. Like I told you, I got it at a liquor store in Chicago. The only time I've seen the marchese and marchesa was in the photograph of them holding me outside the basilica."

Again, the tone of sardonic self-effacement. But Gaetan's

attempts at modesty have an effect opposite the one intended: the more he makes light of his upper-crust background, the more attention he calls to it. Nevertheless, Lisa is charmed. She's always been a sucker for men with glamorous histories. Bill's had been interesting enough—Navy flyer, war hero, son of a two-term state senator and newspaper publisher, grandson of a timber-and-mining magnate—but Gaetan's (it is Gaetan now, not Clyne) was a different order of magnitude entirely. She learns as they graze on dinner that he lived all over the world in his childhood and adolescence—Rome, Cairo, Nairobi, Paris—and later in Washington, where his father had been an assistant secretary of state and Gaetan went to school with the children of illustrious people. He graduated from Columbia University Journalism School, and more globe-trotting followed. He became a foreign correspondent with NBC Radio—that deep-pitched voice made him a natural—covering what he calls "dark events in sunny places." Small wars in Central America. A bigger war in Bosnia. The Rwandan genocide.

It could be a turnoff, all this talking about himself, but Lisa is fascinated. She has the impression, without knowing how she acquired it, that Gaetan is not an egoist; he wants her to know about him.

"Rwanda was the end of my career," he says. "Nineteen ninety-four. I quit."

He gnaws on his second grouse. Lisa, feeling stuffed, leaves hers for tomorrow's lunch.

"Quit why?"

"I was the network's go-to guy for covering wars, and I was sick of it, so I packed it in and eventually got into doing commercials. The money's good, it's a stretch to call it work, and it's a lot safer. Rwanda was what did it. I won't tell you, at dinner, what I saw there. I wouldn't tell you at any time."

The censorship, naturally, is a tease, whetting her curiosity. She asserts herself. She's not some delicate little blossom. She knows what happened in Rwanda. Tribes murdering each other. She forgets the names . . .

"The Hutus and the Tutsis. The Tutsis got the worst of it."

"I saw it on the six o'clock news, the bodies . . ."

"Oh, the six o'clock news. You saw it on the six o'clock news." Narrowing his eyes, he leans over his plate, his left hand cupping the fist of his right. "Did you *smell* anything on the six o'clock news? Hundreds of corpses, hacked by machetes and piled up like trash in a landfill. Rotting in the heat for days. Did the six o'clock news broadcast what that smells like? The stench makes your eyes water and gets into your clothes so you can't wash it out. You have to burn them."

She does not say anything. The change from mellow to severe has been swift and disconcerting. He can be intimidating when he wants to be.

"I'm sorry," he adds, softening. "It's just that . . . It's . . . Oh, hell, it's not the kind of conversation I'd like to have with someone like you."

A flush has come to Lisa's cheeks, not from embarrassment for upsetting him or from the wine.

"All right, then. What kind of conversation would you like to have?"

She's flirting now, a little with her eyes, a little with her voice, subtly but unambiguously flirting.

"I've been wondering about you. And, no, I'm not interested in what sign you are."

"Leo."

"What did you do before you opened this place? Were you born up here? How did you end up here if you weren't?"

The radio reporter in him has come out.

"Boring," Lisa says. "Compared to you, boring as a pair of sensible shoes."

"Oh, come on . . ."

"Okay, you asked for it. I did marketing and publicity for the Northern Suns casino. The one down in Manitou Falls? You know it?"

"I've seen the signs for it. Don't gamble myself."

"I quit for the same you reason you quit your job. I got sick of it. Sick of enticing people to blow their money on blackjack and Texas hold 'em. Made me feel like a shill for a tobacco company. How did I end up here? Not real sure. I had to get out of the house I'd lived in with Bill—it felt haunted, I guess. Want to hear more?"

Gaetan nods.

"You were born in Rome; I was born on a dairy farm downstate, near Port Huron. A small dairy farm. We grew some corn, too. Been in the Williams family since the 1890s, and my parents had to work other jobs to keep it—my father in an auto distributorship in town, my mother clerking now and then at a Walgreens. We had linoleum floors and plywood cabinets and an old pickup truck with parts my dad cannibalized from two older trucks. We ate roast chicken for Sunday dinner, and it was always one of our chickens, just like our eggs at breakfast were from those chickens, because the chickens and eggs at the supermarket were too expensive. But we did have indoor plumbing." She speaks sharply, laying emphasis on words like "linoleum," "plywood," "cannibalized," as if to shame his glittering childhood with the dull poverty of hers. "I was the first one in my family to go to college, and only because I'd won a scholarship.

Michigan State, class of 1991. Married Bill six years later, and seven years after that he was hunting with two of his old high school friends and he tripped and fell and his gun went off and blew a hole in his chest big as a rabbit hole. I think that about wraps up my résumé."

"It's not boring, not the way you tell it. Your husband—"

"We're not going to talk about him. Not the kind of conversation I'd like to have, all right?"

Lisa motions at his plate, on which two grouse carcasses have been picked clean. "Finished? I've got dessert. Blueberry pie with ice cream."

"Sure. I'll walk it off tomorrow."

As Lisa stands to clear the table, Gaetan rises with her, picking up his silverware and plate. She steps over to him and, taking advantage of a chance to touch him, rests a palm on his shoulder.

"Uh-uh. You cooked; I'll do the cleanup."

She signals him, with a light pressure of her hand, to sit down. But he interprets it as a signal of something else, and she knows in her heart that he's not misinterpreting, which is why she doesn't resist when he clasps her waist and draws her to him. They kiss, tentatively at first, then, Lisa locking her fingers around the back of his neck, with the urgency of pent-up adolescents. They hold the kiss until her lips hurt. There is, in her, a sense of the inevitable. From the moment on the first morning when she stooped at the sideboard and her shoulder pressed against his arm and he refused to move, she'd known that this would happen. Not consciously but known nonetheless.

He drops into the chair, pulling her onto his lap. She straddles him and, feeling wild and wanton, bumps and grinds.

"In there," he says in a thick voice, motioning at his room

with his head. She shakes hers. Klaus is in there. She doesn't want to deal with Klaus—he'll break the spell as surely as a knock at the door. Nor does she want Gayle to find stained bedsheets when she comes in to clean tomorrow. Taking Gaetan's hand, she leads him outside, and under the Milky Way's dusty arch, they quickly cross the backyard into Lisa's cottage. Inside, tearing at their clothes, they don't speak, for a word now would also shatter the spell.

She falls onto the bed, he leans over her, his palms flat on the mattress. She is half hypnotized by his body, the muscles in his arms long and tensile, like tree roots under his skin. Gaetan is a skilled lover, maybe a bit too skilled. There is a practiced quality in what he does with his hands, in the way he kisses her breasts, going from one to the other, giving each equal attention, his tongue tracing the outlines of her nipples. Practiced, accomplished, yet he enjoys giving her pleasure, and she responds, grabbing his cock, filling herself with him. Is this the lust of a woman celibate for too long? Of course it is; yet there is more in it than raw desire.

It is she who climaxes first, a shuddering spasm that provokes him into frenzied thrusts. Her nails drive into his back. He very nearly slams her head into the headboard when he comes. She doesn't object to the brutality, because it is needed; the rancor and sadness and Bill's ghost must be driven out. This is exorcism as much as it's sex, and exorcisms are always violent.

He rolls off her, onto his back. Turning onto her side, she feels a warm stickiness under her thigh. *Ah, fluids,* she thinks. Odd, how sex can be as repulsive as it's rhapsodic. They lie there, still and silent, for several minutes. Gaetan's hand rests on her tummy. She is conscious of its bulge.

"I'm a little flabby, I know," she says.

"I'd say you're Rubenesque."

"That's kind of you. Tell me something—why would a guy who's been all over the world come here? Every year for the past ten, you said."

"I like to hunt wild birds over pointing dogs."

"You could do that in a lot of places. The U.P. is a back-water. I've met people who don't know where it is or have never heard of it at all."

"Maybe because I'm familiar with it. Ever hear of the Huron Mountain Club?"

"Sure. Just about everybody up here has."

He turns sideways to face her. Their noses are within inches of touching. She can see, sparkling in the table lamp's light, the stubble of beard that scraped her when they kissed.

"And what have you heard?" he asks. It is his voice that captivates her, more than the rugged face, the athletic physique. He could make a weather report sound thrilling.

"Let's see—it's near Marquette. It's thousands of acres; it's got pretty lodges; you need megabucks to join and it's very exclusive. Just a handful of people belong. It's so damn exclusive that Henry Ford had to wait years to get in."

"Ten years," Gaetan says. "And it's twenty thousand acres and fifty families are regular members. That includes the Clynes. I inherited membership from my father, who inherited it from his."

This revelation impresses her more than the christening in Saint Peter's or the aristocratic godparents, because she can relate to it. Bill's father had tried to get into the HMC and been rejected, despite his prominence and modest fortune. Apparently, the fortune had been too modest.

"My dad grew up in Lake Forest, started going to the club when he was a kid," Gaetan goes on. "When he got posted back to the States, he would bring us there for two weeks every summer. Fly-fishing. Swimming. Sailing. Tennis. The perfect WASP holiday."

He says this with a muted but distinct note of contempt.

"Begs the question," Lisa remarks, even as she thinks: *I've been fucked by an authentic blue blood.* "Why are you here instead of there?"

He rolls onto his back again and, clasping his hands behind his head, stares up at the ceiling fan. Its paddles, she notices, need dusting.

"It's boring, a monoculture," he answers. "Everybody's loaded, votes Republican, thinks and says pretty much the same thing. If you've ever been trapped in a room with a couple of CEO types yakking about which flies work best on the Yellow Dog or the Salmon Trout—when they're not bitching about the corporate tax rate, that is—you'd know what I mean."

"That's an experience I've missed out on," she says, injecting a little acid into the statement. She wishes he would stop flaunting his privileged life by scorning or making fun of it. "If that's how you feel about it, why don't you hand in your membership card? Do they have membership cards?"

"Oh, the club does some good things for conservation, the environment. And we do stay there in the summer sometimes."

"By 'we,' you must mean your family."

He is quiet for a beat. "Does that bother you?"

"Bother me, why? Because I'm a good girl who would never knowingly sleep with a married man? Or because the lonely widow is looking for a husband?"

He lets out a breath, and it seems to her that some of his con-

fidence, his aura of command, leaves with it. Lisa swings herself on top of him and, in a movement more aggressive than
erotic, pins his shoulders to the mattress with the flats of her
hands.

"That's not what the lonely widow is looking for, if that's
what you're thinking."

She believes this declaration to be true and looks down on
him, trying to read if he does, too. But Mount Rushmore's
expression doesn't reveal anything.

"So, is that what's on your mind?" she says.

"No . . . No . . ."

"Maybe we can have an encore tomorrow night," she says,
with a boldness that surprises even her. "And then I'll have other
guests coming in and you'll be on your way home to Barrington
and that will be that."

"Will it? All things being equal, I'll be back next fall."

"And we'll see what happens then." The fog of lovemaking
has completely cleared from Lisa's mind. She feels sure of herself, as sure as she ever has.

*　*　*

Lisa becomes the Other Woman for a week or two weeks for
the next five autumns. She thinks of this as a kind of annual
holiday season, like the period from Thanksgiving to New
Year's. Its discrete beginning and end, and the distance that sep-
arates her and Gaetan the rest of the year, are guardrails against
skids into messy emotional entanglements—the deep ditches
where most affairs wind up. Gaetan lays down a rule: There is to
be no communication between them—no texts, emails, phone
calls, letters, or notes—beyond his making, and her confirm-
ing, his annual reservation. Lisa gladly accepts this regula-
tion. She's in little danger of losing her heart, he of losing his,

and the brevity of each liaison preserves its intensity; passion is not dissipated by routine or everyday cares. Passion is what she needs most. Bill's ghost is a powerful spirit requiring repeated exorcisms, and tenderness is not always up to the task. Passion is demanded, and she doesn't mind, doesn't mind at all, if it involves some roughness. Nothing kinky or perverse—just *rough*.

There is the freakishly warm afternoon—a week into October and it's almost eighty degrees—when, to spare his dog, Gaetan does not hunt and goes blueberry picking with Lisa in a barrens well off a back road. They stoop and pick in the Indian-summer sun until they come upon a swale of the wheat-colored grass called blanket grass for its flannel-like softness. They set their buckets down. She removes her sweat-spotted shirt; he strips off his. They are soon naked, except for their socks, which makes them look ridiculous, but they are too avid for each other to bother pulling them off. She squashes some berries, rubs his cock with the juice, and, kneeling, licks it off, his scent damp, pungent. She brings him to the verge, then withdraws her mouth. His penis, stained the color of dark blood, veins twined around it like tendrils, looks like a quivering root. Then he crushes berries in his hands, nudges her onto her back, and smears the purple liquid on her inner thighs, into her pubic hairs. His tongue almost draws a scream from her, and as her own smell reaches her nostrils, a salty odor like low tide, a scene she's read—Mellors taking Lady Chatterley in the rainy woods, *short and sharp . . . like an animal*—springs into her mind. She turns partway onto her side, only partway to entice him into doing what she wants. Grasping her waist, he flings her over on her belly, pulls her rump into him. A trembling in his loins, his seed leaps into her, short and sharp, short and sharp, yes.

* * *

Mellors the gamekeeper, Gaetan the game hunter. She joins him once in a while, for the exercise and for the enjoyment of watching him stride through the woods, confident and alert. She doesn't carry a gun herself, turning down his offer of one of his—a lightweight 20-gauge. Although Bill had taught her to shoot on a skeet-and-trap range, although she'd grown up around guns—her father and brother were hunters—she doesn't like them and what they do. Gaetan rhapsodizes about the beauty of a well-trained bird dog fulfilling its nature. The dog work, that's what this is really about, he says, claiming that he doesn't hunt in order to kill but kills in order to hunt—an awfully fine distinction. Too fine. Killing is what this is about. She isn't squeamish; she'd seen her mother wring the necks of chickens for those Sunday dinners, her father butcher hogs. She's aware that life and death are not separate but knit as tightly as the threads in a blanket. Yet her heart freezes when Gaetan's shot finds its mark and the wild bird plummets to the ground.

He talks a lot—way too much, Aileen says. She knows him from the diner, where he stops in for lunch every so often and is likely to corner her or a customer and soliloquize on whatever subject has grabbed his attention.

One gray, nippy morning, while he and Lisa tramp down a long-disused logging road, the topic is the financial collapse.

"I saw it coming way before the smartest guys in the room found out that they weren't the smartest guys in any room," he says. They've been walking for forty-five minutes; Klaus hasn't flown a bird. A slow day, when hunting becomes, in his words, "armed hiking," always brings out his inner orator. "I'd been reading in, you know, *Barron's* and the *Journal* about subprime mortgages and credit-default swaps and collateralized-debt obligations, all that Wall Street bullshit. I was long in a helluva lot of bank and financial stocks. So about six, seven months before the house of cards came tumbling down, I called my guy and told him to unload them, like pronto. Harry Taylor, he was with Oppenheimer in Chicago. I called Harry—*Unload!*—and he asked why and I said, *Because they're holding all these sliced-up subprimes, millions of them. Mortgages from people who shouldn't have them, people with credit ratings lower than a sub-way rat's ass. If they default, and, Harry, believe me, they're going to sooner or later, those investment banks will be in a tail-spin and take just about everybody with them.* Well, we'd made some nice profits and Harry was sure that I was making a mistake. That I sounded like a street-corner nut shouting, *Repent! The end is near!* He said, 'It would take the collapse of the whole friggin' system for that to happen.' His exact words. And I said, 'That's what I'm talking about, Harry.' My exact words. So he unloaded. Saved myself from losing my shirt—hell, my socks and underwear, too. I didn't make any money, like that hedge-fund guy, the one who saw the handwriting on the wall and shorted everything and made a killing; he's famous now. I wasn't smart enough for that, but at least I was smarter than the guys who thought they were the smartest ones in the room."

As much as she likes to listen, the monologue leaves Lisa feeling pummeled. The jargon—credit-default swaps, collateralized-debt obligations—might as well be Arabic. A few weeks ago, she'd mentioned to her mother that the North Coast Inn was getting fewer reservations from out of state because of the recession. Gladys sighed into the phone. "Oh, yeah, this Great Recession they keep talkin' about on the TV. All these folks losin' their houses, losin' their money. We haven't noticed it. Nobody we know has. Can't lose what you ain't got, and that's a fact."

While Klaus ranges in the woods, a fat grouse hops out of a culvert onto the logging road. Gaetan snaps his shotgun to his shoulder, and the bird takes flight; but instead of vanishing into the trees, it wings straight down the road, an easy, wide-open shot that Gaetan misses.

"That's your comeuppance," she says, teasing.

"What for?"

"It's a good thing you've got that distinctive voice. Stops people from getting the wrong impression."

"What impression? And what's it got to do with my quote, unquote, distinctive voice?"

"It distracts from *what* you're saying to *how* you're saying it. If you'd made that speech in a normal voice, somebody would get the impression that you were bragging that *you're* the smartest guy in the room."

"Like you, for instance?"

She bumps a hip into his. He lets out a quick, throaty laugh. He doesn't take himself too seriously, thank God.

* * *

Once, not long after their first time together, she googled him. His website came up first, and she learned from a brief bio that his wife's name is Marlene and that he has two sons in college, Richard and Michael. That's all she knows about his family, and even those tiny bytes are more than she cares to know. He never talks about them, not a word about his personal life in Barrington, Illinois. Lisa is grateful. Additional details probably would excite her curiosity about Marlene (*Plain? Beautiful? Bright? Pleasant? A bitch?*) and satisfying it would bring on some weird combination of guilt and jealousy. *Adulteress.* The archaism, a word her grandmother might have used, seems fitting, yet it doesn't make her as ashamed as she feels she ought to be. It carries a hint of scarlet wickedness, even of glamour. It lacks the hard, condemnatory edge of *stalker* or *home-wrecker* or *slut*.

The year 2009 marks the third autumn of their episodic affair. She had turned forty in August. No longer a young widow, she is middle-aged, childless, and likely to remain so. Bill had not wanted children—he'd done his bit, had two by his first wife, and that was enough for him. Lisa went along willingly, knowing that she was too self-centered to be any good at motherhood. Also too much a romantic. Children transformed lovers into parents, the magnetism that had drawn them together neutralized in a bath of nighttime feedings, dirty diapers, packing school lunches, car pools, report cards, parent-teacher meetings, and, when the time for them came, lectures on safe sex. Without kids to worry about and care for, Bill had been the sole recipient of all of Lisa's passion and devotion. With his death, the manner of it, something had gone out of her, and she sometimes felt that it was gone for good: the willingness to surrender her heart with her body. Now she's able to keep heart and flesh separate. It's a trick men manage instinctively; women have to learn it, most women anyway.

With Gaetan it's all *sex*. Sex with him is what she revels in, the high carnal fever. They give each other pleasure, and the reciprocity, she feels, saves her from selfishness. Gaetan has also freed her from the chains of memory. Bill's intrusions have ceased almost entirely. Thinking about him does not evoke the usual ache marbled with bitterness. She feels a wistfulness, nothing more. It isn't that his ghost has let her go; she's let go of it.

Gaetan leaves Vieux Desert, as always, right after the Columbus Day weekend. She will miss his embraces for a while; for a while she will think about him, four hundred miles away in Bar-rington with Marlene or jetting off to some distant location to shoot an ad. But business has picked up and she has a great deal to keep her busy. Preparing and serving breakfast; washing up afterward; helping Gayle with the housekeeping and launder-ing; checking in guests. She has also been elected secretary of the county's chamber of commerce. The position doesn't involve much work, but it fills up what idle time she has. Once in a while, she joins Aileen and Alex for drinks at the Great Lakes Brew Pub. Mostly, at the end of the day, she reads or watches TV, con-tent in her own company, and is asleep by nine-thirty. Widow-hood seems to have brought out a sense of self-possession in her. She doesn't dread loneliness, as she had in the months after Bill's death. She's discovered the difference between loneliness and solitude.

*   *   *

In 2011, the late summer, Aileen publishes a memoir, *Horizons*. "My first book for grown-ups," she enthuses. Lisa has read an advance copy. The parallels between their lives are uncanny—the childhood on a struggling family farm (Aileen's in Wiscon-sin), marriage to an older man (Alex is ten years her senior), the decision to launch a small business in a small town—and deep-ens their friendship into sisterhood.

One afternoon in mid-September, Lisa drops in to the diner to pick up a batch of Aileen's blueberry muffins for the next day's breakfast and to have her copy of *Horizons* autographed.

"I loved it," she says.

"You better have." Aileen smiles. She has small teeth, straight but small, like a child's. She sits down in a booth, takes the ball-point clipped to her sweatshirt collar, and scrawls on the title page. "If my career takes off," she says, passing the book back to Lisa, "that might be worth the price of a pastrami sandwich after I'm dead."

The inscription reads: *Sept. 18, 2011—For Lisa Williams, my dear friend and blood sister. With love, Aileen Earhart (no relation to Amelia).*

"I promise not to sell it after you're dead. I don't like pastrami anyway."

She has news, Aileen. She's been invited to be on a panel at the Traverse City Book Festival next month.

"My biggest gig yet!" she exclaims with uncontained excitement. "That festival has pulled in some major names. My panel is about regional writing. Guess I'm on it for the local angle. They told me we'll be talking to four, five hundred people. Holy shit! Ten, twelve kids in a high school library—that's been my usual audience."

"Congratulations," says Lisa, a little envious, though she's never written anything more complicated than a term paper. "Next month when?"

"First weekend. Saturday, the First. I've reserved a few tickets for people from town. I'll feel more relaxed if people I know are there. Hope you can make it."

Lisa hesitates. "Damn, I've got people coming in then. I'm sorry."

"Don't mean to be pushy, but it's just for one night. You can find somebody to manage things for one night, can't you?"

Lisa slides into the booth, facing Aileen across the table.

"I've been seeing somebody, and I'll be seeing him that weekend," she says in a confidential tone. "We don't get to spend much time together—it's, you know, a once-a-year kind of thing."

Aileen gives an understanding nod. "Well, I wouldn't want to stand in the way, but you'd be welcome to bring him."

"It would be a case of what he wants to do." She feels relieved to have shared her secret yet wary of possible consequences. "I'd appreciate it if you kept this to yourself. The guy is married."

"Uh-oh. Not from town, I hope. Wait. Couldn't be. Once a year you said. Anyway, you don't have to worry about—" Aileen stops herself, recognition flashing in her eyes. "No! Him? The voice of Zeus?"

"I don't know how Zeus sounds, but, yeah, him. If he does come, there might be a problem for me. He knows a lot of people in this town. Some of the ones you're inviting might recognize him, and if we're seen together, well, you know."

"Oh, if anybody says anything, I'll just tell them that I invited him, he's a regular customer and my guest. But . . ." Aileen lays both hands on Lisa's arm. "Be careful."

"We have been. We've been super discreet."

"I don't mean that. Nine times out of ten no good comes of these things."

*　*　*

She hires the night desk clerk from the Hiawatha Lodge, the big motel on the highway into town, to run her place over the weekend. He'd filled in for her six months ago, when she took a couple of days to visit her family downstate, so she knows he's reliable and can fry eggs.

On Friday morning, she checks in a retired man and his wife, then a Canadian couple, bikers riding the Great Lakes Circle Tour on a Honda cruiser. To all four, she explains that a commitment is taking her to Traverse City but assures them that they'll be well taken care of until she returns on Sunday afternoon. Gaetan shows up late in the day. She offers him a more detailed explanation after he's hauled his guns and duffel and dog into his usual downstairs room.

"You're invited, too, if you're interested. Otherwise, you'll have to live without me for a night."

"I live without you three hundred and fifty nights a year, so I suppose I can for one more. But . . ." Wrapping his arms around her waist, he shuts the door with a flick of his foot and kisses her. "I don't want to."

He's fifty but has lost none of his charm.

"Easy, bub," she says, pulling away. "It's still daylight, and"—motioning at the ceiling—"I've got guests."

"Can't help myself. The last commercial I did was a voice-over for Cialis. They gave me a free sample." She throws him an incredulous look. He laughs. "Joking. I didn't take any. Donated it to the less fortunate. So Aileen is a celebrity now?"

"Sort of. Like she would say, a good ten floors down from movie-star celebrity."

"But still in the fame hotel. I'll be damned. I'll find a kennel for Klaus."

* * *

The drive to Traverse in Gaetan's new dark-red Range Rover takes five hours. It's midafternoon when they pull into the Bayshore Resort, an environment more fit for the Rover—ninety thousand dollars on four wheels—than the Best Western Lisa had chosen. No chain motel for Gaetan, who booked a suite at the Bayshore. Private balcony. Splendid view of Grand Traverse bay. In-room spa.

They deliver Klaus to the kennel, kill some time with a stroll along the bayfront and downtown. Traverse City isn't a real city—only fifteen thousand people—but it has a moneyed, cosmopolitan vibe. "Wants to be the Hamptons of the Middlewest," Gaetan says. They eat an early dinner at a bistro called Amical. He orders risotto, Lisa the salmon, done in a blood-orange glaze and dusted with fennel pollen, the waiter declares, rather proudly. Dressed in black pants, a cream-colored blouse, and a linen jacket, Lisa is pleased that she doesn't look like a hick, and she doesn't want to come off as one. She waits until the waiter is gone before asking Gaetan, "What is fennel *pollen*?"

"It's a spice, collected from fennel flowers. Popular in Italy. My mother used it a lot."

The book festival starts at seven in the City Opera House, a grand old place with putti and trompe l'oeil clouds flying across the central dome, an ornamented balcony curving above ranks of plush red seats, almost every one of which is filled. Lisa and Gaetan sit with the half-dozen people Aileen invited from Vieux Desert, but they make sure to sit at opposite ends of the row. Aileen and her co-panelists, onstage in upholstered chairs, flank their moderator, a New York publisher wearing a blazer over a black T-shirt. Lisa is amazed at her friend's transformation: a gray smartly tailored dress has replaced her usual jeans and sweatshirt, high heels her sneakers, and her hair is not bound in a ponytail but tumbles freely over her shoulders. Overall, she looks glamorous and is poised and witty answering the moderator's questions. Lisa notices another change after the panel discussion ends and the authors move to tables in the lobby to autograph their books. Aileen has shucked off the accommodating, welcoming manner she wears at the diner; she's slightly aloof, composed, a frank expression in her chocolate-brown eyes that's strangely alluring. One her invitees, Harry McSweeney (president of the chamber of commerce), can't resist embracing her. Aileen winces when he declares, "Are we proud of our local girl or what?" as though she's a ninth-grader who has won a spelling bee.

Lisa stands back, maintaining distance from Gaetan. Although Harry hasn't cast curious looks at her or him, much less said anything about them, Aileen sees fit to provide cover, just in case.

"Harry, do you know Gaetan Clyne? One of the diner's most loyal customers! So I asked him to come on down for the show!"

"Oh, that's why you were sitting with us," Harry says to Gaetan. "I was wondering what the connection was. Come to think of it, I've seen you around town."

Lisa is grateful for the preemptive smoke-screen. Gaetan appears to be too, but maybe it's not gratitude that moves him to bestow an admiring gaze on Aileen. It lingers a bit too long— far too long, in fact. A prickling, reflexive as a flinch, races across Lisa's cheeks. *You have no prior rights to him,* she advises herself. *You can't afford to fall for him.* But jealousy, like desire, isn't obedient to the will. That night, after they've polished off half a bottle of wine from the minibar, she stages a memorable performance in the spa, making love to him like a madwoman, pressing him against the tub's tiles into the spewing jets. They towel off without speaking and collapse into bed, where Gaetan whispers, "Hey, Lisa Williams, it could be I'm falling in love with you."

She makes no reply, thinking, *I can't afford that, either.*

* * *

They sleep late on Sunday morning and skip breakfast. Lisa is anxious to get home, but it's past ten by the time they retrieve Klaus and start out, heading east through cherry orchards and brilliant woods, then north toward the interstate, forty miles away.

"I could use something to eat," Lisa says.

"Thought you were in a hurry."

"In a hurry and hungry. That means a McDonald's drive-through. An Egg McMuffin."

In half an hour, they come to a town. A billboard on the outskirts displays a hand reaching out of a cloud and the message: DESPAIR? JESUS IS YOUR HOPE. Passing an abandoned factory, its glassless windows revealing pipe and conduit dripping from the ceilings like jungle vines, they cruise slowly down the main street, whose handsome old buildings are either boarded up or repurposed into the sort of businesses that thrive in hard times—thrift shops, payday loan agencies.

Two doors down from a café, on a plywood sheet covering a window, someone has painted a plea in blood-red letters. CLEAN UP TOXIC WASTE, GOVERNOR! TCE KILLS!

"Trichloroethylene," she murmurs.

"Yeah," says Gaetan. "I read about it. A cleaning solvent they used in factories. Poisoned drinking water, right?"

"Hey, there, a McDonald's."

"I see it."

It is across a railroad siding from another industrial ruin, this one larger than the other, covering at least an acre, and of more recent dereliction: the weeds sprouting from the cracks in the parking lot are inches high rather than feet, and none of the letters are missing from the sign at the base of a flagless flagpole. TATE AUTOMOTIVE SYSTEMS, it reads. Teenage boys are tossing a football in the lot, younger children playing tag, their shouts and laughter somehow heightening the atmosphere of desolation. Aileen described a scene much like this in her book. Lisa recalls the line: *like kids cavorting in the ruined temple of a religion no one believes in anymore.*

"McDonald's must be *the* place for Sunday brunch," Gaetan

says, falling in behind a long line of cars in the drive-through lane.

They creep forward, stop, creep, stop, creep, and stop again, alongside a tall, square shipping container enclosed on three sides by a block brick wall. The van in front of Gaetan's car is at the kiosk. It must be fully loaded, because the driver takes a long time relaying his passengers' orders. Lisa glimpses two kids atop the container, a girl in a soiled jacket and a scruffy tow-headed boy. Just as the van starts forward to the pickup window and Gaetan releases the brake, the girl either jumps or falls, crashes onto the Rover's hood with a heart-stopping thud, and rolls off the front end and under the car. "Jesus Christ!" Gaetan yells, slamming the brake pedal. Klaus, in a car kennel in the back, yips once; the girl howls in pain, a cry both chilling and comforting—it means she's conscious. The boy, who is still on top of the container, hollers out, "Kim got runned over! Kim got runned over!"

Gaetan and Lisa leap out of the car. The girl named Kim is lying on her back, her legs spraddled, the right a few inches from the front tire and torqued at the knee at a sharp angle to her thigh. Lisa kneels beside her and strokes her hair and face and tries to quiet her cries. Could the car have rolled over her leg, then rolled back when Gaetan hit the brake? Lisa hadn't felt a bump, though she might not have because they had been barely moving. Most likely, the girl injured herself in the fall. She appears to be eleven or twelve, brown-haired and lanky, and reminds Lisa of herself as she was at that age—a gawky country girl, tall for her age, and maybe a bit reckless. If she had jumped, it had been out of recklessness, perhaps taking a dare from the boy to hurtle over the hood while the Rover sat motionless below them.

"Don't move her," says a man wearing a bomber jacket. He's standing beside the car behind theirs.

"I haven't," Lisa replies, her voice a little shaky.

The man whips out his cellphone. Gaetan gestures to him to put it away. He's called the police; they're on the way.

A patrolman arrives five minutes later, while a siren sounds in the distance—the ambulance, probably. The patrolman, who can't be a day past twenty-two, asks to see Gaetan's insurance card and driver's license, takes down his tag number, gets statements from him and Lisa, then turns to the bystanders, asking if anyone saw what happened. No one did, except the man in the bomber jacket.

"She was up there"—pointing at the shipping container—"next thing, she's flying through the air, right on top of this fella's car."

The patrolman examines the dented hood, then writes on a report sheet fastened to a clipboard. The ambulance pulls in, announcing itself with that awful noise ambulances make to clear a path, part blare, part squawk. The decals on the doors state that it's from the volunteer fire department. Kim's parents are right behind it, in a pale-blue sedan that looks to be ten years old and shows its age. The mother is a heavyset woman with short hair the same chestnut shade as her daughter's; the father is also on the hefty side, but muscle is evident beneath the flab, and his shaved skull and dark beard and bullish gait convey an air of menace.

The scruffy boy runs up to him. "Mr. Parichy! Mr. Parichy! Kim got runned over!"

"Why do you think we're here, Bobby?" he says sharply.

The two people follow the paramedics, a young man and woman, to their daughter's side.

"Mom! Mom!" Kim groans. "My leg . . . my knee . . ."

"Take it easy, baby," the mother says, gripping her out-stretched hand. "Lay still and these nice people will take good care of you."

Neither she nor her husband makes a fuss when Kim yelps as the paramedics straighten her right leg or when they fit an air splint over it, inflate the splint, and lift her onto a gurney. No fuss at all. It's the stoic calm, which Lisa knows well, of country people who are shocked more by good news than bad.

"Munson Hospital in Traverse," the male paramedic says to the father while the woman buckles the gurney straps.

"How's it look to you, Pete?"

"I'd say Kimmy is one lucky little kid."

"If you call gettin' hit by a car lucky."

Kimmy. Bobby. Mr. Parichy. Pete. They all know each other. Lisa is afraid that tribal defenses will go up; she and Gaetan are outsiders here.

"Excuse me, sir, we didn't hit her," she says pleasantly. "She jumped or fell from there."

Her hand sweeps from the container to the bruised metal on the hood above the grille and the chrome letters that spell RANGE ROVER.

"It couldn't be helped, but we feel awful about it all the same," Gaetan interjects. "And relieved that she wasn't . . . That she'll be all right."

Parichy levels his gaze on Gaetan, then casts a longer look at the Rover, which stands out among the beat-up cars and pickup trucks like a man in black tie at a meeting of the welders' union.

"We'll wait and see what the doctor has to say about that," Parichy says.

With a single gulp of its siren, the ambulance rolls out onto the street, Kim's parents' sedan trailing. The patrolman comes up to Gaetan.

"Looks like it was unavoidable, sir. I'm not going to cite you for anything, and I've got all your information in case it's needed. You're free to go."

*　*　*

"What are you doing?" asks Lisa, watching Gaetan punch *Munson Hospital, Traverse City, MI* into the car's GPS.

"We've got to make sure that little girl really is going to be okay."

"What can we do, whether she is or she isn't? And the cop said it wasn't your fault."

"That's beside the point. What's with you? Are you just being practical or are you worried that you'll be late getting back? Gotta get those omelets out on time tomorrow morning."

She governs a sudden urge to smack him. "It's the kid's father. He scares me. You didn't see the way he looked at you? Like he wanted to punch your lights out?"

"He's upset. Who wouldn't be?"

They volley for another minute, and during that minute they are no longer lovers; they're a feuding *couple*.

*　*　*

The ER is quiet on a Sunday afternoon, the waiting room empty except for the four of them, sitting in molded plastic chairs: Lisa and Gaetan, Ken and Nancy Parichy, whose first names came courtesy of Nancy, as did the information that Kim is in radiology, undergoing an MRI for what the doctor believes is a broken knee. Ken says nothing, arms crossed over his bulging chest, billiard-ball head tilted aside, chin cocked—a posture that communicates a mixture of defensiveness and belligerence.

"Thanks for coming in to check on her," says Nancy. "You didn't need to."

Gaetan avers that they most certainly did, they would have been wondering and worrying about her daughter's condition. The least they could do, really. He's a parent himself; he can well imagine how they're feeling right now.

He's in one of his babbling moods, going on too much for too long, trying to show this blue-collar couple that he's compassionate and responsible, not some careless rich guy who drives a car worth more than they earn in a year. His speechifying moves Ken to speak:

"That little girl is all we've got," he says, drawing a quick, surprised, puzzled look from Nancy. "Y'know, if she did jump on top of your car—and I can't figure why she would, but if she did—that jump's not more'n two feet. Don't seem like she'd bust a knee, a jump that short."

Gaetan shakes his head in confusion, not denial. "She fell off the hood right onto the pavement. Could've happened then."

"She was layin' in front of your car," replies Ken, his tone embittered and ominous all at once.

"People can break a leg stepping off a curb," Lisa interjects.

"Is that a fact?"

"Yes, Mr. Parichy, it is," she answers, flint in her voice because she'd noticed the look Nancy had given him—Kim isn't all they've got, there is another child, maybe more than one. He's trying to build a case, at least in his own mind.

They sit in silence for a time, Lisa feeling waves of hostility rolling toward her from Ken Parichy. Then Nancy, attempting to change the tenor of the conversation, turns to Gaetan.

"I could swear I've heard you before. Not too many men talk like you, and I could just swear it."

"Radio or TV maybe. I do radio and TV commercials."

"I knew it! Which—"

"Is there much in that, money-wise?" Ken cuts in, his manner slightly more cordial, if also contemptuous. From his Carhartt jacket to his steel-toe boots, it's obvious that he doesn't consider doing radio TV commercials real work.

"Now, honey, you ought to know better than to ask a man how much he makes," Nancy chides.

"No problem. It's a living, pays the bills," Gaetan replies, but in a manner so jocular and coy that he might as well have disclosed his income.

Worried that he might say too much, Lisa intervenes, politely asking Ken what he does for a living.

Wrong question.

"What do I do? Not a goddamn thing is what I do," he comes back savagely. "I haven't done a goddamn thing since the plant shut down. Tate Automotive. Unless you count goin' to cash my unemployment check, a big fat zero is what I do."

Gaetan attempts to ride to Lisa's rescue. Shaking his head, he says, "It's a damn shame, these companies going to Mexico or China or someplace."

The earnest display of solidarity with the working class earns a smirk.

"Tate didn't go nowheres but under," Ken says.

Just then the doctor enters the room. Identified as Dr. Gupta by the tag pinned to his lab coat, he smiles broadly as Nancy and Ken pop out of their seats. He delivers good news: yes, their daughter's knee is broken, but it's a non-displaced fracture, meaning a simple fracture. No other broken bones. No internal injuries.

Nancy sighs relief and murmurs, "Thank the Lord."

"She will be in a cast for six to eight weeks; otherwise, she'll be fine," Gupta continues. "Very fortunate it happened where it did. The car must have been moving very, very slowly."

Ken crowds him. Though he's not much taller, his hulking frame seems to trivialize the slender doctor.

"Yeah, but it hit her and busted her knee."

Gupta draws back. His black eyes flit around the room, then rest quizzically on Lisa and Gaetan.

"It was our car," she says before Gaetan can speak a word. "The girl jumped on it, or she fell from a container box, and then fell off the hood."

"Oh, I see. The injury is consistent with a fall. In any case, a fortunate child." He returns to the Parichys. "Come, I'll take you to her and you can have a look at the MRIs."

"We're really happy that she'll be all right," says Gaetan as the three people move toward a double door leading into the ER. "If there's anything I can do to . . ."

He withdraws his wallet from his pants pocket and from the wallet a business card. Lisa seizes his wrist before he can present it. Looking hard at Ken, she says, "You don't need this. Anything you need to know, it's in the accident report," then adds, but without a dollop of warmth, "Glad things have come okay for you."

Still clasping Gaetan's wrist, she all but tows him outside.

* * *

"What the fuck was that all about?" he snarls when they're in the car.

"You didn't need to give him your card," she answers.

"Not like it's got top secret info on it."

"It's not necessary. You don't have to give that guy your phone numbers, your address and email." Lisa pauses, gathering her thoughts. "The whole time, you were practically . . ." She almost says "groveling" but checks her tongue. "You were show-ing him how kind and open you are, a real good guy—*here, Kenny boy, here's my card, reach out to me anytime.* But he would see it as a sign of weakness. You telling him how sorry you are, and you're sorry because you feel responsible, no matter what— that's how he would see it and take advantage."

"By giving him a *business card*? You're over the top."

He pulls out of the lot. Sitting stiff and straight, fingers threaded in her lap, Lisa gazes out at the street, a Norman Rock-well painting: large frame houses set back from lawns papered with yellow leaves.

"I don't understand how a guy who's been around as much as you can be so . . . so . . . naïve. You couldn't tell what he's up to?"

"Sure I could. I'm not naïve, all right? And if it comes down to it, I've got a good lawyer and top-of-the-line insurance."

"You acted like you were guilty, Gaetan. I could see it; so could he. When you pulled out your card, his eyes lit up. If he had three of them, he would have looked like a slot machine hit-ting jackpot."

"Holy Christ! You are out there. He's a working stiff who's had a run of bad luck and now his daughter's in the hospital."

"Oh, yeah, salt of the earth," she scoffs. "Stop romanticiz-ing. I know people like him. I grew up around them. They can be dead flat broke, but they'll always find a spare buck or two for a lotto ticket. That's how he sees you, a lotto ticket."

"Thought I was a slot machine," he grumbles, and at a road sign—Jct.: U.S. 31—turns onto the highway.

"No, he's the slot machine," she says.

"Right now I feel like I don't know you. But we've got a ways to go. Maybe we'll get reacquainted."

* * *

What few words pass between them on the rest of the drive are informational—*Still hungry? Yes. We'll stop for lunch next exit. Okay.* In the long intervals between these exchanges, Lisa grows reflective and self-critical. Maybe she'd been tough about Ken because he reminded her of the world and people she'd left behind long ago; maybe he did not have designs on exploiting his daughter's misfortune; maybe she'd "gone over the top" because she did not want to see Gaetan's generous nature taken advantage of, which might mean that she cares for him more deeply than she's been willing to admit.

Returning to Vieux Desert in the early evening, they eat a whitefish dinner at the brew pub—one of the rare times they permit themselves to be seen together in public. Gaetan has always been more concerned about gossip than she. He's been coming to Vieux Desert for fourteen years, knows every bartender, waitress, and shopkeeper by name. Although the chance that a careless word from any of them would get back to his wife is less than the chance of an asteroid strike, he doesn't want to take it. For that reason, Lisa is certain that he's strayed before, gotten caught, and been given an ultimatum: once more and I'll take you to the cleaner's.

They do not tumble into her bed that night; the image of Kim, sprawled on the pavement, is too fresh. And what love they do make throughout the next ten days is furtive and hurried, like the coupling of co-conspirators on the run.

Lisa entertains the possibility, the hope, that this is temporary, but she doubts that it is. For the first time in their relationship—if it can be called a relationship—she fakes an orgasm; for the first time, she is relieved when Gaetan's stay ends and he drives away, back to Barrington. She cannot account for the change in her feelings. All she knows is that there has been a change and that an eleven-year-old girl tumbling off a shipping container in a McDonald's parking lot in a dismal, dying town has been the cause of it. Somehow or other, Kim has torn her, Lisa, out of her fantasy. That may have happened regardless. Passion consumes itself, as every disillusioned romantic has learned for a thousand years; and if an incombustible nugget of love does not lie in its heart, cinder and ashes are all that remain.

* * *

Ice-out on the lake and rivers arrives in early April; the trees begin to bud and are slapped for their presumption by a sudden frost. A second thaw a month later encourages them to have another go; they seem tentative, as if wary of another deception. Taking advantage of the warm spell, Lisa goes on her first shoreline jog of the year. This winter, she'd begun snowshoeing with Aileen and Alex to trim the flab she always put on in cold weather. A segment on the nightly news about the obesity epidemic had provided additional motivation: fat people, it said, were twice as prone to cancer as slim people. She'd had a scare in January, after getting a mammogram at Marquette General. The doctor said he'd seen "something" in her left breast and set her up for an ultrasound-guided biopsy.

"You tell that doctor to take that thing out," her mother demanded during their weekly phone call. "No ifs, ands, or buts. Out it comes."

Lisa, careful not to betray her anxiety, explained why that couldn't happen unless and until the biopsy found a malignancy.

"Listen to the medical expert, will you?" said Gladys. "Are you ever going to get married again?"

"*What?* What's that have to do with anything?"

"Do you want to die alone, like your aunt Meg?"

Gladys seldom failed to inflate a mere concern into a certain catastrophe. Aunt Meg was her youngest sister. Metastatic breast cancer had claimed her, unmarried and childless, at forty-eight. The entire family, Lisa included, had gathered at her bedside the day before she passed, but no husband, no kids. That, to Gladys's mind, was dying alone.

Lisa pounds down the beach to the lighthouse and back. Four miles. Four hundred calories. She cools down with a walk around the campground. A week after the biopsy, the doctor reported happy news—the something turned out to be a cyst. Lisa's life, on pause for an entire week, resumed playing. But she will turn forty-three this August, just five years younger than her aunt had been at the end. One day in the future, some growth somewhere will not be a cyst and the news will not be happy. The words "die alone" rattle in her brain as she walks, and they summon a picture of Aunt Meg, lying in her hospital bed, wasted and drugged. Probably the very image her mother had hoped to conjure up, both to prod her into remarrying and to remind her that disaster was only a diagnosis away.

Her cellphone in her sweatshirt pocket vibrates.

"Hey, Aileen. What's up?"

"I was about to ask you the same thing. Guess you haven't checked the Journeys website this morning."

"Nope. Been jogging. Why?"

"Better c'mon over. The house, not the diner."

Aileen and Alex live in a century-old three-story frame two blocks from Lake Superior in one direction, four blocks from the woods in the other. She leads Lisa up to the attic, which Alex, who is a skilled carpenter, has converted into a writing studio. Two shafts of sunlight, angling through the skylights, one on each side of the pitched roof, meet over a U-shaped desk. Aileen sits down and punches up the travel service's site on her computer. A few keystrokes take her to the customer reviews for the North Coast Inn. She scrolls down to the most recent, a one-star posted late last night. Its author is cryptically identified as *DCR2404. Level 2 reviewer.* Leaning over Aileen's shoulder, Lisa reads it in disbelief.

"What the fuck!" she blurts out, and reads it again.

> I stayed at the North Coast Inn last October and was shocked at the unprofessional conduct of its owner. She—how to put this?—entertains one of her male guests on the premises. They weren't quiet about it, either, keeping me awake half the night. I would have checked out the next day, but no other rooms were available in town. The previous night's activities were not a freak occurrence, because the same thing happened the second night, causing me to wonder what sort of establishment I was in. The owner's private life is her own business, of course, but not when it disturbs her guests. Others who have experienced this inexcusable, inappropriate behavior may have been too embarrassed to say anything about it. Indeed, I myself was for the past few months. No longer! I will never stay there again!

"I came across it by accident this morning," Aileen says. "I'm sorry to be the one to show it to you, but better me than somebody else."

Trolled. Slut-shamed. Lisa's face is on fire, though from anger rather than shame.

"This is bullshit! It's a hoax! Somebody's sick prank! Who the hell would do something like this?"

"Some fat punk somewhere maybe, but it sounds like a woman to me."

"Yeah, to me, too."

"Who knows?" Aileen shrugs, and in the twin shafts of pallid light converging on her face, Lisa sees the same composed, candid expression it wore at the book festival last fall. "You told me you two were being super discreet, so maybe . . . I mean, an affair with a paying guest who happens to be married?"

"Are you judging me?" Lisa snaps.

Aileen gives her a long, searching look. "Not you. I'm judging your judgment. Better contact Journeys right away and tell them it's defamatory and to take it down."

* * *

In her office, still wearing her sweats, Lisa journeys through the Journeys website, landing at the "Management Center," which lists a six-step protocol for reporting a complaint about a review. Following instructions, she selects DCR2404's post and types in the "Comments" box: *This person has never stayed at the North Coast Inn. His/her review is false, malicious, and slanderous. Apparently it slipped through the cracks in your system. I demand that it be removed immediately.*

A few moments later, a message flashes on her laptop screen: *We have received your report and will delete the selected review if we confirm that it violates our guidelines. Please note that we cannot disclose the identities of our reviewers and are unable to fact-check customer reviews. We cannot remove one because there is a dispute about its contents.*

"In other words," Lisa says out loud, "any asshole can post a total lie and you're not responsible."

And why would this asshole, if she was so affronted, wait seven months before posting her commentary?

The review lingers for several hours before it's finally deleted. In cyber-time, several hours equal several eternities. The review is out there long enough to be picked up by Twitter trolls. Lewd and plain-stupid comments appear on Lisa's website and Facebook page. She feels vulnerable, exposed, invaded.

As mortifying are the whispers that fly through Vieux Desert. Like all small towns, it's a cauldron bubbling with rumors and innuendo, which the gossipmongers revise, exaggerate, or otherwise mangle. Resolved to set the record straight, Lisa makes a brief speech at the next meeting of the chamber of commerce. She asks her fellow members to ignore everything they may have heard; the customer review was fraudulent, an attempt to defame her by an unknown person for unknown reasons. She runs her business according to the highest professional standards. Around twenty people are there, seated at a long table in the community hall next to the volunteer fire station. They nod in sympathy; Harry McSweeney declares that they never believed a word of it; they've got her back. His assurance brings on a twinge of guilt; not every word in the post was false. One small part was true, though Lisa would dispute the verb "entertains."

The mystery troll takes no further shots at her, and Lisa soon returns to running the machinery of her daily life. Food must be ordered to restock the pantry with non-perishables, menus planned; a new showerhead has to be installed in room three. Bookings for the Memorial Day weekend, coming up in two weeks, pump her morale: all five rooms are taken.

* * *

She is in the kitchen, emptying the dishwasher, when her phone warbles—the tone for an incoming text. She picks it up from the counter, reads:

>—Will be at meeting of HMC next week. Need to see you about something. G.

Did she have an evil genie, the opposite of a guardian angel, its sole purpose to upset her equilibrium? She hesitates. Gaetan is breaking his own no-communication rule. She types:

>—When?
>—Next Wednesday. Midafternoon.
>—U can't stay here. Full up. (A lie. The place won't be full till the following week.)
>—No problem. Staying at the club.
>—What's up?
>—Prefer face-to-face.

Avoiding a paper trail, she thinks. Or an electronic one.

>—OK. C U then.

She clicks off, feeling like a spy arranging a clandestine rendezvous. Not as far-fetched as it sounds. There is an element of espionage in most adulterous affairs. Among the things Lisa has learned about herself is that she has a capacity for compartmentalizing. When she's been with Gaetan, she's been with him totally; when apart, totally apart. Now, with this text, he has broken the pattern. She is curious about what he must tell her in person, yet she would as soon not see him. He isn't good for her; he may even be dangerous.

Today is Saturday. Four days to wait.

* * *

She is unloading groceries from her car when he shows up on Wednesday afternoon at one o'clock. Accustomed to seeing him dressed for fall weather, she finds his summer apparel— khaki pants, polo shirt, lightweight sweater thrown cape-like over his shoulders and knotted at the sleeves—strange, like a costume.

There is a distance in her greeting, which she doesn't consciously intend; it's simply there.

"I expected you later," she says.

"The meeting let out early."

Her gaze drifts to the white SUV parked across the street.

"A rental," he says. "I flew up for the powwow. Give you a hand?"

"I can manage."

"I insist."

He takes a grocery bag in each hand and follows her into the kitchen, where she orders him around as if he were a delivery boy. The bacon in the right bottom drawer of the fridge; ham and pork sausage in the left; canned stuff in the cabinet above the stove. When the contents have been put away, he presents a restrained smile, pleased with his chivalry. The lines in his face look like grooves etched into clay by a sculptor's fingernails. And is it her imagination or has he lost some height? The impression is so strong that she looks at his feet. He's wearing flat deck shoes rather than his thick-heeled hunting boots.

That must be it.

Then, clasping her waist, he draws her to him to kiss her. She pushes him away, gently.

"Not here, not now."

"You don't seem real excited to see me."

"Oh, it's not . . . Give me a few minutes to adjust. It's early, but how about a drink?"

"If it helps your adjustment."

They go into the cottage, where they had spent so many nights. It's not much larger than a double-wide, but its three rooms have enough space to avert claustrophobia. After pouring Gaetan a shot of his favorite bourbon over ice and herself a glass of sauvignon blanc, she steps into the bathroom, pees, brushes her hair, freshens her lipstick, collects herself. She returns to the living room and drops into one of its two matching chairs. Gaetan is in the other, kitty-corner from her.

"So, here we are, face-to-face," she says, and gives him an expectant look.

"You were right about that guy last fall, the girl's dad."

"Parish."

"Parichy."

"That's it. He came after you?"

Gaetan nods. "I got a letter of intent from some ambulance chaser in Traverse. Right around Thanksgiving. Pitched it to my lawyer. No case at all, he said. It would be dismissed as frivolous in a heartbeat. But I told him I didn't want it to get that far, and I told him why."

Lisa sips her wine. "Because it might have come out in court that I was in the car? You'd have to explain to your wife what I was doing there?"

"Something like that."

"So you settled."

He nods and slouches, so that he looks smaller, diminished, just as he had in the kitchen.

"I hope it wasn't too much."

"It wasn't. Enough to make him feel he'd won one."

She doesn't ask the amount. His definition of not too much and hers are probably not the same. Nowhere near the same.

"And this is what you needed to tell me in person?"

"No. Hell, no." He rattles the ice cubes in his glass. "Are you adjusted yet?"

"Uh-huh."

"Marlene and I are getting a divorce."

She'd intuited that this would be his news; nonetheless, she is startled.

"Oh, Christ, Gaetan. I hope you're not doing it on my account. I really hope not."

"Yes and no."

"Can you explain that?"

"She filed, not me. Three or four letters went between my lawyer and Parichy's, copies to me, registered mail. One of them had the cop's report attached, with your name in it. That happened to be the one Marlene signed for. I was in Chicago when it came, and she opened it and . . ."

Lisa takes a healthy gulp of wine to relax the rubber tube that has cinched around her gut. "Is she in the habit of reading your mail?"

"Not my personal mail. But she saw the law-office return address and figured it was business." He pauses. "To get to it, I thought of a bullshit alibi. That you were just a friend I'd taken to Traverse to see Aileen. But I knew it wouldn't fly."

"Because this wasn't the first time she caught you leaving the dance with somebody else."

Gaetan doesn't say anything, which is as good as an answer.

"It's not that I mind," she says. Leaning toward him, she notices more lines in his face, lines as fine as spider's silk fanning out from the deeper grooves. They make his skin look like crinkled paper. "I never, not for a microsecond, thought I was your first fling. All right, so you told her about me—"

"Us."

"Me. Us. She forgave you the other time, if there was only one. Not this time. She's done."

The whiskey goes down. He reaches for the bottle and carefully measures out another shot.

"It was a weight off my shoulders, telling her."

"I don't like to think of myself as the bitch who broke up a marriage."

"You're not. Don't go theatrical on me."

"Theater? This isn't theater to me." The rubber tube squeezes, relaxes, squeezes, like the band on a blood-pressure gauge. A thought begins to form. "When did this happen?"

"She filed in March. We're legally separated for now. I'm contesting one of her terms—she wants half my residuals till death do us part. Marlene is a Scorpio. The vengeful type."

"Does she have a job?"

"Sort of. She freelances."

"Can I ask at what?"

"Tech stuff. She used to be in IT for an investment bank on LaSalle. Quit when our oldest was born, so now she freelances, contract work for IT departments. Why?"

"Curious, is all."

So now she knows who had the skills and the motive to hijack a registered reviewer's online identity and post the vile review. Maybe she wrote the vulgar tweets, as well. The knowledge reassures her. She has not been trolled since then and is reasonably sure she won't be in the future. It was a one-off, a virtual slap in the face to the Other Woman from the Woman Scorned. Lisa would have preferred the real thing, a good sharp crack across the cheek. There was something weaselly and underhanded about hiding behind the stolen identity DCR2404.

"I've moved out," Gaetan says. "Rented a condo in Lake Point Tower. Do you know it?"

She does. She'd seen it on a trip to Chicago with Bill. Gaetan will not suffer in his single state.

"Well, thanks for letting me know. I'm sorry you have to go through all this."

"There's more."

More. All along, she's been afraid there would be more.

"The first year or two, I thought, *It's just bodies. Two bodies having a great time.* But it's turned into something else for me. I'm wondering if it has for you, and if it hasn't, if it can."

"I didn't think of us as just bodies," she says. "There was passion, real passion. Not many people are lucky enough to ever know it, and we had it, Gaetan."

"Maybe I'm not making myself clear. I'm in love with you, and I—" He stops in mid-sentence, jerking his head, as if he's been interrupted by a loud noise. "Was? You said there *was* passion? That we *had* it?"

"Yes, I did."

Making no reply, he lifts his eyes to the poster on the wall behind her. It's a blowup of the lighthouse that marks the half-way point on her morning runs. She tries to parse the grammar of Gaetan's silence, as he'd parsed the grammar of her words, but she cannot tell what it means, if it means anything.

"I could ask you to think about it," he says at last.

"Please don't," she replies, managing the neat trick of sounding, simultaneously, tender and ruthless.

He resolves things for her as, planting his hands on his knees, he rises from the chair.

"It's gotten late and it's a long drive back to the club. I'd better go."

A tiny rise in his voice turns the statement into a question.

"Yes, of course, you had better," she answers.

* * *

It is the morning before the holiday rush, a fine morning, only a few wispy clouds brushing the sky. Lisa parks in her usual spot in the campground at the mouth of the Windigo. The river runs swift from spring melt-off, tumbling clear and cold over the multicolored rocks paving its bottom. Lake Superior reaches for the northern horizon, a gigantic blue eye in the face of the continent. She goes down the staircase to the beach. In the sand, deer and coyote tracks print the history of the night's wanderings and predations. Gripping the handrail, she stretches her calves and thighs, then begins to jog toward the lighthouse. At this hour, there isn't a soul between her and it.

LINES OF DEPARTURE

Even now, four years after hearing it, I cannot get Devin's story out of my head. I remember the day when Will Treadwell put me on the path that would later cross Devin's. I remember it from beginning to end, one of those exquisite days October produces in the north woods. Across Lake Superior—Gitche Gumee, Longfellow's shining Big-Sea-Water—no horizon was visible in the windless, cloudless twilight of early morning. There was hardly a wrinkle in the lake, its gray perfectly matching the gray sky so that air and water seemed to be a single element. The sun rose, not with a riotous display but with a crimson blush that brightened as the disc bulged out of the lake. Then the horizon was drawn, the sky blued, and the lake darkened to a color mimicking the deep ocean.

The air bit, but not too sharply, just enough to make me greedy for it and suck it into my lungs until I was half dizzy. By midday, alto-cirrus appeared far overhead, some ribbed like beach sand after a tide has run out, some sweeping in thin, multiple threads—the clouds that sailors call mare's tails, prophets of heavy weather. But November is the month for Superior's gales. No storm threatened on that day; nothing was permitted to spoil it. Even the cedar swamps and jackpine barrens looked inviting.

In spite of the high latitude, the sunlight was intense, bleaching birches to the whiteness of paper, exposing nuances in the autumn colors that would have been lost to the eye on a dull afternoon: cardinal red, blood red, maroon, and plum; pale yellow, yellow green; and shades of orange from tangerine to burnt ocher. The hour before dusk was the most enchanting, also the saddest. The sky took on a lilac tinge, a shelf of flat gunmetal cloud formed, and the sun, falling beneath it, illuminated the treetops. They glowed with an unreal brilliance, as if each leaf were a tinted lightbulb. I still wished I could live forever, if only to behold such beauty once a year, even as I knew that my portion of eternity, like everyone's, was a fraction of a fraction of a nanosecond; and yet there was a melancholy in the slant of mellow light, a forecast of ever-shortening days, of things ending, of winter's coming.

Will Treadwell and I were sitting on the tailgate of his pickup, relaxing after an afternoon of woodcock and ruffed-grouse shooting in the woods near Vieux Desert. We hadn't been too successful, but that didn't matter as we looked at those electric trees, hypnotized by their gorgeousness. When you reach a certain age, you tend to treasure small moments that would pass unnoticed if you were much younger. We were in our sixties, mid-sixties, on Medicare and Social Security, "card-carrying geezers," Will said. We had had our big moments, but that account was closed, and in lieu of plunging into self-pity, alcoholism, or senior-citizen grumpiness, we accepted that the small ones were all that was left and tried to make the most of them.

I had met Will through a friend from Connecticut who

raised and trained sporting dogs and knew Will from the hunting trips he made to the Upper Peninsula. He convinced me to join him one year, 1987. I'd never been to the U.P., and I took to it immediately, the wildness and lonesomeness of it—a place that had managed to escape the bulldozing depredations of land developers. I liked it so much that I returned the following year on my own and linked up with Will. I had hunted with him every autumn but three since then. It became a necessary annual ritual for me, so much so that I was willing to drive a thousand miles rather than miss it.

We are very different, Will and I. I'm midsize; he's extra-large, with arms and shoulders that, even at his age, project an impression of superior leverage. I'm a writer; he ran a bar and a local craft brewery until he retired; but we share a passion for tramping through wild country behind spirited bird dogs. There were—still are—sterner strands that tie us: the semi-mystical brotherhood of the Marine Corps and the bonds of war.

We both participated in the misbegotten venture into Indochina, though our tours there did not overlap, and our roles had been as dissimilar as our physical statures. Will had been a grunt, a machine gunner, and I had been a combat correspondent, an accidental Marine, really, the accident being my last name, which begins with a "C." I got my draft notice a month after flunking out of journalism school at Northwestern University (a singular achievement; journalism isn't exactly astrophysics). I reported to the induction center on South Jefferson Street in Chicago (I was born and raised in Joliet, Illinois) and passed the physical, following which a sergeant ordered us draftees to line up facing him. He then commanded everyone whose surnames began with "A" through "D" to take one step forward. We did. "You people are now in the United States Marine Corps," he announced, stunning us all. The fabled corps was a volunteer outfit, wasn't it? The sergeant's declaration struck every one of us as a death sentence. It was 1967; the Marines were suffering casualties on a par with World War Two—the reason we with surnames beginning "A" through "D" had been ordered to take that fateful one step forward. There weren't enough volunteers to fill the corps' depleted ranks; it had to shanghai conscripts.

In a collective state of dread, we were packed off to Parris Island for boot camp. Following that ordeal and an additional month of advanced infantry training (it is holy writ in the Marines that every man is a rifleman first), I was granted what I thought would be a reprieve from the death sentence. Some angel somewhere in the records department noticed that I'd studied journalism in college. I was assigned the primary MOS (Military Occupational Specialty) of 4341—i.e., combat correspondent. With a happy heart, I shipped out to the Defense Information School at Fort Meade, where I graduated top of my class. There were two reasons for this unusually excellent performance: (1) the course repeated much of what I'd already learned during my three semesters at Northwestern; and (2) I was highly motivated. Ignoring the combat part of my MOS, I'd deluded myself into thinking that if I did well at the school, I might not be sent to Vietnam or, if I was, would spend my tour of duty banging out press releases in an air-conditioned office.

"You were a goddamn REMF," Will has mocked, with genial scorn. REMF was the unofficial acronym for Rear-Echelon Motherfucker. In actual fact, I saw more combat than he, sent out week upon week, month upon month, to cover one operation after another. But Will's derision was accurate in one sense—I didn't fight; I only *saw* combat. Not a warrior, I observed and recorded the warriors' deeds. With one exception.

About eight months into my tour, I'd been assigned to cover a search-and-destroy mission near the Laotian border. I flew out on a helicopter and joined up with a platoon from the First Battalion, Ninth Marines, an outfit known as "the Walking Dead" for its off-the-charts casualty rate. The platoon went out on patrol the next morning, me tagging along armed with a notebook, Nikon camera, and a pistol that would probably be good only for committing suicide. We began climbing some nameless numbered hill through the jungle's greenish twilight. Men walking, men who would soon be dead. I was raising my camera to photograph a Marine clutching a tree root to pull himself up the steep incline when the North Vietnamese sprang an ambush. A bullet blasted the camera out of my hand. I bellyflopped onto the muddy slope. The enemy fire ripped through us like a typhoon through tarpaper shacks. The Marine whose picture I was going to take tumbled down and came to rest beside me, the lower half of his face shot away. I picked up his rifle and fired back and saw an NVA soldier fall, though I can't say if it was I who killed him or someone else.

Forty-two of us started up that hill, nineteen made it down, me among them, bleeding from the fragments of a Nikon SLR embedded in my hands and face.

* * *

Now Will and I sat on the tailgate, drinking lukewarm thermos coffee spiced with bourbon while we gaze at the treetops. Their brilliance dimmed as the sun fell behind a flat purplish cloud, igniting a gold fire at the edges that resembled a gilded frame around a blank canvas. I mentioned the sunsets in Vietnam, the spectacular sunsets over the Truong Son Mountains—my only pleasant memories of the war.

Will relit the thin, ropy, stinking cigar he'd been smoking.

"Phil, you remember that guy who bartended for me a while back? Chris?"

The question, seeming to come out of nowhere, puzzled me, but I gave it a few moments' thought.

"Tall guy, scrawny, on the shy side?"

"Him. He didn't last long behind the bar. Bartending and shy don't mix. He was one of us, y'know."

"Us who?"

"A vet. Different war. He enlisted right after nine-eleven, did a tour in Afghanistan, another one in Iraq with the Army engineers." Will dropped the cigar into the dirt, slid off the tailgate to crush it, hopped back up. "A Humvee he was riding in in Iraq hit an IED, and he got a shitload of shrapnel in his guts. They had to cut out half his stomach. The reason he was so skinny. Like that surgery they do on fat people, but he wasn't fat to begin with."

In the pause that followed this, I steeled myself for the hard-luck saga I knew was coming. Will was a storyteller who gravitated toward tragedies, an inclination I attributed to a morbid streak in his nature or to the Upper Peninsula's long, gloomy winters, maybe both.

And the tale of Chris the bartender was as long as it was woeful. I'll try to abridge. Medically discharged, he returned to his hometown, Saginaw, landed a job in an auto-transmission factory, but when it moved to China, he moved to Texas, where he found work in construction and married a woman from Houston. The marriage lasted long enough to produce two children, a girl and a boy. After it broke up, Chris migrated back to Michigan and wound up on the U.P., laying block brick days, bartending nights for Will. He was a terrible bartender and spared Will the heartache of firing him, a veteran, "one of us," by quitting.

It was in the winter when his former brother-in-law phoned with dreadful news: his ex-wife and daughter had been killed in a car wreck, but his son had survived and was in the hospital. Unemployed again—his brick-laying job was seasonal—he had to borrow money for plane fare to Texas. Will loaned it to him.

"I gave it to him, really; knew he'd never pay me back," Will went on. "I didn't see him for a while. A couple of years ago, right when I was in the middle of selling the bar, getting set to retire, he showed up again. The dude was in tears."

What had happened was this: By the time Chris got to Texas, his ex's sister and her husband had taken legal custody of his son, spirited him out of the hospital, and brought him to Massachusetts, where they lived on a farm, a religious commune. They'd convinced the authorities in Texas that Chris was a bad father who'd deserted the family and missed too many child-support payments. They would not allow him to see the boy.

"What Chris wanted from me was another loan to pay for a lawyer and for me to help him find one so he could fight this thing," Will said. "But like I told you, I was in the middle of selling, setting things up to retire. I didn't have time for Chris. And if you want to know the truth, I felt he was a hopeless fuckup. Iraq had fucked him up mentally as much as physically. Even if I had time to do what he wanted, he'd be back with some new soap opera, so I pulled a hundred from the till, gave it to him, and blew him off. I didn't hear anything from him or about him till this past summer."

"This being a Will Treadwell story, what you heard wasn't good," I said.

"It could've been a whole lot worse." He removed his stained baseball cap and brushed his thin ginger hair with his fingers. "He found where this commune was and got there somehow or other and tried to kidnap his own kid. He had a handgun on him. That's what I heard from a guy I know who knows Chris. The cops got there before he shot somebody . . . or himself. He's in the Massachusetts state prison and is going to be there a long time."

Will's English setter, Samantha, curled up with my dog in the car kennel behind us, began to whimper. Will turned to check on her, but there was nothing wrong. She was dreaming.

"If you meant to ruin a beautiful day by depressing me, you succeeded," I said.

Will gave a caustic laugh. "I was leading up to something."

He hopped off the tailgate again, rummaged inside the truck, and returned, handing me a mailer printed on stiff, grainy paper. *The Stiggs Wellness Center,* read the front side, above a cheery logo showing a sun rising over pine trees. Above the sun, a comet streaked across a royal-blue sky, with the slogan *Where New Lives Begin!* riding its tail. A block of promotional copy filled up the rest of the space: *Located on ten private acres adjacent to a state park in the dramatic Huron Mountains of Michigan's Upper Peninsula, the Stiggs Center is dedicated to individual and group renewal and empowerment.*

"What is this?" I asked.

"Look at the back side."

It listed the various programs by which renewal and empowerment were to be achieved, with the prices alongside, like a menu. The last one was in bold black caps: **A 4-WEEKEND PROGRAM FOR COMBAT VETERANS. VETS MENTOR VETS. FREE!**

"I volunteer there," Will said. "I'll be there this weekend."

"At a spa?"

"It's not a spa," he replied testily. "It's a kind of clinic. I'm one of the mentors."

"You mean you do counseling?"

"Mostly, I listen. I'm good at that. You run a bar for thirty-odd years, you learn how to listen."

"Let me guess. The way Chris works into this is, you didn't listen to him, you blew him off, he landed in jail. You felt guilty, so you got into mentoring vets."

He flapped a hand. "More or less."

"Okay, you'll be gone this weekend. I'll miss your company, but I think I can manage all by myself."

Will gave me a soft punch in the shoulder. "You're coming with me."

"Oh, come on."

"Hear me out. They use your book in the vet program. Charlie reads from it sometimes at the group sessions. Charlie Stiggs. He started the center with his wife. Her name's Laura." He threw me a quick, almost shy smile. "You're a famous guy, eh."

Will was flattering me, and I was flattering myself earlier when I claimed to be a writer. Actually, I'd been a newspaper reporter all my career and had written only one book, title: *Lines of Departure: Memoirs of a Combat Correspondent.* It had made me famous for a brief time but not famous in the way the word is commonly understood, that is, celebritized. Most people had never heard of the book or me.

"I mentioned to them that I knew you, that you were going to be here and we'd be seeing each other," Will continued. "So they asked me to ask you if you'd drop in this weekend."

"Didn't sound like you asked. It sounded like an order."

"Yeah, it was. You never got above lance corporal; I finished up as a sergeant E-five."

The sun was down; the sky had darkened to violet, the air grown colder.

I said, "I could go for a beer and bowl of chili. You?"

"Sounds good."

We started toward town, lurching down a rutted logging road through a recent clear-cut littered with slash piles, broken branches, stumps. It looked like a bombing range, but the absence of trees afforded a view of Venus, bright as a headlight, and a pinpoint to its lower left, Mercury. The moon shined above them, the first full moon of October, a hunter's moon.

"What am I supposed to do?" I asked, sounding a bit whiny. "I'm not a trained counselor."

"Neither am I. Do what I do. Listen. And talk to the guys about . . . y'know, stuff. How you got through your PTSD. Stuff like that."

He nudged the truck through a wide hole that resembled a meteorite crater. I maintained a strategic silence. I have an aversion to that term, "post-traumatic stress disorder," partly because I dislike the clinical, bloodless sound of it, preferring older terms like "shell shock," "battle fatigue," "soldier's heart"; mostly because I don't consider it a disorder so much as a normal reaction to an abnormal experience. Anyone who emerges from months of combat the same person as when he went in is the one with the disorder. Which isn't to deny that war lacerates the soul. For a long time after I came home, I was afflicted with a sensitivity to loud noises, with outbursts of anger at the slightest provocation, with an unusual form of insomnia—I could not sleep without a light on and a loaded shotgun at my bedside.

Over our beers and chili in his old bar, Will talked me into obeying his orders, presenting it as something like a civic duty. He and I were elders, obliged to dispense our hard-won wisdom to younger members of the soldier's tribe. That I didn't have much wisdom to dispense seemed beside the point.

* * *

We left Vieux Desert on Friday afternoon. While Will drove, I acquainted myself with the Stiggs Center by reading its online newsletter on my iPad. Upcoming events: a three-day session for people *in transition,* featuring an *experiential process to build a dream structure within your life cycle.* Cost, $300. A Women's Pilgrimage celebrating female roles through *ancient rituals* carried a $350 price tag for single occupancy, $250 each for double. A Wellness Weekend that included a *wisdom quest to a sacred forest* was going for $380 per person.

I tapped to the next page, which described the four-weekend Veterans' Program in the same moony lingo. But it was offered at no cost, owing to a grant from the Michigan Department of Veterans Affairs. *We begin the journey to restore wholeness with a welcoming drum circle. . . . We learn how to let go of the war experience and build the dream of a new life. . . . Guiding warriors to bring meaning to tragedy through cross-cultural ceremonies.* It was the sort of prose I had been trained to avoid like Ebola. Phrases like "bring meaning to tragedy" rang obscenely hollow compared with statements of unadorned fact.

The troops in Vietnam had a saying they uttered when a best friend died for no good reason, when a Dear John arrived at mail call, or when forty-two men went up a hill and only nineteen came down, a mantra hymned in response to the lies they heard from generals, politicians, chaplains: *Don't mean nothin', don't mean a thing.* Wisdom? To reject all comforting illusions, to embrace the war's absurdity—that was the beginning of wisdom and the most effective vaccine against going crazy.

I closed the iPad, feeling that I had been shanghaied once again.

"Will, tell me you haven't drunk the Kool-Aid. Drum circles? You don't buy into this mumbo jumbo, do you?"

"You have to ignore it. But the program does the guys some good. Maybe it's just a placebo effect, but if stuff like this had been around back in the day, you and me wouldn't have been as fucked up for as long as we were."

I wanted to say, *Speak for yourself,* but I kept quiet. I was aware that with unending wars in Afghanistan and Iraq, retreat houses and sanitariums like the Stiggs Center had sprung up all over the country, becoming as common as snake-oil wagons once were. To say that I was skeptical that war's hidden wounds could be healed by well-intentioned amateurs spouting New Age psychobabble would be an understatement. When I thought about that grant from the VA, I caught the whiff of a hustle.

* * *

The Upper Peninsula is the wildest part of Michigan, and the Huron Mountains are the wildest part of the U.P.—a thousand square miles of steep forested slopes, rock bluffs, ravines, and crevasses sculpted by Ice Age glaciers. They aren't true mountains, the tallest topping out at two thousand feet, but their ruggedness has spared them from the logging and mining that ravaged the rest of the U.P. in the past. From the worst of it anyway.

Despite the claim its brochures made—*located in the dramatic Huron Mountains*—the Stiggs Center was on the verge of the range, a short drive down an all-weather road to a pine-shadowed meadow overlooking a lake. Through the trees, I made out a large building faced with half logs, three or four white-framed cabins, and two shingled bungalows that looked like old-timey motels. The center had been a summer Bible camp before the Stiggses bought it, Will told me. The bungalows had been the boys' and girls' dormitories, now converted into guest rooms. A volunteer, a young blond woman wearing hiking boots and Lands' End togs, escorted me to my room. Will knew his way around and carried on by himself. The young woman gave me a key and a map of the grounds and said that we were invited to dinner with the Stiggses. She took my overnight bag inside, while I carried the rest of my gear: a metal case containing a pair of 70-by-20 astronomical binoculars and a cylindrical canvas holding a tripod. I had taken up astronomy in my retirement, following Marcus Aurelius's advice to *look round at the courses of the stars, as if thou wert going along with them . . . for such thoughts purge away the filth of the terrene life.*

"Are you going to do videos?" she asked, indicating the cases.

I shook my head. "Hope to do some stargazing if the sky stays clear."

That wasn't completely true.

"Dinner is in the main building, the log one," she said.

The dining hall where Methodist adolescents once refueled after a day of hiking, swimming, and hymn-singing had been downsized into a cozy dining room accommodating six round tables, each with four chairs. A stone fireplace helped create the feel of a rural inn. Will, showered and changed into fresh clothes, introduced me, likewise cleaned up, to Charlie and Laura Stiggs. If he'd been standing on a medicine ball or any large round object, Charlie would have looked like a human exclamation point. Everything about him was long and thin: his face, his neck, his torso, his legs. But my second impression, taking in his white eyebrows, trim white beard, and white hair curling over his forehead like foam on a wave, was of an ascetic, somewhat underfed monk. Laura, brown-haired, round-faced, smooth-skinned, must have been twenty years younger than her husband. She wore a pair of oversize glasses, the copper-tinted eyes behind them holding a benign and vaguely dreamy expression. She shook my hand firmly and presented a warm smile that struck me as not entirely sincere: professional, rather, the kind of smile you might get from a saleswoman behind the cosmetics-and-perfume counter in a department store.

We sat down to eat (no cocktails, no wine, alcohol prohibited). My fears of a vegan meal were unfounded, and I silently thanked the chef (whom I never saw the whole two days I was there) for the meatloaf, mashed potatoes, and peas.

The Stigges proceeded to stroke my ego, praising *Lines of Departure*. My glance pivoted to Will. In all the years I'd known him, he'd never offered his opinion about the book. I'd often had the feeling that he disapproved of it, not for its literary flaws but for its very existence. To him, the experience of battle was incommunicable to those who were strangers to it. All war stories were therefore false to one degree or another; to publish an entire book of them was to commit a kind of fraud. That is what I thought he thought, probably because I sometimes thought it myself.

"I was intrigued by the title," Charlie was saying, his hands clasping his glass of iced tea. "It's a military term for . . . for . . ." He fumbled, trying to recall the definition, and looked to Will. "You told me once."

"For the start point for an attack on an enemy position," Will explained. "When a unit crosses the line of departure, it's committed to the assault. No turning back."

"Yes, I remember now," said Charlie. Then, to me: "But you

use it in a metaphorical sense, don't you? The lines can refer to the lines you wrote in your reporting, the departures to . . ."

Again, he struggled, his slender fingers plucking the air. Now it was my turn to help him out.

"Do you know a Hemingway story, 'A Way You'll Never Be'?" I said.

"Nope."

"You go into combat one thing, you come out something else, if you live through it. You aren't you anymore."

"That's what we do here!" Laura chimed in. "I never thought of it before, but it's what we do. We provide a line of departure." Her fixed smile deepened into something near beatific. "From one mode of life to a new and better one."

"We open them to the possibility of one," Charlie added by way of refinement. "To the dream of one. And we hope you can help our guests make that transition."

I scooped up some mashed potatoes before they got cold.

"Tomorrow starts the first of the four weekends for this session," Charlie said. "There'll be five guests, all vets from Iraq or Afghanistan. Adam, Alex, Bruce, Larry, and Devin."

"I don't see how I can help them make this transition you're talking about," I said, and I should have inquired as to the nature of the transition. Something more concrete than from one mode of life to a new and better one.

"Much of that will be up to you," said Laura. "But we would like you to read from your book at tomorrow afternoon's group session." She dipped into a tote bag at her feet and pulled out a paperback copy sprouting Post-it notes as bookmarks. "These are the passages we think would be most effective, but feel free to choose your own. It's your book after all!"

She passed the copy to me. I squeezed a little more ketchup on my meatloaf.

"Since it'll be up to me, what would you say if I took them out stargazing tomorrow night? If it's clear enough."

"Stargazing?" asked Charlie.

"I do some amateur astronomy. I've got a pair of binoculars with me. You can see the moons of Jupiter with them."

Laura, who so far had hardly touched her food, looked perplexed. "The purpose being?"

"It puts things in perspective."

The couple traded glances, then nodded their approval.

* * *

We assembled in the dining room next morning at eight. We sat while Laura stood by the stone fireplace, dressed as if for a hike, in cargo pants, a flannel shirt, and a down vest. Will introduced himself to the vets; Laura presented me as a special guest. There was an awkward moment, more awkward for her than for me, when the announcement of my name and the title of my book was greeted with silence and blank looks. Evidently, my great fame had not reached any of the five men. This prompted her to give them a brief biography, with encomiums to *Lines of Departure,* which elicited a slightly more animated response.

Her round face—it really was almost a perfect circle— beaming a tyrannical benevolence, she then welcomed her guests to the program in a mellow, hypnotic voice and took them through the steps they would follow to their eventual recovery. "We will begin this morning with a welcoming drum ceremony. This will prepare you to learn how to build a dream structure for a new life. . . ."

What was a dream structure? I tamped down an urge to grimace at this drivel and studied the others to see how they were reacting. To a man, they looked befuddled but attentive, like students on the first day of class in differential calculus.

Adam was from Wisconsin and, like the others, in his late twenties. He had cloudy green eyes—cloudy but hard, like agate marbles—a wide mouth with thin lips, and flaxen hair nearly as white as Charlie's. He was the biggest of the bunch, tall and broad, and sat with his legs apart, both arms hanging between them. Even when still, he emitted waves of tension, a belligerence easily provoked.

Next to him was his friend Alex (they'd come together)—skinny, dark-haired, a sharp nose and cheekbones, garbed in biker black, serpentine tattoos twining around his neck.

The other three were Michiganders: Bruce, whose pudgy body and receding hairline prefigured him in middle age; Larry, with a wiry build and an angular face; and Devin, whose story was to take up lodging in my brain. His peculiar look caught my attention right away. He'd kept his high-and-tight military haircut and wore a shadowy brown beard, but his large soft eyes, with their long lashes, had a feminine quality and shone with a gray autumnal light, producing the impression of a deeply held sorrow.

". . . and each day we'll conduct exercises to release toxins from the body, the mind, and the spirit," Laura droned on. She was a practiced public speaker, making eye contact with each one of her audience before shifting to the next. "Under the guidance of veteran mentors"—motioning at Will and me—"you will learn to identify and release the triggers of the combat experience and how to reorder your life priorities."

Showing anyone how to release the triggers of the combat experience was beyond me. I had no idea what she was talking about. I thought, *Thank God,* when she wrapped it up.

* * *

In the building of dream structures, Charlie's and Laura's construction methods followed the principle: *if you try just about everything, something might work.* The center's regimen was cobbled together from Native American rituals, yoga, New Age mysticism, scraps of Eastern religion, and stuff I'd never heard of, such as "emotional-cleansing energy sessions." The Native American part began with an uphill walk past the lake to the sacred forest. Charlie, with a tom-tom slung around his neck, led us there. He claimed to be a certified Ojibwa shaman. I wasn't aware that the Ojibwa Nation granted shaman certificates, especially to white men; neither was it clear to me to whom the forest was sacred or what made it so—its pines and pointed firs looked no different from the rest of the woods.

We came to an open space beneath the trees that was surrounded by a low, circular rock wall. We filed into the enclosure and stood in a circle facing a pile of smooth stones. Each of us, our shaman explained, was to pick up three stones, representing what we hoped to be rid of, hoped to take in, and what we were grateful for, then toss them back into the pile one by one, voicing our wishes and gratitude aloud. Charlie beat on his tom-tom as we gathered the stones.

"We'll start with Phil and go clockwise," he said.

If I'd been forewarned that Will and I were to participate in this ceremony, despite our mentor status, I might have ginned up a list of things I wanted to be rid of, to take in, and be grateful for. But I wasn't, so I froze, like a high school kid tongue-tied by a pop quiz. Charlie, however, didn't seem to care; he went right on drumming—*boomthudboom*—and as a result, I missed much of what the others had to say. Except for Devin. I heard him in an interval between a *boom* and a *thud*.

"I'm grateful I didn't off myself."

A cleansing ritual followed the drum circle. Charlie must have learned it in shaman school. He lit a pile of cedar boughs and wafted the smoke over us with an eagle feather, purifying our spirits. We then marched to the gym in the main house, where the blond volunteer, now wearing spandex tights, put us through a series of stress-taming exercises. She bubbled with good cheer—*positive energy,* she would have said—explaining that these movements had been developed by a prominent yoga master. They opened valves in the brain, allowing stress-inducing toxins to flow to one's extremities and thence out of one's body. I needed a break from this nonsense. One of the exercises, involving bends and stretches beyond the capacity of my sixty-six-year-old body, allowed me to leave, pleading a pulled muscle.

Lying down in my room, I cussed myself for forgetting to bring a book or magazine. The only reading materials available were promotional pamphlets and brochures, two of which were capsule biographies of Charlie and Laura. Neither had had any training in professional counseling or psychotherapy, but Laura had graduated from the Body and Spiritual Medicine Institute, which granted her a diploma in Healing Touch Therapy, while Charlie, in addition to being a certified shaman, had been ordained a Minister of New Thought by the Center for Spiritual Awareness and New Thought (whatever and wherever that was). The scent of a hustle grew stronger, but I decided to take a kinder view of the couple. People had been flocking to health resorts for centuries, seeking miracle cures for every ailment from bad digestion to polio. Taking the waters at Bath or Baden-Baden or Warm Springs probably had never healed anyone, but it didn't hurt them, either. I assumed that the Stiggs Center's nostrums would likewise prove as harmless as they were ineffective, and at least the veterans' wallets wouldn't be any the lighter for it.

* * *

My newfound tolerance was tested that night. After dinner (fried chicken—again I wanted to embrace the cook), Will and I finally played our mentor roles. Charlie had arranged chairs in a circle in front of the crackling fireplace for a group session, Laura presiding, and the veterans talked about the monstrosities they'd witnessed and the damage their witnessing had inflicted. Will offered words of advice, words of encouragement; I read a passage from *Lines of Departure* about my own shaking, shuddering reentry into civilian life, for whatever good that did.

What balm could stress-taming yoga offer Adam, who had fought in Fallujah and could still smell the corpses rotting in its streets and had, just a month ago, been arrested for assault for flattening a guy who'd made the mistake of bumping into him from behind? What dream structures could be built to replace Alex's bad dreams of the night the Taliban overran his platoon, so that now he had to check the perimeter around his house every night before going to bed? And could the Minister of New Thought minister to Larry's mental wounds, bleeding afresh whenever a loud noise summoned memories of the bullet that splattered his best friend's brains across a floor in a village near Kandahar? I was growing angry, so much so that when Laura asked, "Would you say you have anger-management problems?" I thought she was addressing me instead of Adam.

He was leaning forward in his chair, his big hands clasped. "Yeah, so what? You had to be angry to be what I was, an angel of fucking death."

She flinched.

"I loved going out on night raids, I'll admit it, loved it. I loved kicking down doors and killing fucking hadjis."

"Hadjis?"

"Sand niggers; Arabs. Middle of the night, kicking down a door, a hadji on the other side with an AK, you don't want to manage your anger, you go with it and kill the fucker. That's how we took Fallujah, kicking down doors, house by house."

Two things were obvious to Will and me: Laura had never encountered ferocity like Adam's, and he was leading us on a mental return to Fallujah.

"Easy, bro," said Will. "Stay frosty; we've all been there, we get it."

Will's physicality lent authority to his words. He summoned Adam back to the here and now from the there and then. Laura, relieved, turned her attention to Devin, who sat very stiff and straight, as if he were in a church pew.

"Do you have anything to add? We haven't heard from you."

He, too, seemed to be somewhere else and did not respond right away. "I was in motor transport, but I didn't drive a truck," he finally answered, his lips barely moving as he spoke. "I drove a wrecker, weighed seven tons. We chained up disabled trucks and Humvees to tow them, and . . ." Devin trailed off.

Laura encouraged him to go on, but he shook his head. "Maybe some other time, okay?"

"Of course. You're under no pressure here," she said in a palliative tone, and called an end to the session. "Oh, I almost forgot. Phil has brought some powerful binoculars to do some stargazing. Anyone who wants to is welcome to join him. I believe I will."

The only takers among the five were Bruce and Devin. In the moonless dark, Laura leading the way with a flashlight, we trooped up to a fork in the same trail we'd taken to the sacred forest. The right-hand fork climbed to the flat, bare top of a pillar of Paleocene rock looming above the lake. We couldn't see the lake; it looked as though the rock plunged into a bottomless pit. The moon had set, the skies were dark. The viewing session wasn't going to last long; the night was as cold as it was clear. Devin gave me a hand extending and clamping the tripod's legs. I fitted the 70-by-20s to the mount and swept across that immense, magnificent sky to train them on Orion, hovering just above the mountains' rim in the east.

"Who wants to go first?" I asked.

Devin stepped up and, bending his knees, looked into the eyepieces.

"You should see four bright stars surrounded by what looks like a cloud."

"Uh-huh."

"That's the Orion Nebula. The cloud is gas and dust that will form stars eventually. It's kind of a star nursery."

"Yeah? Hey, cool," he said.

"It's about fifteen hundred light-years away. In other words, the light you see started our way fifteen hundred years ago. You're looking at the Orion Nebula the way it was around the time the Roman Empire fell."

"Really cool," said Devin.

The others took their turns. I showed them Jupiter's four Galilean moons, low in the west, and the Pleiades, a glittering brooch in the heavens; the blue furnace that was Sirius and the glorious Hyades and Aldebaran in Taurus, the red eye of the bull. I saved the Andromeda Galaxy for last. In the binoculars, it showed only as a faint grayish smudge, for it was so distant that its light began voyaging to Earth when Lucy planted her footprints in Africa's primordial mud. And all that out there, I said—stars being born, stars dying, galaxies turning—had been going on for thirteen billion years and would keep going no matter what happened on our speck of a planet.

"We aren't as important as we like to think. We shouldn't take ourselves too seriously. Microbes on a grain of sand in the Sahara, that's us."

I was trying to stretch Devin's and Bruce's imaginations, to present the beauty and vastness of the cosmos to get them out of their own heads. I knew from my own experience that the psychic pain of war's aftermath could be as isolating as acute physical pain; you are locked up in the prison of your memories, a kind of solitary confinement where no light shines.

"If we don't take ourselves seriously, who will?" said Laura. It was a rhetorical question. "Shall we conclude? This microbe is freezing to death."

We walked back. As I started toward my room, she tugged my sleeve.

"I'm not sure that was a good idea," she said in the darkness, her breath pluming. "The stargazing, fine. What you said might not have been a good thing. These people feel like hell; they don't need to hear that they're microbes."

* * *

It was a pleasure to hear her speak in plain language, and I explained my intentions as plainly as I could.

"Like I told you yesterday, it's to put things in perspective. We get too caught up in ourselves. The vastness of all that out there"—motioning at the sky—"gets us out."

"Oh, I know you meant well. But I question your word choice. Good night."

Right after she left, I heard Will's shrill whistle, the same one he used to call his dog, and saw flames shoot up from the fire pit near the main house. I went to him. He was sitting by

the fire in a camp chair, smoking one of his awful cigarillos—
the reason he was outside on such a frigid night. I took the
chair next to his. He asked how the astronomy lesson had gone
and I answered that it had gone okay and told him about Laura's objections.

"She's got her own ideas how to run things."

"Mind if I hang with you guys?" It was Devin, bundled up in
a parka, a watch cap pulled over his ears. "I could use a smoke."

Will waved at an empty chair and Devin dropped into it and
lit a cigarette. We were silent for a little, content to sit and stare
at the flames flaring up, dying down, flaring again. Then Devin
said he'd enjoyed the stargazing.

"That one thing you showed us, it began with 'P.' That was
beautiful."

"The Pleiades. It's a star cluster."

"I was thinking about that and the galaxy you showed us,
and what you said . . ."

He fell into another silence. It was plain that Devin hadn't
joined us merely to smoke; I asked if there was something on
his mind.

"If you want to hear it," he said.

"We're here to listen," said Will. He reached for a log in the
woodpile and tossed it into the fire pit; the rising flames made
a circle of quivering light.

"Well, I'm here because I tried to off myself," Devin said. "It
was in my room at Northern. I'm in mechanical engineering
there. I was in my room and looking at myself in the mirror. I
had a handgun stuck here"—indicating his temple. He confided
this without any vocal inflection; a voiceprint would have shown
a nearly flat line. "I was going to give myself the death penalty.
Don't know why I didn't go through with it. But I'm glad I
didn't."

The next day, he went on, he called the VA's crisis line, saw a psychiatrist at the hospital in Iron River, and spent two weeks in the neuropsychiatric ward.

"Hey, I'd appreciate it if you don't mention any of this to the other guys. Or even to Charlie and Laura. I'll do that when I feel like I'm ready."

Will assured him that secrecy would be no problem and asked Devin what he'd meant, that he was going to give himself the death penalty. What for?

"I said I drove a wrecker over there? A recovery vehicle? One night—this was in Anbar—we got a call that there was a disabled Humvee down the road. It had run off the road and got stuck and we had to pull it out."

It was difficult to hear what he was saying because of the quiet, tight-lipped way he spoke, but Will and I did not impede him with questions, sensing that any interruption might stop him altogether. Devin's wrecker and two trucks left their base in a convoy. The rule was, he said, never stop or slow down for any reason, because insurgents could set off an IED or spring an ambush.

"Sometimes the hadjis would force civilians—a lot of times they were kids—to run in front of a convoy or flag it down, but you had to keep moving. We were rolling through a village that night when something like that happened. I had my eyes nailed to the taillights of the Humvee in front of the wrecker. I thought I saw a kid at the side of the road, waving his arms, and then he ran at the Humvee, and it looked like it clipped him, and he fell right in front of our vehicle. If he fell under the treads, he would have been squashed flat, squashed like a bug you stomped on; that wrecker was one heavy piece of machinery. We rolled and rolled. I hoped that he fell between the treads, because there would be enough clearance for him not to get crushed to death.

"We got to the disabled Humvee and set up to haul it out of there. It was buried to the axles in some kind of mudhole, like a little marsh in the desert. We got out and went to the back for the tow equipment, and holy Jesus, there was the kid, wrapped up in the chains. We saw him in the headlights of the Humvee that was following us. Don't ask me how the fuck that happened, because I don't know. We always kept the chains secured; maybe they'd got jarred loose and the kid grabbed them. They were wrapped around his arms and chest, his head even, and there was blood and hair on the chains. We'd dragged him five, six K's; one of his feet was hanging on by just a few strips of skin. This was my second deployment to Iraq, I'd seen some shit, but that was the worst. It wouldn't have been, if he'd been dead."

Devin halted his narrative. He wasn't looking at Will or me but into the fire, and I knew the fire was not what he saw.

"He was still alive?" asked Will.

"He was, yeah. A mess, but still alive and moaning. A really weird moan—it sounded like the muezzin. You ever heard that, the muezzin?"

Will shook his head.

"It's the guy who calls Muslims to prayer. The kid sounded like that. Sergeant Jackson—he was in charge—Sergeant Jackson ordered us to get him out of there and we did, and we got blood on our hands doing it, and we laid him down at the side of the road, and you couldn't believe he was still alive, parts of him looked like strawberry jam, Jesus, they did.

"We hooked up and dragged the Humvee out of the mudhole and now we've got to tow it back to base, and I said to Sergeant Jackson, 'What about the kid?' and he said he must be dead by now and we'll have to leave him. Except he still wasn't dead. He made one of those moans again. I said, 'We can't just leave him here like this in the middle of the fucking desert in the middle of the fucking night,' and the sergeant said, 'McIntyre, get your ass behind the wheel and let's move.' I'm standing over the kid—he was maybe twelve or so—and in the headlights I can see him looking back at me through the strawberry jam. It was that sound he made that got to me. I took my pistol and I shot him. I shot him in the face just to stop it. Or maybe like you would a wounded animal. I don't know. I do know I couldn't leave him to die out there.

"When we got back, the sergeant told us to hose the blood and hair off the chains and said that I'd better be a top soldier from now on, that I'd best watch my step and never give him any shit, because I could be court-martialed for murder. What do you think of that? He was going to leave that kid to die like roadkill and he called me a murderer. But you know, I started to call myself one. I kept seeing that kid's eyes in all that red mess and I could hear my pistol go off and I went to the chaplain and he sent me to the division shrink and he diagnosed me as bipolar. They were going to give me a medical discharge for psychiatric reasons, which would have fucked me up for life. But my enlistment was almost up, had two months to go, and the army cut me some slack and let me out on an honorable."

His cigarette had burned down to a butt in his hand. He flipped it into the fire pit and lit another. "All of that was seven years ago, and sometimes I still see and hear that kid. Maybe that's why I put the handgun to my head, so I wouldn't have to anymore."

The fire had died down to embers, shrinking the circle of light. Long shadows fell across it, threatening to engulf it in darkness. Will stood and dropped another log into the coals, and as the tongues of flame licked skyward, expanding the bright circle, he moved behind Devin's chair and laid his hands on the younger man's shoulders. The pose reminded me of a sponsor standing behind a confirmand. I sensed that Will felt he had heard a true war story—no heroics, no excitement, and no redemption. Devin was as much a casualty of war as the nameless boy he had shot. Perhaps he felt forgiveness in Will's touch, but of course he would have to find a way to pardon himself. I hoped he would. There was nothing Will or I, or Laura, or Charlie, or anyone, could say to make a soul so wounded whole again.

* * *

Will and I stayed on till late Sunday afternoon. We kept Devin's secret. Laura asked me for a contribution, whatever I could afford, and I answered that I'd left my checkbook in Vieux Desert but would be sure to mail her and Charlie a few dollars. Then we left, arriving in town at nightfall. I took a walk on the jetty, a long steel-and-concrete finger poking into Vieux Desert bay. A light breeze blew, and a ridge of black cloud rimmed Lake Superior's northern horizon. Snow was forecast for after midnight; it was probably snowing already on the Canadian shore, but the skies above me were clear for now. Orion glimmered in the east, and the Pleiades, visible to the naked eye, sparkled bright as ever.

ABOUT THE AUTHOR

PHILIP CAPUTO is an award-winning journalist—the co-winner of a Pulitzer Prize—and the author of many works of fiction and nonfiction, including *A Rumor of War*, one of the most highly praised books of the twentieth century. His book *The Longest Road* was a *New York Times* bestseller. His novels include *Acts of Faith, The Voyage, Horn of Africa, Crossers*, and *Some Rise by Sin*. He and his wife, Leslie Ware, divide their time between Norwalk, Connecticut, and Patagonia, Arizona.